NOT A
SELF-HELP
BOOK

Praise for *Not a Self-Help Book*

"An expert combination of humor and deep feeling...Digs deep into the particular challenges of defining and asserting an artistic identity in the world." —*PANK Magazine*

"A breezy and charming tale...Anyone who's grown up immersed in a profoundly rich old-world culture and feels its constant pull will commiserate—and be entertained." —Cheryl Lu-Lien Tan, author of *A Tiger in the Kitchen: A Memoir of Food and Family*

"Ceaselessly surprising and entertaining...Lai's debut is an unexpectedly radical book on our deeply complicated relations with parents." —*Hyphen Magazine: Asian America Unabridged*

"Both harrowing and incredibly funny." —*Small Press Picks*

"From New York to Taiwan and back again, Marty Wu will make you laugh, make you cringe, and make you hope for the best even when it seems impossible." —Miriam Gershow, author of *The Local News*

"Adopts an exhilarating, almost manic pace from the start and never lets up." —*Tahoma Literary Review*

"A heroine for a new era, a wacky, wistful, hyped-up version of our own inner anxieties." —*Start with a Story*

"By turns humorous and harrowing, *Not a Self-Help Book* displays Yi Shun Lai's astute observations of family conflict and cultural complexities." —Anjali Banerjee, author of *Maya Running, Haunting Jasmine,* and *Imaginary Men*

"Gives voice to a generation of immigrants caught amidst multiple ways of being in the world." —*Books, Not People*

"Quirky, hilarious, and continually surprising, *Not a Self-Help Book* takes us across the world and back on a breathless search for personal meaning." —Tiffany Hawk, author of *Love Me Anyway*

"One part joy, two parts laughter, and three parts I-can't-believe-she-just-did-that, Lai's dynamic narration introduces us to voices as surprising as they are satisfying." —Camille Griep, author of *Letters to Zell*

NOT A SELF-HELP BOOK

THE MISADVENTURES OF MARTY WU

YI SHUN LAI

Shade Mountain Press
Albany, New York

Shade Mountain Press
P.O. Box 11393
Albany, NY 12211
www.shademountainpress.com

Lai, Yi Shun
Not a self-help book : the misadventures of Marty Wu / Yi Shun Lai
ISBN 978-0-9913555-8-7
1. Taiwanese Americans—Fiction. 2. Mothers and daughters—Fiction.
3. Children of immigrants—Family relationships—United States—Fiction.
4. Family secrets—Fiction. 5. Immigrant families—Fiction.

Printed in Canada by Hignell Book Printing.

10 9 8 7 6 5 4 3 2

Shade Mountain Press is committed to publishing literature by women.

For Jim, Candace, Nasrine, Jo, Bor.
Friends like you make books like this.

NEW YORK

May 1, 1:30 p.m.
In office

My mother will not let me off the phone. I'm not going to make it to the museum. Also I'm about to be late for my two o'clock.

The Language of Paying Attention to YOU (Strand Bookstore, used-book section, $1.25) says I'm supposed to write down everything that annoys me in a sharp little notebook, with neat ruled lines, the better to stay on-task, or something.

It also says that I'm supposed to "give myself permission" to be annoyed, since this helps "clarify my goals."

Day one of diary: starting out frustrated.

Mama is still talking to me. I can hardly get a word in edgewise. Why am I not used to this by now?

Oh. I'm supposed to *report* the things that annoy me. Here's the conversation, almost verbatim. (Mama and I have the same one every week. I can practically write it from memory, except I don't need to, because it is happening *right now*. TLPAY says that writing annoying stuff down "takes away its power." I'll try anything.)

ME: Marty Wu speaking.
MAMA: Well, aren't we professional.
ME: Hi, Mama.
MAMA: What are you doing?
ME: Working, Mama, like everyone else is. (*Looks at watch; actually about to scoot off for lecture at museum.*)
MAMA: Aren't you important!
ME: Well. I *do* have a lunch appointment I need to get to soon. (*Sees self as lady who lunches and then goes to lecture, only without lunch.*)
MAMA: What kind of appointment?
ME: (*caught unawares*) Uh. Uh. Just a sales thing.
MAMA: Too busy to explain to me, I guess.
ME: No, Mama. Just...it's hard to explain.
MAMA: Is it one of your "clients" again?

Oh, I know. I know. It's impossible to hear air quotes. But from Mama, anything is possible.

3

Me: Well. Kind of.

Mama: (*switching to English so she can—what, berate me in two languages? I don't know*) You know, you maybe catch one of those clients, marry him, be rich woman, never have to work.

Me: I *like* work, Mama.

Marginal lie here. I like *some* work. *Some* men at work. But not this work especially.

Mama: Well! Work isn't everything. (*Sighs.*) At least you leave that illustrator job you had before.

Me: I liked it there.

Mama: You never go anyplace, no promotion.

Me: (*at a loss for words*)

Mama: Wait a minute. You not taking time off to go to that museum again, are you? You spend way too much time at museum, that's why you never go anywhere to begin with. Everything you do is waste of time, everything, everything! I so ashamed of you. Did you know, whenever my friends ask what you do for living, I must say I don't know? You buy friends, you know, that's what people who work in advertising do. On television, they never talk about people in advertising. They talk about editors and writers. Why can't you be one of those? At least then I hold my head up high.

Me: Well, that's why I took this job. To try and make you happy, so you wouldn't seem so unhappy. And also so I could make enough money to quit in a blaze of glory, and then open up my own little costume shop, just like in the old movies, and so maybe you can tell your friends that I own a little shop on 18th Street, right next to the bookstore, and you can come visit and have tea with me some days.

No, just kidding. I did not say that. But *TLPAY* also encourages daydreaming and writing down of pipe dreams, so I thought I'd write down what I really wanted to say. And anyway, Mama has shifted seamlessly into Taiwanese, is yelling much more fluently now, and my head hurts. (Taiwanese always sounds urgent. I don't know why I never noticed this before. Maybe it's because we don't have verb tenses.)

I never actually get to say these things out loud. But Mama is always yelling. No one knows why, although we've tried to ask. Dad didn't know, I don't know. I only know that stopping her—or even trying to stop her—is even harder than having to sit through the yelling. At least I can, um, meditate my way through the yelling (*Meditation for Morons*, on-street bookseller, $1).

Okay. I am not going to make it to the lecture. I have a little over a half hour to get to the 2:00 appointment. Which takes half an hour to get to. Why? Why does MediaStar have to be so far away? All the way across town, from my glossy offices here at *Retirees' Review*—Third to Lexington, Lexington to Park, Park to Madison, Madison to Fifth, Fifth to Sixth, oh god, still Sixth to Seventh and Seventh to Eighth— fuck! I'm never going to make it.

Oh. Oh. *The Language of Paying Attention to YOU* says I should not agonize over things I cannot change.

But I'll tell you what. I'm definitely allowed to agonize over the fact that I'm still on the phone with my mother. And probably I'm allowed to agonize over the fact that I'm not going to get to that lecture on time.

And I'm most certainly allowed to be angry that it's the last time this particular expert on fashion and Impressionism will be speaking. (I can't believe how dorky that looks when I write it down.) Oh, Met Museum! Why? Why can't you offer these lectures in the evening, when normal people go? Why do you always think it's little old ladies who lunch who want to attend these lectures?

Some of us are young, up-and-coming costume designers —I mean, advertising account executives with pipe dreams— who want to see these things on our lunch hours.

Boy, I'm firing on all cylinders: *TLPAY* says I'm sup- posed to write down my aspirations, things that annoy me, and that I'm supposed to give myself permission to be whatever I want to be. Maybe I wasn't supposed to do that all at once.

Mama is still yelling, even though I haven't said a single word back to her yet. The clock is ticking down, and now, not only do I not get to go to the lecture, I also am going to be late to see Chris.

I have to get out of this job. I won't last much longer.

I really hate this notebook, by the way. What the hell is the point of a notebook with lines? How do you imagine anything, in a notebook with lines?

Oh, good, she's hung up on me. Gotta jet. Chris is supposed to give me a huge deal, and my review's next week.

May 2, 2:17 a.m.
At home

So very, very late. But cannot get to sleep. Feel as if have screwed things up so badly; must tell someone. Jody out partying and probably met some guy at party and so is probably indisposed—well, anyway, I called her earlier tonight and her phone went right to voicemail, which is Jody's equivalent of the sock-on-the-doorknob—you know, code for "I'm busy with someone right now and really more interested in him than I am in talking to you."

Anyway. So here's what happened. After Mama hung up on me, I quick quick threw everything in my bag and then grabbed my coffee cup, which had been on my desk for, oh, four days and was therefore more coffee yogurt than coffee anymore, and therefore needed to be brought to the staff kitchen sink *pronto*. Then I bolted out the door.

And then. Wouldn't you know it. Stafford was right there, like the brick house he is, blocking my way. Crash! Sploosh! Glop! All over both our suit jackets.

Stafford. Stafford is so put-together. Drives me nuts. Even when we were dating, he would always sit there, looking like a smug, fat cat (except Stafford is *not* fat; Stafford is gorgeous and cut, with pectorals like bowling balls), while I dashed around and got ready for work. Even now that we're broken up, he never fails to make me feel so *not* put-together. It's like a talent.

Like, how come his collar points always look so neat? How come he always has an extra suit, no matter how many nights he's been out on business? How come he always knows just what to say to people? Argh!

Anyway. Stafford. Standing in door. Now covered in coffee-yogurt mess, just like me. Except he's just standing there, and he only says, "Oops!" while I flap and fling yogurt stuff around and smear it into my lovely worsted wool and manage to get some on our office carpet.

Feh.

Stafford. Glances only once at his own messy suit coat and then at mine, and says, "Here," and unbuttons my jacket for me and takes it off. Folds it in on itself, wipes his fingertips on a somehow-not-messed part, straightens my collar, and says, "There. Just go like that. I've always liked that blouse on you. You'll be lovely. Seeing Chris, are you, today? The Irving Liquors account, is it?"

(The British accent makes everything sound better than it is, doesn't it? Stafford could drop the eff-bomb fifteen times in a row and it'd sound like Keats.)

"Yeah. Yeah. Seeing Chris."

"Okay. Good. That's almost a ringer; I've seen the way he looks at you. And remember, we should schedule your review for next week. How's next Monday? First thing?"

"Yeah. Yeah. That works." I sound like a parrot, but that's mostly because I can't believe what I've just heard: Stafford actually thinks I'd use the fact that Chris may like me to earn the pages toward my quota for next year's issues.

"Right. So breakfast Monday for your review. And Marty..."

"What, Stafford?"

Stafford is really close now, and I'm remembering what it was like to wake up next to him: Nice, but always with a little frisson of—I don't know, uncertainty? Impending doom? Ugh.

"You need to close this thing. You're not the only one with a ton of pressure on, you know."

I'm remembering why we didn't make it past four months of dating. Aside from the whole his-taking-me-on-to-work-for-him thing.

"I hired you out of the blue, as you know," he says now. It sounds like he's on a roll, and I'm trying to exhibit some body language that says *I need to go*, but he ignores me. "No one would have ever guessed an illustrator would make a great salesperson, but you do have such a way with people. We invested a ton in you, and we're expecting a lot back, aren't we, love?"

Oh! Plummy vowels, rolled around in the mouth, leisurely, before they finally come out, all Eton and right-side-of-the-tracks. It's no wonder most of the world listened for so long, even if they were constantly being threatened, which I'm beginning to figure out is what's happening here.

I have to work to hold his gaze. (I think, if this were the movies, Stafford's gaze would be labeled "gimlet," or something.) "I'm pulling my weight."

He shakes his head and drapes my jacket over his arm. He's still standing there, dripping coffee mess, and he's still talking to me.

"Takes more than that in this world, sweetie. You know that. But close this deal and I'll consider us even, okay?" He winks, and finally steps back.

I narrow my eyes. "Bite me, Stafford," I say, and "You weren't ever *that* good in bed."

No. No, I don't say that. I tell him I'll close the deal, don't worry.

Okay. So then I'm bolting across town, wondering exactly how I'm supposed to close the thing. I mean, I *like* Chris. But I'm thinking he may not have the clout I need to close it. I'm asking him for a three-, maybe four-page deal, which will meet my quota, for sure, but Stafford sounds like maybe he wants more, and what the publisher wants, he'd better get.

By the time I get there, I'm late, sweaty, and annoyed. I mean, not too much more than usual with this job, I guess, but it's not the best way to start a meeting. It's probably more honest to say that I'm frazzled. Really, really frazzled. If I had curly hair, like Jenny in the sixth grade, whose curly hair I wanted so badly, I'd have been a hot, frazzled, *frizzy* mess.

Fortunately, I have limp Asian hair. Not as big a deal, except I know I've sweated right through my top, so I stand outside for a while, in the unseasonal heat, and hope to cool off.

I get into the lobby. It's still middling warm in there. And in the elevator too. But then I reach the sixteenth floor, where Chris's office is. A wall of air-conditioning hits me and my body makes a, um, *pointed* remark, if you get my drift.

And wouldn't you know it. Chris is hovering there, at the reception desk, where he's totally not supposed to be.

I *know*. Faaaack.

So Chris. Chris is standing there, with his mouth in a little pout of an O—cute!—and the receptionist, Jeannie, who I like a lot, is avoiding looking at my chest, and I'm totally regretting the day I decided to buy a "lightly padded bra" to wear with this top, and then I think to myself, Oh, Marty, just *own* it, will you?

I throw my shoulders back and give Jeannie kind of a rueful shrug and a brief eyebrow waggle, what I hope is an exasperated "Sucks to be girls some days," inside-joke kind of waggle, and then I turn to Chris and blow air up through my bangs and laugh what I hope is one of those devil-may-care laughs you always hear about.

Actually, I'm pretty sure I did none of that. I'm pretty sure I looked and sounded like a stressed wildebeest, but whatever, because I saw Chris swallow, swallow big, looking a little nervous, maybe, and that's when everything went horribly awry, because some part of my reptile brain latched on to what I saw and went:

HE LIKES YOU HE REALLY REALLY LIKES YOU.

And I don't remember what happened after that.

Okay, not true. What happened is that I made the conscious, female-praying-mantis decision to do the Stafford thing. You know, take what I can get, play up the feminine wiles; do whatever I can do to make the sale and close the deal.

Oh, hell yes. I did. I batted my eyelashes and said, "Aren't you going to ask me in, Mister Christopher?"

And he said, "Oh. Yes. I was just about to ask Jeannie to phone you, to see if you were okay, since you were so late."

"Oh, well." I waved my hand carelessly (sloppily, I mean, almost catching him in the face). "Some days a girl is busier than others. *Really* sorry to have kept you waiting."

I swept past him—careered around the corner, rather—totally aware that maybe I was not leaving behind a wafting, lovely scent of gardenias or whatever it is girls like Rosalind Russell in *His Girl Friday* wore, but was instead probably cutting a swath in the rarefied air of the sixteenth floor with eau de New York hot-dog vendor, since by then I felt about as fresh as a bun left on the steamer too long.

But I did not fail to notice that Mister Christopher had his hand on the small of my back, and no, it's not something I imagined, because I remember wondering if it was as sweaty down there as I felt.

Fabulous.

So there I am, in Chris's cubicle. I'm standing in the doorway and he's hustling, moving huge binders and stacks of papers from the one guest chair so I can sit down.

I swear, he's such a gentleman. Makes sense, though: Rumor is that he only really has this gig because his family is majority stakeholder in the company that makes up the bulk of MediaStar's business. That's "company" as in "blue chip, goes back years and years" kind of company, so I guess he'd have learned his manners—but I don't care. He's sweet and nice and he's always been willing to do everything with me, all of those client events I'm supposed to fill my calendar with so it looks like I'm out selling advertising pages all the time.

(I guess Mama is *kind of* right: I am *kind of* selling my friendship. Whatever. I'm supposed to save that topic for later, according to *TLPAY*.)

Anyway. So Chris finally clears a spot and then he glances at me—my chest—and says, "You're freezing. Here, put this on," and he pulls a suit jacket off a hanger by the cube entry and drapes it over my shoulders.

He smiles. "Your arms have goose bumps on them."

Hunh.

He sits down and goes, "So. The pages."

I feel better for the jacket. Plus, it's got some lovely woodsy dreamy smell on it.

Mmmm. Woodsy.

"Marty."

"Yes."

"The pages."

"Yes. What about them?"

"I think we can get them."

Part of me jumps into my throat and I barely remember in time to play it cool. "Oh?"

"Yeah." And then he says, "Only—"

Oh, hell.

"What, Chris? What do you want? Isn't it enough that we go places together, and hang out, and that I take you to see all the shows, and that you're always my choice for when we have big client events? What about the Springsteen concert last year? Or Cirque du Soleil?"

Apparently I am no longer playing it cool.

"Plus, our magazine has the majority share of the over-fifty eyeballs!" I go on, feeling lame. Hey! Way to shoehorn in those selling points, Marty!

Chris does this thing where he draws his eyebrows up and his eyes get really big all at the same time. It's a look that evokes instant sympathy. It was aimed at me, turned on full force, and it was all the worse because I knew he wasn't doing it on purpose.

"Sorry."

He shakes his head. "No, it's not that. It's that I always thought you took me on those things because you knew they were things I'd like to see, not because—"

There's a long, ugly pause.

"What?"

"Never mind. Look, I was only about to say, I think we can get Irving to dedicate a big chunk of their advertising budget to pages in your magazine. A full year's worth. And they're interested in the back page for all twelve issues."

My heart's up in my throat again, but I stay quiet this time, which is kind of unbelievable (self-help books say I should acknowledge the things I do right). It's unbelievable for two reasons: One, I can never really stay quiet around Chris; and two, twelve freaking pages is triple what we were going for, and also (okay, three reasons), holy *shit* that's a lot of money.

Chris waits a beat, maybe because he sees I'm not really breathing. "But I'll need you to help me sell Marcus and Elroy on it. They want to see the magazine in action."

"Wait, what?"

Chris looks embarrassed. *Uh oh.* He roots through the pile on his desk until he pulls out a big glossy brochure that looks familiar. "You know. Vegas," he says, pushing it across the table, and then I see it's something I dropped off for him nearly two months ago, a piece on the big expo we throw for our subscribers. We dangle it out to advertisers as a perk, so they can get a taste for the magazine's demographic, presumably, but really, it's the New York advertising world's version of a wine-and-dine.

Worse, it's the one I've filled all my slots for, because the show is *four days* away and because Chris had said he didn't think the account was ready.

I don't say any of this. But I do stare at Chris, long and hard. I think I even knot my brows, whatever that means. Actually, I have no idea what to do now.

Chris waves his hands in front of my face. "Marty? Can you make it happen? This is a huge deal. Marcus and Elroy are willing to give you the bulk of next year's advertising budget if you can make it happen. It's just that they haven't had much success with the demographic before. They believe the numbers you've sent over, so this would just be—well, the next logical move, anyway, for a deal this big, wouldn't it?"

"Yeah, but—it's next week."

He's quiet for a while, and then he leans forward, across his desk. "I've been working on them for months," he says. "Looks like they're finally biting. I just didn't want to give you false hope yet, you know?"

Oh, he's so sweet. Part of me flashes forward to me and Chris on movie-ish, New Yorky dates involving Central Park and snow, and reading newspapers in bed on lazy, coffee-fueled Sunday mornings.

I finally manage to say something intelligent, although I can't remember what, now, and then I thank him, and then I hear myself saying that I can make it happen, and then I hear him telling me that he has faith in me, and that there's a lot on the line, and then I give him back his jacket and I walk down the long hallway to the elevator, thinking. Twelve back pages will put me over my quota, and net me a massive prorated bonus, bigger than usual because Stafford went easy on me and gave me a lower goal than everyone else.

Which, of course, would allow me to quit. Like, right after the convention, if everyone signs the right papers and stuff. I'll get the commission for the first few insertions even if I'm not still an employee. I can afford to walk away from the rest of it.

All of which would make a tiny little shopfront *so* within reach.

But how the hell am I supposed to get Stafford to give me three plane tickets to Vegas, three tickets to the convention, three rooms in our swish hotel, and a full weekend's worth of entertainment for three more clients?

Diary writing: Good for filling time. Not good for solving problems.

Crap. Is 4:00 a.m. Have breakfast meeting. Must sleep.

May 2, 3:05 p.m.
In office

Ohhhh, dude. What a day, and it isn't over yet. Still have to go to two more meetings and boring Women in Advertising event, where we'll stand around sipping cheap white wine and pretend we're not trying to out-deal each other.

Anyway. So after my breakfast meeting (7:00 a.m. ridiculousness), I go in to see Stafford. He's knee-deep in something on the phone, listening to someone's problem with a most sincere expression, but he waves me in. I take a minute to admire: he's wearing another gorgeous suit, scribbling notes, looking casual. He winks and gestures at my suit coat, which is hanging behind his office door. He's had it dry-cleaned, like the perfect gentleman he is, even though it was me who'd spilled on us.

Yep. Perfect, more or less, until he hangs up and I ask him for the three extra slots.

He leans back in his chair and stretches. I hear his sternum bone pop, and I have a crazy-ass flashback to a nature program where the silverback gorilla gets up on his hind legs and bangs on his chest right before he rips the jugular out of a younger, presumably errant gorilla.

Shit.

"I don't have them, Marty."

"Stafford—"

"No, Marty, really. No. All of the slots are taken. I haven't anything else for you. I'd have to find the money someplace else."

This can't be happening. I was so close. "Please, Stafford."

Stafford lifts his upper lip by a fraction and wrinkles his nose. It's something he does when he's thinking. It makes him look like he's snarling, but he only does it for a split second, and only someone like me, who's spent so much time with that lip, would notice.

"Twelve pages, right?"

I swallow. "Chris says it's a near lock. And I think it's too good a chance to pass up."

He Stafford-snarls again and picks up the phone, waving me out with his other hand. "Fifteen minutes," he says. "I'll come find you."

I go back to my office. Ten minutes go by while I gaze at the ads on my bulletin board, my shoot-for-the-stars board. It's just a *skosh* ironic that I want to go into costuming, but haven't even managed to get a meeting with any of the big fashion advertisers. That gets me thinking about my little imaginary costume shop again, so I open up real estate listings, looking for available shopfronts in Queens someplace. I don't care what size; the smaller, the cozier, the better. But close, within walking distance of my apartment.

(I've always loved the idea of wandering down the street to where I work, picking up a coffee from my regular guy on the way over. He'll ask how it's going. While he's prepping my coffee I'll tell him about my day, the fun clients I have lined up to fit; the consultation meetings where people tell me who or what they want to be for a night, those meetings where they tell me their pipe dreams, and the hours I'll while away, sketching those same dreams out and stitching them into reality. Then he'll give me my warm cup and send me off, and the next day he'll want to hear again, ad infinitum.)

Another ten minutes go by while I'm daydreaming. I clear up my desk and am on my way to walk yesterday's coffee mug (just day-old, not at all yogurty) to the kitchen when it almost happens again: Mr. Brickhouse is in my way.

"Marty."

"Stafford! Dammit, you almost had to dry-clean another jacket."

Understated twitch of the lips. "Good news first or bad news?"

I back into my chair, and he takes the one opposite me. "Good news."

"I got the slots."

Yes!!!

"And now, the bad news."

Oh.

"If this thing happens, you have to stay on."

I start. "Wait, Stafford, what?" Some overdramatic part of me is yelling, "Foiled again!" and shaking my fist at the sky. In fact, nothing so exciting is actually happening, except for the slow sinking feeling I recognize as my pipe dream, uh, going down the drain.

He snorts. It's unattractive on him. "Oh, Marty, please. I *know* you. From day one you've been itching to move on to something you like better, although I won't even pretend to know what that is."

I'm blushing a little, and a lot annoyed that he can't even remember what I told him about my life's aspirations while we were dating. He shakes his head. "Anyway, I can't have it look like I gave you the slots because we used to go out and then I let you just go off. Loyalty, Marty. It's not just a buzzword around here. We want our employees to have loyalty to us. And I don't need to remind you of the flak I got for hiring someone everyone knew I was dating."

I'm wondering how I ever got the idea that Stafford was the warm, tender, dateable sort. Really I'm listening for the telltale clicky robot noises that androids, even perfectly humanoid ones like Stafford, must still exhibit. Nothing.

I bark, "We were already breaking up! Our relationship was falling apart! And anyway, you said I had natural sales talent!" I sound shrill.

"Yeah, but *they* don't know that. They just know that you used to appear on my arm, and suddenly, you were in the office, and with your *own* office, too."

Stafford's teeth look bared, but I'm only imagining things. He's grinning, but I don't think it's even close to funny.

Then again, he doesn't know that I only took the job so Mama could stop worrying—and stop yelling about worrying.

You know what would be funny? If Stafford suddenly decided hiring me after all was a terrible decision and decided to let me go.

Of course, he'd have to wait until after the paperwork was all signed, I mean. After the money was in my bank account. After the first print ad appeared in the magazine.

Oh, hell. Never mind.

Later, same day
Grand Central Terminal

Best friends are supposed to be your north stars, right? They're supposed to be the people who guide you and support you and make sure you're not making yourself crazy, right? I looked it up in *Women Who Love Men Who Love Themselves* (Barnes & Noble Bargain Books, $4). Even *that* says best friends are supposed to be the ones who make sure you feel loved and smart and pretty, even when the guy you're sleeping with is making you feel ugly.

I digress.

Jody is driving me *nuts*. Sometimes she can be so self-righteous. I mean, Jesus *Christ*, just because she has a perfect relationship with her perfect mom doesn't mean she's the end-all, be-all of maternal relations, does it? And sometimes, dammit, I just don't want to talk about my mother. And some days, furthermore, one's mother needn't play into anything at all. There are some things, in fact, that one's mother doesn't *ever* need to know.

Say, for instance, if one is on the verge of a maybe-successful deal? One would not tell one's mother, just in case said deal falls through. Say, further, that one is on the verge of a successful business deal that would potentially set her free from having to work at something she dislikes most days. One would also not tell one's mother, for the same reason.

Say, even further, that one is close to the biggest deal ever in the recent history of a publication. One would also not tell one's mother this, just in case one's mother is apt to say that such a success is impossible for her loser daughter. In fact, one would not say anything until said deal is signed. One might not even say anything until one's little shopfront in Astoria is well stocked with lovely fabrics and patterns and mobbed with patrons. Then one might invite one's mother in to partake in the afterglow. But not before.

But if you're Jody, you cannot fathom such a thing. You put up arguments that sound reasonable. You say to your beleaguered best friend, who is trying in vain to eat her ice cream cone uninterrupted, "But Marty, these are all good things. These are wonderful things. These are things your mother would be proud of. Why wouldn't you tell her?"

And then the beleaguered best friend, who only wanted to enjoy an ice cream cone on a park bench with her best friend in relative peace and quiet, says, "Well, Jody, not all mothers are the same. Not all mothers will be supportive, even in times of seemingly fail-proof joy. Not all mothers can be depended on to react as one thinks they should react."

That's not actually what I say. What I say is, "You don't even want to know, Jody," and then I clam up, because no, she really can't understand.

Jody says, "You need to be more generous, Marty. Just because she's screwed up in the past doesn't mean she'll do it again."

I shake my head. Jody's pretty far off the mark. It's not that Mama *screws up*, exactly. In fact, she does precisely what she wants to do, which is rain on my parade.

Little things, like when I brought Stafford home, feeling certain that she finally would like this one, since he had a great job (publisher at twenty-eight!) and was good-looking and had a posh British accent to boot. Littler things, like when I bought my first shirt from Thomas Pink on my own earnings ($200 a pop!) and wore it home to show her.

Big things, like when I took the job at *Retirees' Review*, hoping a more stable income would help her to worry less about my career, and maybe even allow me to sock away enough money to carve out a little space of my own in the costuming world, something she'd never have to know about until I was good and ready.

Every single time I gave her something to nibble on, she bit hard. Stafford was too handsome for me, and he'd eventually leave me for another, prettier girl. I'd spent too much on my shirt and was too stupid to know it. Advertising was for fools and spendthrifts, and could only lead down the road to perdition.

So—no, it's not really screwing up. It's full-on stormclouds over every potentially sunny day. So I lie. Jody knows this. I lie all the time. I never tell Mama where I got those shoes, or that bag, and I never tell her how much I paid.

I never tell her exactly what I do for a living. Everything is a possible landmine. So I make it as hard as possible to find them. I hide them under layers and layers of silence. (Note to self: I *must* stop doing this. All self-help books say that lying to others is akin to lying to yourself.)

"Tell me again," I say. "Tell me again why you think I should tell my mother anything."

"You owe it to yourself," she says, after a little while.

I can't think of an answer to that.

"This is not you. You don't want this kind of relationship. You want someone to behave like a mother, and you're dying to be a daughter."

"Yeah," I say, "but this is not that woman, so I can't be that daughter."

"Try it."

I look at her. Bright green earnest eyes, the beginnings of crow's feet from squinting at the computer screen—Jody's a freelance writer and, okay, I admit it, has seen and met all kinds of people. She's a really good judge of character, and I'm a really good judge of Jody: she's not going to let me go until I give, at least a little bit.

I try another tack. "You know, most Asian mothers are like this. Most Asian girls have this problem."

Jody lowers her chin, levels a squint at me. "Oh, yeah?"

I *could* be just imagining her combative tone, of course.

"Yeah!" I say, maybe a little too loudly. I'm practically verbally flailing here.

"You know this because all your Asian friends have the same problem?" Jody's really sinking her teeth in. She knows I don't have a lot of Asian friends. I think it's because so many Asian women I even know tangentially, like the ones I went to school with, went on to be doctors, engineers, lawyers. Not salespeople, and not illustrators, for sure. No lie. Stereotypes exist for a reason.

"Well…"

Jody cocks her eyebrows at what she thinks is my hesitation, and I start babbling.

"I read about it. It's, like, a tiger mom thing. Like, you know, really high expectations, and Asian culture saying you shouldn't, like, praise your own kids too much. You know." (Note to self: Strike "like" and "you know" from conversation.)

Jody shakes her head. "That is *such* a load of horseshit. No one should treat their kids the way your mother treats you. It doesn't matter what color you are."

"But it does," I say, "if every single other Asian girl has this problem."

"Well, you're the only one who can't stand it, then, and that's pretty piss-poor."

We both are quiet for a bit.

"Fine," I say. "I'll tell her. But later. I don't have my mobile phone on me."

Jody rolls her eyes and holds out her own phone. "Here."

I wave her off. Mama on the phone is too much. "Oh, never mind. I'll just go up there."

"What, now?"

"Now."

"You don't *have* to go *now*."

"No, I'd better go now. I think she's headed off to Taiwan next week sometime, anyway, so I'd better go see her before she leaves. Might as well get it over with!"

Jody quirks her lips. "You don't have to finish the workday? And don't you have that thing with the Women-in-Bad-Suits group?"

"Women in Bad Advertising Suits, thank you very much. And no. Both afternoon appointments cancelled on me, so that means I get to cancel on tonight and on one other thing."

Jody rolls her eyes.

Isn't that the way karma works?

Train is here. More later.

May 3, 4:50 a.m.
Own apartment

4:00 a.m. is not my usual time for my daily jog. But there's something very peaceful about being out on the streets when no one else is awake. Some of the bodegas are open, and there is one Korean grocery that stays open at Ditmars and 37th, where some of the bars are in Astoria, but otherwise, everything is sleepy quiet.

When you get to the East River, you can hear the lapping of the waves, and the water pushing the gravel on the shore around. It rustles, like crinoline. One late night, I heard a lot of tinkling, like wind chimes, and I stood there for the longest time before I realized it was the waves pushing seaglass around. I wish I had never figured it out. I should have left before I stopped imagining seahorses with bells on, messing around in the water.

The bakery up the street is open. I could smell the croissants as I passed it. Was going to go get one but then remembered why I snapped awake at 4:00 a.m.—because I am scared stiff due to horrible mistake and resulting nightmares (*Dreams, Unwoven*, Strand, $14).

Ridiculous! Am grown woman with grown-up job! Clearly am somewhat good at job; otherwise would not be in this predicament!

No need to be scared stiff!

Anyway, newly acquired book on unleashing own creativity (Strand, $17) says writing in mornings is good for you. 4:50 is totally morning.

So. I went to visit Mama yesterday, fuming at Jody all the way up to Bronxville. (I hate Bronxville. I hate the precious little shops, the precious little town square, the ridiculous Manhattan prices for not-in-Manhattan and only semi-talented bartenders.)

Bronxville is even on the wrong train line. Harlem line: yuck. Much better: the Hudson line, where you can look at the lovely Hudson River all the way up and away from the city; up, up to Poughkeepsie if you want; up, up, but you always know that you can find your way home by following the Hudson.

Anyway. Bronxville. Mama moved here after she got her messy divorce finalized from Dad, and after Dad's move west. Way west. So far west that it's east again—South Korea— someplace he always wanted to see. Okay, whatever. (It's obvious he was escaping from something. But must not project own motivations on others. *The Language of Paying Attention to YOU* says this not healthy or productive.)

My heart was in my throat like it always is when I go see Mama. I didn't have time to go home to change, so I was wearing a work suit. It's a good thing I didn't spill the coffee again.

At least I knew I looked semi-sharp. I checked myself for lint before walking around the corner and up the street to Mama's house. Made sure my shoes and bag were spotless.

I put my finger to the bell, but she was already there.

"You don't call before you come by? Bad manners. What you do to your hair? Look like dog chewed it. Don't you pay arm and leg for haircuts down there in fancy city?"

Crap. My hair. I fluff at it. "Oh," I say, "long day."

She holds the door open, half-blocking it. I'm trying to decide whether I should try and get inside or what when she starts talking, moving into Taiwanese like she does when she's on a roll.

"Long day, hunh? Doing what? Partying? Flirting with men so you can sell pages? That's not far off from what prostitutes do, you know. Even that stupid job you had before was better than this. Drawing with crayons was better than this. Why can't you do something to make me proud of you? Why can't you, for once, think about my happiness?"

Whoa. On days when I show up 75 percent put-together and she talks to me in Taiwanese, I usually have a pretty good chance of getting inside before she lets me have it. Something has gone wrong today: a misplaced piece of jewelry; a spot on the white carpet in the living room; a stilted conversation with my faraway brother—it doesn't matter what, only that it's happened recently. (I have lots of cues for Mama's temper. Someday I will write them down.)

Why, why, why didn't I call ahead?

My heart is hammering even worse now. I switch to Taiwanese, too. Maybe it will help her to remember that I'm a good daughter who can still speak the native tongue. "A-bu! A-bu!" I say, "Mama, guess what happened today!"

She steps aside, and I must hesitate, because she says, "Get inside. You're so ugly today I can't stand to think the neighbors might see."

I double-step, trying to move quickly, and trip.

"Sloppy," says my mother, only in Taiwanese it sounds like more than that, like you haven't just tripped, but that you're a tripping, drooling shadow of a functioning creature. I swallow. "Go say hello to your ancestors. Pray for better luck."

I shuffle past her, and make my way to the altar most Asian families keep in their homes. Pictures of ancestors from my father's side are lined up on it, along with incense and fruit, so that the ancestors don't go hungry and never feel alone. (The divorce, highly American, doesn't change the emotional fact that my father's family still has a place in this house.) I tap out three new sticks of incense and look around for the lighter.

I can't find it, and start to panic—I can feel Mama getting impatient behind me. "Mei Mei," she says, and I steel myself, both against that pejorative-feeling word for "little sister" and what I know is coming. "Why can't you even find the lighter? A good daughter who visited her mother every day would know where it is. No wonder you can't find a husband."

She shoves past me, precise and small, and plucks a lighter from a dish behind some peaches. I reach for it, and she slaps my hand, hard. "You can't do this right. You can't find anything."

I hold out the incense and she grabs the sticks and lights them, finally pushing them back at me. "Pray," she says.

I'm not religious by any means, but I love the idea of talking to my ancestors. I just could never do it with Mama standing over me, and today was no different. In my head I make the standard offerings of thanks for my safety and the good things that have happened, and apologize for having not visited much. I sneak in a plea for an unfettered road to my own costume shop, and reach forward to press the sticks into the urn that holds the incense while it burns down.

I back away and bow, pressing my palms together, trying to quell the nervousness that always springs up around my mother, and turn slowly around, hoping her annoyance with me has lessened.

No such luck. Mama is walking away, fast, toward the kitchen. I follow.

"Well?" she asks, over her shoulder. "What fancy news is it? Did you finally get smart, apply for grad school like I told you to? It's not too late to become a lawyer. I can support you, you know." She sniffs. "You argue with me so much anyway, you should become a lawyer."

Oh, crap. I'm grabbing mentally at things, trying to derail her from an all-too-familiar track, and then I do this: "I did it," I blab, sliding onto a kitchen stool. "I landed the biggest deal in all of the magazine's history. I'm quitting next week. And the bonus is huge. So big that I'll be able to open up a shop, and I've found the perfect place and everything. It's going to be amazing, Mama. You'll see."

Yes. Yes, I really say that.

Shit, shit, shit.

I watch her, hoping this will—what? Make her happy? Appease her? I don't know. A lifetime goes by while she runs her gaze over me. Through me. I resist the urge to fix my collar. "We'll see," she says finally. "Your brother said he wanted to be an art professor, and he is one, so I guess dreams do come true every once in a while. We'll see."

She fills a teapot with water and sets it before me, along with a cup.

I start to breathe again. She might ask about the shop. I start making stuff up that I think is pretty decent. But she says, "Woman with shopfront—not a job for ladies. You want to stand outside your store, yelling for someone to buy your things, buy this, buy that? This is not an elegant job."

I wait for her to go where she always does. Something about women hawking meat on the street. I *want* to laugh, because I know she's picturing the street markets of her childhood in rural Taiwan, where women who had things to sell—vegetables, fruit, shoes—really did stand by their wares, yelling for people to buy. But I bite my tongue, for fear of upsetting even this delicate equilibrium.

(Surely, this abject terror isn't normal.)

She goes on, headed right down the track I know she's already thinking about. "Women in Taiwan with shops— always so rough, always begging for anyone to buy."

"But Mama," I say, "I am talking about a shop here in New York."

She waves me off and switches back into English, underscoring how much she knows about America. "You think I don't know? New York shops even worse. New York shops have bad reputation. Rent so high, everything so small. Better off in Taiwan."

She turns her gaze on me again, and I flutter shut my eyes, feigning an eyelash in my contact.

"When was last time you go to Taiwan, anyway?"

"Uhhh..."

"Can't even remember! Weak brain. You don't remember I am going back again, do you?"

"I do, I do, but when exactly did you say?" I'm trying to visualize myself in the mindset of being in an office and asking someone to remind me when my next appointment is (*Visualize Your Way to Career Success*, ShopRite, $8.95), so as to take the danger out of the situation, but it's not working.

"Bah! Bad daughter! Good daughters know. Good daughters know when their mamas are going places. Good daughters even go with mamas. But not mine. Mine is too busy *selling* things. Maybe even herself, I don't know."

Oh, geez. Things have really passed the tipping point now. I know there's no stopping her, so I just let her spin out, slowly, another fifteen minutes, until she notices something else wrong—a loose thread on my jacket, maybe—and then I can go.

This, at least, is a predictable track, and she doesn't seem overly angry or worried or upset at my, uh, "news." Now maybe the rest of the visit can go okay, and it does. She feeds me soup, complaining that I'm too skinny (last week I was too fat; the week before I was too sickly) and that I probably drink too much. She even gives me a little around-the-shoulders hug on my way out the door by way of actually finding a loose thread off my jacket and snapping it off, which makes me feel so pleased that I'm confused at the terror I felt before.

I'm not sure if writing all that down helped. Now it's on paper, in black and white, and I have to admit it happened, and also admit that I don't know why, or how to fix it. And, also, that it happens all the time.

If everything goes well in Vegas, maybe this will stop.

6:00 a.m. now. Perfect time to get to the gym and get to work. And get a croissant.

May 4, 12:34 p.m.
Office, lunch at desk

Was just listening to a podcast interview with a costumer-to-the-stars. I'm supposed to be filling out a travel-and-expense projection for the trip to Vegas, but something this woman said keeps rattling around in my brainpan. She said, "Costuming is like a conversation without words. I don't have to talk to you, but I can start a conversation with a pair of pants, and the cut and the way they fall, and look."

In my office, communications and conversations are all around me. I can hear one side of the negotiation Stafford is in the midst of next door; I can hear the gossipy sales assistants nearby; the mockups I have on my bulletin board for next issue's ad layouts are all barking about quotas; samples of my shoot-for-the-stars clients' advertisements cover another bulletin board, talking talking talking of money and exchanges and getting people to buy things. The ads themselves aren't subtle by any means, but the clothing and models *in* the ads are: "Look at me," they say. "You're not me, but imagine what *you* can be in these things I'm wearing. What would you make of yourself, in these clothes, carrying these bags, literally in my shoes?"

Costuming speaks quietly, indeed. It can tell you who the person in the costume aspires to be, maybe. Who she believes she is on the inside. Maybe who he hopes to attract, or the impression he wants to convey.

Halloween is our one night a year to dress up and feel okay doing it. What if my shop, my little storefront, became the place where people came to see what it was like to slip into another skin? What if we made costuming something that people did, a leisure activity, just like we go out to dinner? What if masquerade balls weren't something only one-percenters did? Wouldn't that be fun, to let people try on someone else's life? Wouldn't it be *awesome*, to let people imagine themselves as someone else, more than once a year?

A shop like mine—I could make this happen for people.

Such subtlety! Such quietude! It's so close I can taste it. If only everything would stop moving, everyone stop talking for a bit, so I can figure out how to get there.

Phone is ringing. Figures.

Same day, 8:30 p.m.
At home

Next week is Vegas. Chris was ridiculous when I told him Stafford was able to find space for everyone. Like a puppy. I took him to Collins Bar for drinks this evening, where they serve the good stuff from Irving.

I swear, I had it all set up in my head, and he still exceeded my wildest expectations while somehow making me all flummoxed at the same time.

I order us two whiskeys, neat, and pass one to Chris. "Guess this is all I'm allowed to drink now, isn't it?" I say.

"Why's that?"

I pause. Dramatic effect, etc. "Well, you and me and Elroy and Marcus, we're going to be in Vegas together, so I'd better start practicing now. Bad form to order from any other client when mine is the biggest liquor distributor in my world."

Chris is on me before I know it, crushing me in a fantastic cedar-smelly hug, and I spill half of my drink before I can put it down. "Marty!" he yelps. No kidding. Yelps it. "That's so exciting! I'm so excited!"

He settles back into his chair, and we toast.

He takes what I think I'd call a healthy slug of whiskey.

"Heyyyy," he says then.

"What?"

He bumps my glass with his again. "This means you might be able to leave the company."

I don't register at first.

"What?"

"You know, this could be the thing that allows you to leave *Retirees' Review*. Oh! Oh!" He sits straight up in his chair. "Holy cow, Marty. If we get this thing inked, you could be on your way to a new gig soon!"

I'm still confused. How would he know I wanted to leave?

He squints at me. "You don't remember telling me? We were at the Johnnie Walker event? That thing they did around their ad campaign? The tasting?"

"Sorry, no." I'm desperately hoping he's thinking of someone else, except I totally remember the tasting, and I remember thinking that "tasting" four different varieties of blended whisky was a little much for a weeknight.

Sure enough, Chris says, "You were a little drunk when you told me. Do you think that storefront in Brooklyn is still available? Probably not. Real estate in New York..."

Oh, god. I must look horrified. Thankfully, he picks up on the cue.

"It's okay!" he says. "I think it's great. Heck, we're in our mid-twenties; we should have dreams beyond our day jobs, don't you think?"

The gerbils that make up the bulk of my brain matter are struggling to find something sensibly professional to express. "I like it here okay," I say, and "I hope you don't think this means I'm any less dedicated to you as my client." Go, brain gerbils!

He treats me to a long, searing gaze, and then he bursts out laughing. "Don't worry, I won't say anything."

"Anyway," I say, "cheers!"

"Yeah!"

Goodness. I wonder what it's like, to be enthusiastic about *everything*, all the time, like Chris is. Must be exhausting.

Anyway. Gotta go. Am late to meet Jody.

May 5, 2:12 a.m.
Jody's apartment

Am drunk, am very very drunk but book says must write especially when intoxicated because then have fewer inhibitions. Am not much interested in inhibibbiations now because am too busy thinking about Chris bothersome boy. Sweet thing very pestery about shop and stuff and also very persistent. Why need to know about secret bothersome aspiration? Is pipe dream! Is own business.

Why so drunk? Let's see: Only had one martini before dinner. Then split bottle of wine with Jody. Then had port and after-dinner sugary cocktail yum. Oh.

Lines in book very silly tonight. Pointless to have lines when very drunk.

Jody annoying again. Don't want to hear about perfect mothers! Don't want to hear about squishy mother-and-daughter days! Am not interested in sitcom-like relationships! Wanted to go home but so much easier to crash in East Village than Astoria. Don't know why since is same train time same number stops same miles.

Oh. Know why. Astoria completely different borough. Feels far!

Why best friend so annoying? Why? Why?

Never mind. Sleepy. Jody yelling to turn out light.

Same day, 6:30 p.m.
Own apartment

Spent all day hungover. Don't even know how I managed to drag myself back to Astoria. Drank *a lot* of grape soda before I actually felt okay enough to get on the train. Jody swears by it. Something about the combination of food coloring and simple sugars. Whatever. Seemed to work, because I was able to get home without feeling too bad.

Jody was gone before I woke up. She had an appointment at the trapeze place at Chelsea Piers, something about a story on acrophobia, and the best ways to cure it.

She left me the wackiest note. Something about how she was sorry we'd argued but that some things were worth arguing over, and that she knew I'd eventually see that deception—

Oh. *Oh.* I *knew* I was pissed at her last night; I just couldn't remember why: I went and told her what I told Mama. Won't I ever learn to keep my mouth shut?

I totally remember now. Jody was all excited to hear how things went with my mom, and I was feeling loose and reckless after getting an email from Chris (halfway to flirty!), and she was all like, "How'd it go?" looking dewy-eyed and expectant, like what? Like my life was going to suddenly be some kind of CW show? Or worse, some ABC Family rig?

And damned if I didn't come right out and say it, almost anticipating the way her face fell into her cantaloupe amuse-bouche. "Well," I said, sounding really mean, even to myself, "it went so well that I had to lie my face off to her to get her to knock it off. Ain't that a kick in the pants."

"Knock what off?" said Jody, and then, on the heels of that, "Holy shit, Marty, what did you have to lie about?"

It fell apart from there. Jody'd ordered a bottle of Margaux, hoping to celebrate something—what? gushy family scene?—and we drank until we were both too blitzed to see, but we were still talking at each other—over each other—her with her infuriating examples of how things could be, how she and her mom had solved whatever infinitesimal miscommunication they'd ever had, and me trying to explain to her what the hell it was like, to live in—well, to live in hell.

Bronxville. Whatever.

In the end: Crying. Weeping. Apologizing at and over each other, just the way it should be when one is blotto with one's best friend. I'm sure the guys at Le Bateau Ivre have never seen anything like it. Right. Oh, I don't know. The more she talks, the more it's apparent that her way won't work. Talking, honesty, grown-up relations—those are not for me and Mama.

Review is Monday morning, isn't it? Why? Why? Why agree to a 7:00 a.m. breakfast meeting? A review, no less? And I have to leave for Vegas on Wednesday afternoon. Ugh. Better pack and clean and stuff.

LAS VEGAS

May 10, 3:34 p.m.
Bellagio pool

Chris is napping next to me.

Hee hee! Just wanted to see how that felt written down. *The Language of Paying Attention to YOU* says it's good to daydream. Their flights just got in, and the first thing Chris wanted to do was bake by the pool. Dry heat is something New Yorkers don't get a lot of.

He promptly fell asleep, so yes, he really is napping next to me.

I just wish I could get him to talk about what our next steps are. He seems to feel like it's all nailed down, but I don't buy that, not one bit. I haven't always enjoyed my time at the magazine, but I know a thing or two about sales, and I don't feel at all like this is sealed.

I mean, I've only ever met Marcus and Elroy once, and while they're great people, it's not like they know me all that well. It just seems too good to be true. Plus, the head of Irving is old Captain Markham, literally, like he used to be in the military and stuff kind of captain, and I'm not sure that he's bought in to the whole thing yet. Marcus and Elroy have never mentioned him, so it's not like he needs to be part of the process, I don't think, but still. Rumor is that he's nixed a couple of deals in the past, for seemingly inexplicable reasons.

You can never tell with military folks, anyway. Stiff upper lip and all that.

So yeah. When I tried to pester Chris about it, he got defensive and even looked hurt.

"Aw, c'mon, Marty, I just got here."

"True. But can you give me some idea of what Elroy and Marcus will be expecting when they get here?"

"You're going to be awesome, Marty. Just be your own awesome self. Hey, did you order drinks? Perfect."

"Chris—"

"What's in this cocktail, anyway? Pineapple something?"

"Yeah, or melon or something. So listen—"

"Can we talk about it later? I'm kind of sleepy."

Then he actually *closes his eyes.*

Maybe I *should* just enjoy it here, before all the madness

starts tonight. That's when the convention really kicks off, anyway. Meanwhile, there's plenty to look at here in Vegas. The heat is like an immediate wall rising off the pavement. You actively question the sanity of going out onto The Strip because there are no gigantic pools for you to wander into or step through when the heat gets to be too much. There are people of different shapes and sizes around the pool, standing around with their hands on their hips, looking for their kids or maybe actively posing for whoever it is they want to attract next, or slouched on chaise longues and in deck chairs, absentmindedly sipping at enormous drinks, or engaging in loose conversation. The temperature makes everyone seem languid, loose, slow, and if you squint you might even spot some heat waves just over someone's figure, like an overlay.

It's an artist's dream, especially one who dreams of putting all these different people in costumes that might best suit their individual personalities. I'd put *that* girl in a one-piece maillot, high-neck, haltered keyhole back, as opposed to the tiny two-piece she has to keep readjusting. And *that* man, the one with the Marine crest tattooed on his forearm, I'd put in a lovely linen shirt with the sleeve rolled up just enough to show the end of the crest, and a pair of flat-front seersucker shorts. And *that* girl, who looks like she's just discovering what it means to be a pretty girl at a Las Vegas pool, I'd put her in a full-length maxi-dress, in a jersey fabric that lets her feel gorgeous but doesn't make her prey. The lady in the muumuu? The one who probably came from Minneapolis? I'd like to see what she looks like in a wrap dress cover-up type thing.

And away from the pool, on the casino floor—the costumes there! I don't mean the stuff on the showgirls, I mean the stuff the tourists are wearing, although we did walk past a bunch of showgirls on their way to a show, and boy, it was unbelievable. Luxe, rich fabrics, amazing color, even up close; sequins everywhere, so many they make your eyes go numb and starry, all at the same time. So fun. So many possibilities.

Who *are* these showgirls, when they take off their feathers?

Chris caught me staring at all the people, right before we took the elevators up to our rooms. He winked at me. I hate him.

No, I like him. He's adorable. It helps to have adorable clients. Makes being extra sweet in order to get more information—I mean, in order to be my own "awesome self"—way easier.

Oh. My review. Review was just breakfast. Stafford said he should have postponed the thing, since it was clear that everything hinged on this deal anyway, but that we should just eat together anyway. Fine. The magazine picked up the bill, so there's nothing wrong with that.

Later
Own room, Bellagio

Oh, hell. Was just picking a piece of imaginary lint off of Chris's perfect cheekbone (really? really? who ever gets lint on their cheekbone? when they've been sitting by a pool? and have just come out of said pool? come *on*, Marty) when Stafford came by, all strutty.

I could swear he pulled himself up a bit taller when he saw us. He nodded at Chris and gave him a big handshake and then winked—*winked!*—at me. The gerbils in my brain were working overtime. Something was about to go amiss. I started packing up, hoping to avoid too much interaction between Chris and Stafford.

Sure enough, Stafford said, "*Great* meeting the other day, Marty. I do *so* miss seeing you in the early mornings."

Oh, geez. I mean, who does that? It was like I was in the middle of some kind of testosterone war, and I was waiting to see who was going to whip out the bigger you-know-whatsit.

Brain gerbils were spinning madly in alternating directions on their wheel, careening between *Act indignant!* and *Stand there with your mouth open!* I shrugged at Chris. "We used to date. That's why he's being such a silly-willy," I said, mock-punching Stafford on the arm. Kind of mock-punching. Okay, a little harder than mock.

"Ah." Chris looked from me to Stafford and back again.

Stafford winked at Chris now. What the frick? "Don't let her get too close now, Chris. I got too close, and I ended up hiring her!"

I think Chris's pupils dilated a bit.

"But, no, in all seriousness, she's lovely, isn't she?"

Chris made some kind of vague *uh huh* positive noise, and then he focused on a spot in the distance and pretended he saw a familiar face, just to change the subject.

What the what? I still can't figure it out. I told Stafford firmly (okay, my voice was shaking a little) that we were all going to be late for the first big group dinner if we didn't get a move on.

Now am really going to be late. Oh well! Fashionably late? Yes.

May 11, 7:30 a.m.
Own room

Oh, man, oh man. I can't believe what happened last night at dinner. Am so embarrassed.

It was already feeling bad. I was wearing my best, my prettiest dress, the one Jody says stops the room, but I could tell Chris wasn't having any of it. He kept on looking away from me, and when he did catch my eye, it was only to meet me with one of those tight-lipped, worky smiles, you know the kind, like you've just met the person and you're not sure of them.

Maybe that's it. Maybe he's not sure of me. Ooh, I wish I were the kind of girl to give Stafford a real talking-to. We were doing just fine until Stafford came along. I mean, what was he thinking? Maybe he was trying to warn me. Maybe he was trying to make sure we stayed professional. Whatever it was, it definitely made Chris frosty-icy-cool.

Like, okay, so I finally get a clear line to Chris, working my way through all the clients we've invited out to Vegas, getting high off the energy. When I get to him I bump him with my shoulder.

"Oof," he says, kind of awkwardly.

"Hiya," I say, and "Howzit?" and already I'm kicking myself for talking like a comic strip.

"How are your other clients?" he says, taking a step back.

I take one back too. I know when I'm being told to back off, and it feels like crap. It's, like, embarrassing and angry-making all at the same time, especially when you know it's something you've done *and* you can pin it on someone else. I wish Stafford were around to glare at.

"They're okay," I say. I try one last time, trying to project all sorts of sincerity. "But you guys are the only ones that really matter this week, you know that, right?"

"Sure, Marty," he says, and I think he sounds kind of sad.

I see Stafford swooping in like a bird of prey, or—okay, more like that big chandelier in *The Phantom of the Opera*, when it finally comes crashing down on all those partygoers. He's larger than life, in his element, and he says, "Chris! Marty! Together again!"

"As usual!" I say, bumping Chris again with my shoulder, only I've forgotten we've each taken a step back and almost fall over. Chris catches me by the elbow. Hardly warm.

"Oops! Don't get too close now, Marty! No saleswoman ever closed a deal by being too pretty or too attractive, right, Chris?"

"Right, Stafford." Chris sounds like he's just barely able to be civil, and I'm trying to quell the rising panic in my chest as I see my pages slipping away with what I think is the diminishing interest in Chris's voice.

"Chris?"

He shakes his head, and my hand off his arm. "I should go see what Marcus and Elroy are doing. Be back later," he says, and leaves me with Stafford.

Stafford is chuckling. *Chuckling!*

"What do you think you're doing, Stafford?" I'm livid, but I'm trying to keep my voice down.

"Take it easy," he says. "I'm just reminding you to keep it professional, is all."

I can hardly breathe. "Keep it professional! You're the one who suggested I use my feminine wiles to close the deal!"

"Don't be ridiculous," he snaps. "I'd never have suggested such a thing." He really does look surprised, and I keep my mouth shut. Now I'm trying to remember exactly whose idea it was and it's just making me more frustrated. "Look," he says, "all I'm saying is, you've come this far; let's not screw it up with anything extraneous, okay? Close the deal, Marty. Then we'll both be happy." He lifts the corners of his lips in a smile—I think?—winks again, and waves over my shoulder at someone else. "Gotta go," he says. "Go do something good."

It sounds reasonable. But god, did he have to be such a jerk about it? After that, dinner was all pins and needles and me keeping an eye on Chris with every course. I *think* he warmed up by the end, but I also think that was probably the bottle service. We like to pull out the stops for these events.

Anyway. Gotta go. Time to meet everyone down on the floor. Today's the big selling day. Today's the day Marcus and Elroy get to see the magazine's demographic in full flood. If the convention doesn't knock this out of the park, I don't know what else I can do, especially now that it seems my, uh, feminine wiles are out of the game.

Same day, 11:34 a.m.
Sands Convention Center, Exhibit Hall C, bathroom

Oh, god. Must compose self. Things not going well at all.

They started out okay. Well, on one end, anyway. Chris met me at breakfast, just like we'd agreed. I had to show him my game plan to show Marcus and Elroy the floor. Wanted to make sure they saw the advertisers who were exhibiting that are on scale with Irving Liquors. I was feeling pretty smug, kind of like cruise ship directors must always feel when they have excellent plans on tight timetables.

I wore my best summery linen pantsuit, which was a total *chore* to pack, by the way. You gotta roll a linen suit. It's not going to arrive looking anywhere close to decent otherwise, not even in one of those silly suit carriers.

I know Chris noticed, because he kind of lit up when he saw me. He even leaned in for a little buss on the cheek! Distinctly flirty again. Ridiculously happy-making and also confusing. Maybe he decided we make a better team if he's not playing Ice God?

I don't know. I didn't care. After last night's confusion, I would've been happy with a change in either direction, so long as I had a better idea of what was happening.

Elroy and Marcus met us after their own breakfast meeting, right on time, and we all went over to Sands to see the show.

I could feel Marcus and Elroy looking at me as we walked over. They were sizing me up, or something. I tried to look as professional as possible, even if I did get a little hot and bothered when Chris guided me around corners by my hip, maybe leaving his hand there a little longer than was strictly necessary.

So. Sands. I knew Marcus and Elroy had never seen anything like it. Imagine! Twenty-five thousand excited folks over fifty, fully aware that everything in these huge exhibition halls is catered to them. A good number of the exhibitors are advertisers in *Retirees' Review*, and the noise is more than you might think for some demure people verging on senior and the folks who want their money.

It's Vegas, so there are Elvis impersonators standing around, and Lucille Ball lookalikes. Marilyn Monroes are a dime a dozen. Marcus and Elroy, though, are more interested in the attendees, like the huge group of motorcycle mamas and their beaus, fresh off their Harleys, leathers over their arms and looking like they want to spend some money on dream vacations, gifts for their grandkids, second homes, RVs, or, even better, monthly wine clubs.

Chris and I take Marcus and Elroy around all the big booths, and I see Chris pointing out to them the vibrancy of the people who are here, milling around—*Every single one of them is a subscriber*, I overhear him saying, and *We want these people to know we're thinking of them. It's too big a demographic to overlook. We'll be the first advertiser of this type in the magazine, ever.* I know these lines because I fed them to him. He sells the magazine better than I can, almost.

But then it happens. Chris looks at me, excited and grinning, and he absolutely *beams* at me, so warmly that I feel like it's just the two of us in this huge convention hall. (Reasonably sure I blush.)

And then I see Marcus and Elroy exchange a worried look. And then, when Chris is busy greeting someone he knows from the Ad Club for Men, or whatever, I see Marcus pull Elroy aside, and I sidle close enough to hear him say it.

It: "I'm not sure Chris has our best interests in mind here."
Shit.

Must go. Have been in here way too long for "just a visit to the powder room." Better get back.

```
Later
Own room
```

So the scene went something like this:

Scene: Bellagio coffee shop
Setting: MARTY, *at a table all by herself, looking glum.*
STAFFORD *walks by the window and spots her. He waves.*
MARTY *flaps her hand at him.*
STAFFORD *stops short, checks watch, enters coffee shop.*
   Takes seat across from MARTY.
STAFFORD: Hi?
MARTY: Hi.
STAFFORD *looks around.*
STAFFORD: No Chris? Marcus and Elroy?
MARTY: Tour of Hoover Dam.
STAFFORD: Ah, right. I'm almost afraid to ask why you're
   looking so sad. Is it because Chris isn't nearby?
MARTY *narrows her eyes.*
STAFFORD *holds up his hands.*
STAFFORD: Okay, okay, sorry. Just trying to make you
   smile.
MARTY: Please stop.
A moment of silence.
STAFFORD: Seriously, what's the matter?
MARTY *swallows.*
MARTY: I think I really screwed up, Stafford.
STAFFORD: Oh, dear. What is it?
MARTY: I overheard something that feels like they're
   not going to give it to us.
STAFFORD gets out his smart phone and starts typing.
MARTY: Oh, come on, Stafford, I'm serious. Put away
   your phone and pay attention, okay?
STAFFORD *waves his phone at her.*
STAFFORD: I'm taking notes, Marty. (*beat*)
MARTY: Oh. (*She swallows.*) Sorry.
STAFFORD: (*impatient*) Well? What did they say? And
   who?

MARTY: Elroy and Marcus think Chris is trying to sell them on our pages just so he can get in good with me.

STAFFORD stops typing.

STAFFORD: Oh, for fuck's sake.

MARTY: I'm sorry.

STAFFORD: What did you say to that?

MARTY: Nothing, I just overheard it. They don't know I overheard.

STAFFORD: Well, what happened after that?

MARTY: I just took them around the rest of the floor, like we'd planned. And I tried to stay as far away from Chris as possible.

STAFFORD: Do you think it's salvageable?

MARTY: I dunno. They felt—guarded. Maybe you could—

STAFFORD: What? What do you think I could do?

MARTY: Well, maybe if I take myself out of the equation—maybe if they're just dealing with you—

STAFFORD: You're asking me to close your deal for you? I presume you still want the commission?

MARTY: I just need you to help me a little bit.

STAFFORD: Okay, first of all, I wouldn't dream of taking your commission from you, or even credit for the thing. You're my salesperson, and you deserve the credit. But Marty—

MARTY: Anything, Stafford. What?

STAFFORD: If this thing works, you must promise me that you won't see Chris.

MARTY is silent.

STAFFORD: I'm serious, love. You can't see him socially, okay? It would be awkward.

MARTY: Okay, fine.

END SCENE

Am on tenterhooks. And also a little bit heartbroken, because I've started thinking of Chris a little bit more than I ought to have been thinking of him lately, anyway.

Typical.

Anyway. I'm going to sleep. Have to see to other clients tomorrow. Must somehow keep mind off of Irving, failed deal, own *huge* part in failure.

One great thing about lying my head off to my mother: she never needs to know what a total hash job I've made of this whole endeavor.

May 11/12, midnight? 1:00 a.m.? Dunno
Own room

Really really bad nightmares.

Stafford, in his best suit, the dark gray one with the pinstripes, chasing me on a broomstick. Chris, flying away on another broomstick, equally fast. Me, on a broomstick with a really rotten, really loud engine (???). And—typical!— Mama, waving tapery-type fingers topped off by long, glittery nails and chanting bizarre incantations that seemed to jerk my broomstick here and there. God, how obvious can I *get?*

Why does everything I do turn out wrong?

Maybe it's ridiculous to want more. Maybe I'm like Eliza Doolittle, wanting above her station. Maybe my desired station is way above my paygrade, like they say; maybe a little shopfront of my own, making a select clientele happy, no matter how small, is always going to be too far out of reach.

I didn't think it would be so hard to get there. Lord knows it's not so hard to imagine. Picture it: a narrow place, with a loft for storage, not one of those scary cellars that opens onto the street that unwitting passersby can fall into. Fabric and trimmings everywhere, neatly displayed, and a big worktable in the back where people can consult with me on whatever they want designed. I'd only work with a few customers at a time, so I could better pay attention to their needs, and I'd hire a good seamstress, one who knew what she was doing and who's better than me. Together, we'd give people the skin they needed to become someone else, if even for just one night of pretending.

The clientele can be tiny. I don't care. They'll only hear about me by word of mouth. I can see it: well-heeled types who maybe already attend masquerade balls and big benefits, talking to one another: "What are you wearing to the big 'do' next month? Really? Not yet? Well, have you *been* to Marty's place? You *must* go. She made me so happy. But don't tell everyone, and you'd better book her now—she's *terribly* busy."

It seems to be all slipping away, bit by very little bit. I waited around all night for Stafford to come back to me with details, but it didn't happen. He swooped Marcus and Elroy out for dinner—dinner with the publisher is always a big winner, and that was four—five?—hours ago.

Chris is out with a friend. I'm not jealous or anything, but the waiting is killing me.

I only just had to ask Stafford for help last week, didn't I? I can't do anything right.

Maybe my mother is right to worry. Maybe I really can't do anything properly. Maybe I need to be looked after, every possible turn I take.

No wonder she makes herself crazy thinking about me.

No wonder I make her so sad. And she doesn't even know the half of it.

May 12, 7:30 a.m.
Own room

Oh, joy! Just got text from Stafford. It seems deal is back on right side of the tracks. Looks like I'll get my twelve pages after all.

Although—Chris. Meh.

In fact, very sad.

Same day, 8:06 p.m.
M. Fina, bathroom

Thank goodness for bathrooms. What would I do without them?

We just had our monthly over-cocktails sales meeting. I was hoping Stafford wouldn't want to say too much about the Irving deal, since I had to be bailed out, but I ought to have known better. Anyway, when I asked him if we could be on the DL about it, he said that it'd be good for morale if the rest of the crew heard that the newest salesperson had closed a most elusive account. I was still hoping he'd be a little bit discreet about the thing, but—no.

It was like a Friar's Club roast, actually: People laughed, and I laughed, or at least I did a reasonable approximation of it, but—oh, here:

Scene: Monthly sales review
Setting: Bar at M. Fina's
PERSONAGES: STAFFORD, MARTY, REST OF *Retirees' Review* SALES STAFF

Glasses clinking, general bonhomie. STAFFORD stands up and taps his glass for attention. Down the table a stretch, MARTY presses her lips together and white-knuckles her glass.

STAFFORD: Well, we are in a most appropriate place to celebrate this month's Big Win. Look around you! Here we are, in Vegas, at the nation's largest convention for our magazine's demographic. We're in the place where nothing seems impossible and everything seems within reach, and, perhaps most important, we're in *a bar.*

Cheers erupt; widespread drunkenness seems inevitable. STAFFORD bangs on table for attention.

STAFFORD: Marty, will you please join me at the head of the table?

MARTY smiles weakly and goes to join Stafford. Someone hoots; someone else yells, "MARTY and STAFFORD, sittin' in a tree!" General laughter.

MARTY: (*internally*) This can't be happening. It's okay. Just put one foot in front of the other; it'll all be over soon.

STAFFORD grins and takes her hand. More hooting from the crowd.

STAFFORD: Our girl here, in her year with us, has never closed a deal as large as this. We've never had this account even come close before. But due to Marty's hard work, and her extremely close working relationship with Chris Lincoln, the account's primary gatekeeper, we're proud to announce that Irving Liquors has agreed to a full year's worth of back-cover advertisements!

Stunned silence from the group.
STAFFORD barrels on.

STAFFORD: What a humdinger of a deal, folks. A big hand all around for Marty, who most definitely didn't sleep her way to the top on this one!

A beat, then finally cheers and laughter all around. MARTY's grin looks like a rictus.

MARTY: (*internally*) Holy *fuck*. I cannot believe what he's saying.

STAFFORD: But wait, there's more! We know our Marty is multi-talented, and we know she has other fish to fry in this life of hers, but because of the enormousness of this deal, she's decided to stay on for a while longer, just to make sure we can maintain the smooth path this deal has taken to reach its brilliant apex. Three cheers for Marty!

MARTY: (*internally*) No. No. No. Please don't.

MARTY takes a step toward STAFFORD and almost gets her hand on his arm, but it's too late.

STAFFORD: Hip hip, hurrah! Hip hip, hurrah! Hip hip, hurrah!

EVERYONE cheers. Marty looks like she's discovered a hairball in her throat.

Ugh. I know, right???

Because that's when it hit me. I am going to be stuck here, with this bunch of jokers, for at least the next few months. I'm going to have to work with these people who already think I was hired under weird circumstances whispering about the way I closed this deal. And Stafford—Stafford will look like the perfect gentleman, on the outside, but I will always know that Stafford stepped in to close the deal at least partly because Stafford. Likes. To. Win. At *everything*.

I did the math: I can just sock away the bonus and commission money into an account and not use it until I can dedicate full time to the shop.

It *looks* like good news. Part of me thinks it *is* good news. It's just—not *exactly* what I wanted. Or exactly *how* I wanted it to happen. Or even remotely close to what I told Mama was going to happen.

Must go. I can hear people moving into the dinner space. Gah.

May 13??? Def. May 13, though sometime after midnight???
Own room

Haha!!! Kissy Chris is in my bathroom!!

Hahahaha Stafford.

Am shit-faced. Is okay. Am deserving woman! Am spearheader of deals! Am now high-profile sales executive with fat bonus. *Am winner. Am celebrating!!*

Ooo. Chris just flushed. Better go pay attention to him. Hee hee!

May 13, 7:00 a.m.
Own room

WTF happened last night?

And *why is Chris sleeping in the armchair???*

OMG.

Later

Chris just left. The news is not good. Apparently I am a complete and total nincompoop. Apparently I:

- Drank something like three whiskeys in the space of an hour and then followed with wine through dinner.
- Flirted like a sex-starved woman with at least four men, one of whom was not even part of our group and had wandered in accidentally.
- Shrieked, "Fresh meat!" upon seeing said person, who Chris says was not even attractive. Is okay, because apparently I also frightened off the fresh meat.
- Ignored Stafford to the point of being rude.
- Ate off my neighbor's plate.
- Eventually decided to home in on Chris (big surprise there).
- Yammered about the importance of dress and costumes in eighteenth-century French society and how they contributed to class discrimination. Whaaaaat?
- Also yammered about the great deals one can get at fabric stores.

46

- And where to shop for patterns.
- Apparently became so drunk that Chris and Stafford had a confab—*I know!*—and agreed I should be escorted upstairs. Chris did the honors.
- Also apparently after I'd written the above awesomeness about Chris being in the bathroom waiting to be attended to, I passed out.
- Snoring.

I can't believe it. What a wreck. Our very last meal with the clients before we send them home is the big luncheon coming up in—eep!—an hour. I'm both dying and terrified to find out what everyone else saw. At the very least I need to get downstairs and apologize to Stafford straightaway: Chris says Stafford worked really hard to keep Marcus and Elroy as far away from me as possible, not that that could have been too hard, since I was very good at throwing "Go to hell" vibes in Stafford's general direction. Ugh!

Feel very guilty for having been rude to him even if he does say stupid things. (All self-help books say acknowledging one's weaknesses is a key marker on the road to recovery—from what? I don't know.)

Oh. Also apparently sent Jody a drunk text. Is unintelligible. Something about being a winner.

God! Can you imagine if Mama ever found out about this? She'd probably have a heart attack. At the very least, she'd go entirely off the rails, and everyone would blame me. (I think I had a dream about this one night last week. It was me, standing in front of a one-cell building with padded interior and exterior, with Mama in it, screaming obscenities from the barred window. I stood outside, trying to balance the big plastic red *A* that had grown out of the top of my head, while the entire sales staff gathered around me waving oversized pointy pencils, screaming, "Shame! Shame! Shame!" It was fantastic.)

They wouldn't be wrong, either.

For once, just for once, I'd like to do something without considering my mother. I mean, for fuck's sake. I am in *Las Vegas*. She is in *New York*. And I work in *sales*. People in sales get shit-faced every day!!!

My mother would say, "You should know better," and "We raised you better than that."

She'd be right, too. Worse than my having zero recollection of what actually happened last night, I have no idea how I let myself get so schnockered at a work function. I mean, deals get closed at these events. We represent the company at these things. Our clients see us at these things!

God. This is the equivalent of a hostess getting hammered at her own party.

Plus, getting obliterated on the company's dime never feels very dignified.

TLPAY says to not beat yourself up over things in the past, even if you're fully aware those things were your fault, but this is beyond the pale.

I'd better eat something and get going. I feel the beginnings of a slow hangover coming on. You know the type—the kind that burns all day long? Flying back to New York tomorrow morning isn't going to be fun for either me or anyone sitting next to me. Ugh.

Still May 13, Longest Day on the Planet, 11:42 a.m.
Own room

Feel as if have been awake forever. Feel simultaneously old in epically world-weary way and also stupid in manner of wet-behind-the-ears naif.

Overall, want to die.

Also, am so sick of this room by now but cannot show face anyplace else. All self-help books say that writing shit down helps. I am hoping this is true. God knows I can't possibly get any lower than I am now.

I chewed up two Advils right before I got out of bed, hoping to fend off the hangover. There isn't any grape soda on the room service menu, so I ordered the next-best hangover cure: gobs of virtuous-looking foods. Cobb salad, for variation on nutrients! An extra-large orange juice, for fluid! Eggs and oatmeal, for protein and fiber, apparently.

While I was waiting for the food I hopped into the shower and turned it on as hot as I could stand it, imagining I was burning all the booze fumes off my body and steaming them out of my pores, and then, feeling very slightly better, I came out all pink and scrubbed and somewhat cleansed and tried to get ready, only I had to sit down while I was putting on my makeup because my head kept on threatening to explode if I stood for very long, and that funny face women make—you know, where you make that idiotic *O* with your mouth while you're doing your mascara and look down your nose at your reflection?—made me nauseated and dizzy. Very annoying.

I ate like a horse when the food came, and not even in any organized order, either, which may, on further thought, have been the root of the problem.

Then I thought maybe I should get the blood moving, and I did some jumping jacks, and when I thought I looked healthier, and not covered in blotchy post-boozing pale patches, I got dressed and went down.

The elevators. At the Bellagio. OMG. I think they bonded the paint there to old-lady perfume and then turned off the ventilation. My reflection in the mirror looked peaked. I closed my eyes. Biiiig mistake. Newsflash: The movement of an elevator, especially a speedy Las Vegas elevator, is not one that is natural to the human body.

I quick opened my eyes again, just as the thing jerked to a stop and the doors slid open, and lurched out the doors into more old-lady-perfumed air, but at least in a bigger space.

Wobble, wobble, down the hallway and following the crazy-ass patterned carpet (1970s-ish brown floral and checkered and maybe even paisley nonsense) down to Jasmine, and finally through the double glass doors and into the bright, searing, ouch-ouch-too-much sunlight of the main restaurant floor.

Whoever said greasy Chinese food is an excellent hangover cure never had eggs, oatmeal, Cobb salad, and jumping jacks on top of it. I started seeing blue spots once I hit the buffet.

And then I spot Chris, who lifts his eyebrows at me and then pulls them way up: *Are you okay?* God, I could love that man. I give him a tiny, tiny nod, so as not to rattle any remaining brain cells. Salesperson training takes over and, totally independent of any will on my part, my head starts rotating, scanning the room, looking for my clients. There are Kathy and Jeff from La Petite Shoppe de Vitamines.

There's the RV account guy, Rick. There's Marcus and Elroy, headed for Chris—good, I don't think they see me yet—and oh, finally, there's Stafford.

Stafford is with someone. Who is Stafford with? Oh, *fuck*—Stafford is with Captain Military himself, the scion of the Irving family, the head honcho with the deal-killing Sword of Doom. And Stafford has seen me. Holy caca. This guy—this guy with the dinky broomsweep of a mustache; this guy with the razor creases in his pants; this guy with the white hair and the suit cut for a twenty-five-year-old on his mid-fifties, military-precision body—this guy is headed straight for me, guided by Stafford.

This guy—this guy cannot see me. This guy, who knows booze like the back of his hand, is going to smell the day-old Irving whiskey on me, eggs and oatmeal and OJ and Cobb salad and jumping jacks and hot-ass shower notwithstanding. This guy is an old hand, and can probably parse a hangover right down to the very hour you became drunk—and then hungover.

Worse, I am incapable of anything but hungover babbling. My hands are already shaking.

I am in deep shit if our vectors manage to cross, and so I execute the only evasion tactic I know:

I pretend not to see them.

I turn right around and go upstairs, in a maneuver I'm sure Mister Military would admire if only I were not so evasive that he didn't even see me.

Except now I'm convinced I can't be sure he hasn't seen me. And I already know Stafford has seen me.

I feel like crap. But I am going to have to go back downstairs.

Worse, I am going to have to do the stupid Vegas-elevator-ride-of-nausea all over again.

Day That Will Not End, 1:31 p.m.

Ohhh. God. It's worse than it could ever have been if I'd never gone back down there. I feel incredibly Victorian: battling dramatic disease while also having to combat symptoms of hysteria.

Deep breaths, now, deep breaths. Could try to meditate (*Meditation for the Rest of Us*, New York Public Library book sale, $1), but my brain is in way too high a gear.

So. I went back downstairs. Soldiered on (read: held breath; closed eyes) in stuffy old-lady-smelling, vertigo-inducing elevator, and went back into restaurant. Brain gerbils thought it'd be smart to make Stafford come find me, so I immediately started speaking to the first person who crossed my path, the magazine's editorial director. She was already deep in conversation with another sales person, who in turn made a nasty face at me. I didn't care.

Could sense Stafford getting closer and somehow decided more evasion was called for. I took a couple of steps to the right after hurried goodbye to editorial director. Inserted self in conversation with—oh. With buffet table. Faaaaack.

Now have trapped self in *V* between buffet table and drinks (ugh!) table and have run out of places to go. Stafford and Markham approaching. Blue spots start to appear in my line of sight, just like ambulance lights. (Christ, what I wouldn't have given for a medical emergency!) I blink hard, once, twice, feeling the sweat start to break out under my armpits and the sleek black silk shirt with the bell sleeves I've chosen to wear—why silk? is hot! why bell sleeves? are hard to maneuver!—and then they're there, in front of me, and then I am barfing.

Barfing! Yes! Barfing!

Holy shit am I barfing, a great torrent of eggs and Cobb salad and oatmeal and OJ—I imagine I can see each of the colors of each of the foods I have consumed that day, and what color would jumping jacks be?—

I see the stuff all over my sleeve, which I've thrown in front of my mouth to—what? Catch the stuff in the bell?— and all over Markham's perfect suit, and then, finally, all over his—yes! yes! it's true, now they really are—spit-shined shoes.

Faaaaaaaaack, faaaaaaaaaack.

I want to black out. I do, I do.

But I never get my wish lately, do I? So I don't. I stand there, dripping, smelly, feeling annoyingly clearheaded and clear of bile.

I hear Markham sigh. I can't bear to look at him.

Stafford—Stafford says nothing. Stafford is free of my effluvia.

Stafford closes his eyes and a consternated line appears between his brows, but I think even that is calculated. Stafford opens his eyes and he points one staffer—the staffers here are in mock Mandarin outfits, can you believe that?—to one side of him and another to another side and one of them whisks Captain Markham away.

The other pinches my elbow, standing as far away from me as possible, and pinch-guides me into a dark, dark bathroom, where I can rinse myself a little bit and Think About What I Have Done.

I stay there for a while, rinsing myself.

A single rap at the door.

"It's Stafford," says a voice just the wrong side of cool.

I open the door a crack.

"Okay?" he says.

I nod.

"Go to your room," he says. *Bad dog.* "I'll send for you."

Which is where I am now. Which is where I should have stayed to begin with.

They sent me up in the freight elevator, by the way. Better all around.

Day That Will Not End, 3:06 p.m.
Own room

When I got into my room, I got into the shower with all my clothes on. Eventually I took off all my clothes and scrubbed myself really good, but I still couldn't get the smell of vomit out of my nostrils.

I am thinking that maybe I imagined the words I thought I heard Markham say just as the mock-Mandarin-coated person guided me out of the room.

I am thinking I only *imagined* him saying to Stafford, "Jones, I will not have the Irving name aligned with that woman."

But even if I could convince myself of this, I know I didn't imagine the look on his face, the one that says, "What a wreck of a human, a catastrophe," and, perhaps more clearly,

"How did I ever land myself in this person's orbit?" and then, "Get me out of here."

I know this look. I saw it in high school, when I was auditioning for a part in *Arsenic and Old Lace*. As I left the house to audition, Mama shot me a look and then illustrated it with some choice words: "They don't want you, you know. They want blonde, they want white, they want Marilyn, they want Elizabeth Taylor. They won't want you."

In high school drama productions, they want people to succeed, and so when it was my turn to audition, they gave me a small cloche hat with a demure half-veil, maybe the better to hide my sloped eyes and straight black hair, and thus allow me to feel a little bit more a part that had been played time and again by Marilyns and Elizabeths and Courtneys.

I think some part of me must have realized then what power a small thing like an old ratty cloche hat can have. I lost myself more easily in the character than I did practicing the lines in front of my mirror, or even with Dana from English Lit class, and the words came more easily, loosely. A part of me became sweet Elaine Harper, the only young woman in the cast. Part of me understood her better. And part of me rejoiced that such a small item could loan such freedom, if only temporarily.

I finished my audition, with no real expectations, but they did want me for Elaine, after all.

Later, as rehearsal after rehearsal went by, and opening night came and went, and then our run of four productions, and Mama never turned up in the audience, I finally begged her to come to our final show, and there, there it was, that same look I'd seen on Markham, that pitying destructor of a look, and then her accompanying verbal judgment: "Why would I pay to see an Asian girl in the role of a young white girl? Ridiculous."

In Taiwanese, "stupid" and "ridiculous" both sound like they're tinged with pity. Translated literally, the phrase for "ridiculous" is closer to "I'ma laugh so hard my mouth is gonna explode right off my face and blow up in yo' face" than just the simple one-word treatment it gets in English.

In my small life, I am forever reimagining things. Would it have been different if I had landed a starring role in that high school play? Would she have come to see me then? And, later that night, after I'd returned from the wrap party and I was kneeling on the floor, shielding myself from the slaps and kicks that came because I'd ostensibly told Mama I was coming home right after the play, instead of after the wrap party, I'd wonder if it really would have made a difference if I was an A-list star and she were afraid to leave hand-shaped marks on my cheeks.

Not, I decided. It would not have made a difference. But that doesn't stop a girl from hoping, from freshman year of high school all the way into freshman year in college, and then, finally, all the way up until the ugly reality that is the life I'm looking at right now.

God, won't this headache go away?

And where the hell is Stafford?

Maybe I'll call him.

Later

It rang once and then went to voicemail, and then a text came almost right back:

Just wait.

I know: I will charge downstairs in an incredibly indignant mood. Is always a good thing, the indignant move. I've seen lots of sitcom episodes resolve themselves this way: If you believe something to be so, it sometimes turns out to be so, just for you.

Hm. Feel have read this somewhere: If you wish for a BMW, it will somehow come to you. But you have to really feel it: the supple leather, the slick enamel paint, the weird combination rumble-roar that a Bimmer's engine makes.

So maybe if I wish that I had never gotten so drunk that I can't even remember what happened, it might come to pass that this was all one ugly nightmare. I will have awakened and I will have a big fat deal under my belt and I can quit and then Chris and I will go to dinner at Chez Eux in Paris. Of course I will have also miraculously opened a little shopfront à la *The Shop Around the Corner*, probably in the 5th arrondissement, of course, which will obviously be frequented by Bridget-Bardot-status-type people, just as my mother decides that she should pop in for a visit.

So picture this: Me, charging downstairs, in non-barf-stained new outfit. Me, pointing a finger at Stafford and saying something witty yet cutting, like:

HEY, YOU. EXCESS CONSUMPTION OF ALCOHOL NOTWITHSTANDING, WE BOTH KNOW I'M THE BEST DAMNED SALESPERSON YOU'LL EVER HAVE. NO ONE ELSE COULDA CRACKED THIS NUT.

Then I will say something self-effacing like:

SO A GIRL CAN'T HOLD HER BOOZE. SO WHO ISN'T ALLOWED TO MAKE A MISTAKE EVERY ONCE IN A WHILE?

And then I will follow that up with something really ballsy, like pointing at Markham and saying,

YOU DON'T HAVE THE GUTS TO WALK AWAY FROM THIS DEAL. YOU NEED US TO BREAK THESE GRAYHAIRS. YOU WANT THE PEOPLE WHO READ THIS MAGAZINE, AND YOU KNOW IT.

Ohnevermind. I'm doomed. Doomed.

Later

Chris just called. Was too embarrassed to pick up phone. Couldn't stand to think he might want to yell at me. Or worse, be kind.

By now rumors must be spreading like fungus, even if he didn't get to see my gastric explosion himself.

Oh, hell. He didn't leave a message. Must have just been calling to yell at me. Or something. Oh, god, what if I've really screwed up *his* career too?

May as well stay here for a few days. Then maybe will become Vegas legend or musical: *The Displaced Recluse*, or *The Vegas Hermitess*, or some such likeness.

Later

The Language of Paying Attention to YOU says it's a good idea to take a self-inventory once in a while. Seems like a good exercise. I am supposed to rate my perceived success in each category from 1 to 5, with 5 being wildly satisfied.

- Platonic relationships: Let's see. Angry at best friend; cannot comprehend own mother: 0.
- Romantic relationships: Have slept with boss; primary desired dating prospect is, at best, off limits: 0.

- Career: −1.
- Environment: Am locked in expensive hotel room that I did not pay for: 3.

Am going nuts waiting for Stafford.

Day That Will Not End, 6:25 p.m.
Own room

I don't think I've ever been so royally fucked in my life.

7:45 p.m.
In cab

So Stafford finally gets back from dinner. He's sitting there, in my hotel room, on the poufy fancy easy chair they have in every Vegas room, it seems, and it's like we're a long-married couple having a conversation before heading out to dinner together, except for the tight line between Stafford's eyes again.

"Hear from Chris?" he says, like nothing's happened, like he's bantering with me.

I want to scream at him that maybe right now isn't the time to be the perfect businessman that we all *already know he is*, thank you, but instead I just look at the message light on my mobile phone and shake my head.

Stafford nods, one of those things you might call a "curt" nod, and leans forward, hands between his knees. I swear, do they teach you things like that in business school? *Deliver bad news by looking worried and concerned for the person's welfare, even if it sets off all the alarm bells in their head?*

I'm sitting on the bed, and I scoot all the way back, as far away from him as possible.

"We lost it, Marty."

I'm not really capable of parsing what this means, and the words are out of my mouth before I can stop them: "What did you lose? Can I help find it?"

The line between Stafford's eyebrows deepens, and he closes his eyes, as if he's finally, finally tired beyond belief. "Don't be daft, Marty. We lost the deal."

I go immediately light-headed. The blue spots are back in force, and I'm seriously glad I'm already on the bed, because I can't feel any of my limbs and I feel like I want to throw up again, only there's nothing left in my tummy to throw up. I gag and lie flat.

"Did you hear me, Marty?"

I'm shaking my head, but not because I don't hear him, only he thinks it's because I'm not only daft now, but also deaf, so he says it again. "Dammit, Marty, we lost the whole fucking deal, okay?"

I finally say something. "What happened?" *Idiot!* And then, "Is Chris going to be okay?"

Stafford tightens his lips. "Chris. You want to know about Chris."

"Oh, Stafford, just tell me."

"I told everyone you had the flu, but I'm not sure anyone believed me. Markham got taken straight to the washroom, to get cleaned up. Elroy came over, wanting to know what happened, so I gave him the same flu story. You know what he said? He said, 'Oh, please, Stafford. I'll tell Markham she had the flu if you like, but he's been around. He can see a hangover from a mile away.' And then he said something about Markham being more annoyed by people who are inconsiderate enough to spread disease than he is by sloppy drunks."

Stafford glances at me. I close my eyes, and he goes on. His voice sounds faraway, tinny. I get under the covers.

"So then he says, 'He won't want to work with your outfit, Stafford,' and that's when I know it's over."

I open my eyes. "Did Markham tell you that?"

Stafford shakes his head. "No. He sent for Elroy, and when Elroy came back, he told me Markham never wanted to hear from us again. And Chris—Chris is going to be fine. No one blames him for your indiscretion."

Jesus.

Stafford scoots closer and moves to the bed. He puts his hand on my shoulder, squeezes. "Marty, I have to let you go. It's really better if you can get back to New York tonight, don't you think?"

I nod. "I'm sure I can get a flight out tonight. I guess I'll see you on Tuesday, right, when you all get back?"

He laughs. It sounds light and a little silly and there's an unpleasant sensation in my brain, because the brain gerbils have glommed on to something I don't know yet, and then he says, "No, Marty, I mean I have to let you *go*. You're going to have to leave the company."

"What—" I say, but of course that's stupid, because it's the only thing that makes sense.

No job. No bonus. And probably not even a severance package, because no one will ever be able to say that this wasn't my fault.

Stafford didn't stay long after that. He left me with some new flight information and told me to put it on my corporate account, which won't be shut down until tomorrow.

So there you have it.

It's Monday tomorrow, but I won't be going to work.

What the fuck am I going to tell my mother???

Day That Will Not End, 8:30 p.m.
McCarran Airport

My brain is like a Dalí painting lately. Nothing seems to make any sense. Remember that crazy scene in *Spellbound*, with the random playing cards and the weirdo skiing? Yeah, that's about what it feels like. I don't know which is up or down.

I almost just called Mama for a ride home from the airport.

I think either Jody is getting to me or maybe I am just going stark raving mad or maybe I am actually still drunk, because by the time I got past the gate agent and through security and was sitting at my gate, all I wanted was my mother—maybe just *a* mother.

I executed every procrastination technique I know. (There's a self-help book on *that*, too, although I'm pretty sure it was meant to *stop* procrastination, not teach you ways to procrastinate. Oh well.) I used my phone to check on my bank accounts and spent some time freaking out, because there's really only enough in my accounts to hold me over for a couple of months, never mind putting anything down on that skinny little dream of a shopfront.

Never mind eating out, never mind seeing a movie, never mind even a $2 ice cream with Jody on the park bench. Heck, I'll be counting pennies getting into Manhattan from Queens before I know it.

Then I went to the bookstore, where the pile of business and leadership books only reminded me of how I couldn't buy them because I don't have any money.

Then I tried to call Jody, because I thought to myself, oh, Jody, Jody will be able to tell me something cheery, even if I do have to admit to her that maybe lying to my mother wasn't the best thing ever, except she doesn't pick up the phone, and then I remembered she's flown to Montana to cover some wolf biologist and his latest effort to get some definitive data on Yellowstone wolf cubs, or something. I ignored the invitation to leave Jody a voicemail and dialed my brother in Taiwan, thereby using up even more precious pennies, but who cared? I didn't have anyone else to talk to at the moment, but just as the thing rang for the second time, I realized that he lives on the other side of the world and can't *do anything* for me, even if talking to him might make me feel better.

And then some primordial part of my heart whispered that I should call my mother, because I remembered that day I was stuck at school, after a fight with boyfriend-I-was-dating-secretly-because-Mama-only-wants-me-to-date-other-Asians and he drove off and left me, and all my other friends had already gone.

That day I only had my mother to call, really, and I remembered what it was like, she feeling loose and happy because she'd been out to lunch with her friends instead of being left all alone in the house playing society wife with no events to plan, and how nice it had been to get into the car on an unseasonably hot late-May day, how solid and real the door felt, a barrier between me and boyfriend-failure. I remember even now the blast of air-conditioning, the supple leather under my legs; how Mama had Rachmaninoff's "Variations on a Theme of Paganini" blaring at top volume, like she was a punk version of a classical enthusiast, and how quickly I felt better, seeing her in such a good mood.

That day, she'd let me off lightly: "Only want to hang out with Mama when you need something, right?" and she threw a small smile at me, the crow's feet only then setting in and her teeth Chiclet-even, somehow perfect, notwithstanding the tiny sprig of green between her canine and incisor, left over from a salad lunch.

Maybe today could be the same.

But then I remembered I could write in this book and now the plane is boarding so I can't phone her anyway.

Close call.

NEW YORK

May 14, 7:00 a.m.
Own apartment

Day-after-hangover is possibly worse than the day of hangover, because you start remembering all the things you might have done right, instead of crash-and-burning. Also, crap red-eye flight makes everything worse.

I wish I could say it was nice to be back home again, but it's not. I'm looking around at my expensive little pad, trying to figure out what I can afford to part with, thinking about eBay and subletting and even renting out my living room, and thinking equally about what my next move is going to be.

I call Jody again. Straight to voicemail. Probably still on the plane back.

And then I open my email and there it is, the contract from work for me to sign that says that they are severing my employment due to "intentional misconduct"—ouch!—and that I agree to leave the company. Well, that's just what the doctor ordered, isn't it?

I close my laptop and wonder what to do next.

7:38 a.m.

I mean, I *could* go to Taiwan.

With Mama, I mean. Things *are* cheaper there. I could clear my head, try to manage a subletter from there, take the two weeks to regroup. And then come back and file for unemployment. Ha! Ha! Ha!

Oh, god.

Later

Chris called again. I let it go to voicemail.

But then Jody called.

Conversation went like this:

"Hi."

"Marty!" says Jody. She's sounding so thrilled to hear from me that my heart hurts. "Hi! I saw you called! I'm back! Just landed! Where are you? How did things go? I have something so exciting to tell you!"

I can't think of much to say, so I just grunt. I want to tell her to cool it with the exclamation points. Anyway, my silence seems to say enough, because Jody says, "Ohhhh nooo."

"Yeah, well."

There's a pause, and then Jody sighs. "Oh, Marty," and then she makes it worse. She says, "It could only have ended one way. That kind of lie never works out."

I can't think of anything to say at all—I am stunned that she can be so sanctimonious at a time like this, so I just stay quiet. On the line, the silence vibrates.

"Anyway," I finally say, "I'm batting around going back to Taiwan with my mother for a while."

Jody practically leaps down the airwaves into my apartment.

"Oh, Marty, is that what you really want?"

I tell her I don't think I have a choice, since I got fired.

There's a great vacuum on the phone line, then, and I am partially relieved that Jody seems to have finally *heard* me, but then she says, "That is a *crap* reason for going home to Taiwan. With your mother."

Jody is dying to find out why I got fired. I know this. But the connection is bad—it sounds like she's in a subway station—and sure enough, Jody says, "Oh, no. The train is coming. I can't hear you. Gimme an hour, okay? I'll be there in an hour, and I have something to tell you."

So now I'm waiting for Jody. Lately I am always waiting for people to Tell Me News. I think somewhere in one of my books it says that I must be a Protagonist, like characters in novels. Protagging is *hard*. Characters in novels never have it easy.

Where did that book go, anyway? I think I chucked it.

Later

You know, somewhere in one of my books (*Proactive Lists for the Low-Activity Procrastinator*, Kindle ebook, $1.99) it says that pro/con lists are a vastly underused tool for career guidance. I mean, I have no career, so maybe I'll just make a pro/con event guidance list. Here:

Event: Visit Taiwan with Mama

First, the pros:

- Escape New York
- See, stay with, friendly relatives (hang with brother!)
- Delish local cuisine
- Check out local costuming customs (bucket list)
- Avoid Chris
- Avoid impending doom
- Avoid New York

Uh.

Cons:

- Two weeks with Mama

Welllll.

Taiwan! Land of my birth! Land of a huge, friendly house—a compound, really—with friendly cousins visiting almost every day, and land where my brother lives now, land where my old-maid aunt lives and a land so different from where I am now—so different from where I'd be going back to—that maybe, just maybe, it could be a chance to start over.

Plus: No need to worry about possibly bumping into Chris and my colleagues and my former (!!!) clients on the street. No abject terror at having to knock around my expensive little apartment by myself while my money dwindles and I look for another depressing gig just to make it through the next few months.

Hm. Oh. Jody is here. Better put some pants on.

Later

So Jody just left. I'm reasonably sure I am now at my absolute lowest. I don't think snakes have bellies as low as I'm feeling now. Here's how it played out:

> CLICKING *heard from inside Marty's apartment. Someone is using a key to open the door.*
> MARTY *runs in from the bedroom, buttoning her jeans. She opens the door and* JODY *gets dragged in by the key she's been using to open the door.*
> JODY *leaves her keys in the door, drops her gigantic handbag and luggage on the floor, and hugs* MARTY.

JODY: Hello! I'm *so* excited to see you.

MARTY hugs her back, but doesn't say anything.

JODY pulls back and takes MARTY's face in her hands. Inspects her. Shakes her head.

MARTY: (*internally*) Wow, I must look like shit.

JODY pulls her key out of the lock, shuts the door with her foot, and picks up her handbag. She rummages through it, talking.

JODY: So, listen, this thing I hunted down for you.

MARTY is already turning away.

MARTY: Yeah?

JODY holds out a business card.

JODY: His name's Phil. He's starting an artist's workshop, and they're going to produce a series of one-act plays, and he needs someone to direct costume design for their first show.

MARTY: Hunh.

JODY peers at MARTY; waves business card at her.

JODY: Anyway, I told him all about you. He said you sound great! Plus, he likes me, so I talked him into it. It doesn't pay much, but you can stay with me and we can sublet your apartment and you'll have enough to get by with the stipend, right? It's...uh...

JODY excavates a notebook from her bag; riffles through it.

JODY: Four hundred dollars for the month. And, get this—here's the best part! He needs you to start *tomorrow!* You don't have to go to Taiwan!

JODY looks around for MARTY, who has retreated to the couch. She grins.

JODY: I mean, I was going to say, you could do this in your free time, after your day job, but you don't have one of those now, so this is perfect!

MARTY starts laughing hysterically. Meanly. Whatever.

JODY starts laughing along with MARTY, but then realizes they're not in on the same joke.

MARTY flaps her hand.

MARTY: Oh, wheee-ooo. Sorry. What was that you were saying about a crappy off-off-off-Broadway production with practically zero payback?

Jody blinks, turns away, closes her notebook.

JODY: (*Beat.*) You could brush up the résumé? Go back to illustration?

MARTY sighs, sounding deeply annoyed.

MARTY: No. I can't go backwards. That's stupid. And it's not what I wanted anyway.

JODY: You could—

MARTY: No. No. Just no.

Yyyeaaaah. It was like that. The rest of the conversation isn't worth recounting. Basically, I was an asshole while Jody was trying to be awesome, but I really could not see being happy at a tiny little dusty theater production. I mean, what the hell kind of job is that?

If Mama thinks owning my own shop is a cheap shot at life, what the hell would she think of me playing dress-up flunky to a cut-rate fleabag theater? God.

After that, Jody said "Fuck you" a couple of times, told me to call her when I got my head screwed on right, and then said she loved me and left.

Whatever. Am not going to speak to Jody until have got awesome success story in vein of opened-own-shop/big-contract-with-theater/celebrity-endorsement type success. Taiwan is the answer. I need a clean break.

(Gee, Marty, did you ever stop to think that your journalist friend might be good to keep around while you're launching this imaginary business of yours? Frick.)

Very, very sad. Luckily I have things to do. First of all, must notify Mama that am interested in going to Taiwan with her. Maybe should nap first, shore up energy.

No. Must get this cleared up. Otherwise am afraid will start to feel very stupid about not taking job with Jody-director-person.

Midnight, sometime between May 15 and Tomorrow-Is-Supposed-to-Be-Better
Eva Air flight BR 05

So Mama couldn't get a seat next to me. Probably a good thing, because I am really unsure of my footing around her now.

The Language of Paying Attention to YOU says one should admit when one has made a mistake. Well, I'm not doing that, because I don't think I've made a mistake. I am on a plane with Mama, and there is no point in looking back and regretting things. (That's from another book I can't remember now.)

So I called Mama after Jody left. Tried to be all natural and casual.

"Hi, Mama!" I say.

"What," she says, just like that, and my tiny resolve to be cheerful dies to zero.

"Ma," I say again, trying to keep from sounding pathetic, and add, "So I thought I'd go to Taiwan with you, if it's not too late. It will be fun!" And then I want to take back those last words, which I know are just a step too far, because I have never used the words "fun" and "with you" in the same breath.

And then she does the thing I really didn't want her to do, which is to feel immediately sorry for answering my phone call with a curt "What," *and* latch on to my over-exuberance, and she says, "Why you suddenly want to go somewhere with me?" And then, because she's really smart *and* really defensive, she says, to fill the blank space I leave hanging like a big, fat pomegranate for the picking, "What happened? You get fired? No one want you here anymore?" and I lose it and start crying, and tell her the truth.

All of it.

Oh, god, all of it.

I don't even think to stop and check what her reaction might be. I just talk, and talk, and talk, and toward the end there I really want to just hang up, because I can't stand to think that she might ruin it with what she says next.

It was the most I'd said to my mother about my life in nearly a decade.

I don't think I've ever been so absolutely utterly desperate for someone to talk to.

Also, I am tired of lying. Just a little bit. Not that Jody's right or anything. I still think you can get a lot done with a good lie, but that assumes you have something to lose, not that you are sitting at the rock bottom of a very deep hole, like yours truly.

Okay. So I've totally dumped all this information on her, right? And then part of me regains equilibrium—is that even a thing?—and there's this deep, dark silence on the phone line, and I start to think that maybe she's gone catatonic, or maybe she's just taking a moment to get ready to start screaming at me.

"Mama?"

And all she says is, "I knew it. Flight's at midnight tomorrow. Pack for two weeks. I'll get your ticket, since you obviously don't have any money yourself anymore. You can find your own way to the airport." And then she hangs up on me.

Part of me is wondering if she only switches to Taiwanese when she has something mean and snappy to say to me, or if I just make her so angry that she can't think of the English quickly enough. Either way, I think it's making me hate my own native language. Never mind. All I need to do now is get through the next twelve hours without Mama coming to see what I'm doing. The last time she peeked in my notebook, she paged through my drawings and then said something about drawing being for children. (Not that my notebook is filled with drawings lately, which might be part of the problem.)

Being in the air feels funny. It's like I'm not connected to anything, really. In another few hours we'll be in yet another time zone, winging over the Pacific Ocean, which, at that point, is so empty that there's no real need to count time zones unless you happen to live on one of those tiny little islands. I think only animals live there, and when was the last time an animal needed to know which time zone it's in?

My mama is nine rows up. She's in an aisle seat, too. I can see her, every once in a while, craning her neck to check on me. For this reason I keep my seat upright and my shoes on, just in case she finds something to complain about, like bad posture or slovenly behavior.

I don't even have anything glamorous like a sleep mask to slap on—I'm hoping she doesn't catch me snoring, with my mouth wide open and drool cascading down my chin, sleeping the sleep of someone who's just been through a really harrowing experience and suddenly finds herself in a position to not be a part of real life.

So I managed to get up the balls to call Stafford before our flight boarded. Well, I left a message at the office, anyway. I don't think he needs to hear in real time that I'm leaving the country to escape the shame.

Still May 15. Or maybe 16.
In-plane limbo, physical space limbo, between time zones

Also, emotional limbo: Cannot decide between indignant that have been fired and pathetic for getting self fired.

Gah. Last thing I remember is wishing for sleep and also hoping that my mother would also sleep. Because trying to stay awake to make sure she was asleep before I went to sleep was fucking tiring.

The dreams! I have to find that book on dream interpretation. Filled with weird aspirations and scary villains that made no sense whatsoever, but then again, since when did dreams ever really make sense? Still, these were equal parts things-I'd-like-to-happen and things-I-hope-never-happen.

Witness:

Chris and Stafford, duking it out with swimming-pool noodles and yelling things like "Marshmallow Fluff!" and "You'll never win her over with that kind of crap!"

or

Jody, whaling away at me with a burp gun. Like, I mean, beating me over the head and shoulders with it, not shooting Ping-Pong balls at me.

or

My little shopfront, on 30th Street in Astoria. The shelves are filled not with rolls of fabric, but with various types of bubble wrap. I'm behind the counter, wrapping a package in bubble wrap, when Captain Markham walks in and yells, "Off with her head!" to and about no one in particular. He's not even really looking at me. Then he leaves and I go on wrapping things, only this time it's a teakettle made of chestnuts and I'm wrapping it in a god-awful appliquéd fabric, because someone has requested a tea cozy.

What the hell. I don't even think I've ever seen a tea cozy in real life before. Only on episodes of *Miss Marple* or *Downton Abbey* or something.

But now that I'm awake, I'm thinking that things really are cheaper in Taiwan. And it's where I was born. And, on top of that, it's where I have all kinds of potential support, like my brother who's an art professor and my aunt who's a painter, that I didn't really have in New York. And my family is well-known in our town. I hear my brother and my aunt are popular, kind of celebrities, if you can have celebrities in a small place like Rueitai Township.

I might actually be able to lean on my family for a little bit, but I might not even need to, if I can manage to sublet my pad.

I mean, it's a lot easier to get a leg up in a small island nation than it is to get a leg up in New York, or, frankly, any place in the United States. If I can just manage to make my mother—

What? What am I thinking? If I can just manage to make my mother see that a boutique costume shop is still a good idea? If I can somehow make it over the barrage of verbal abuse that I just know is going to come my way before I even can get a foothold in this place?

And then there's "this place"—it's her place, right? She spent at least some of her adult life there, and it's her childhood home. Me? I left when I was five, and even a visit every other year isn't enough to make me feel as comfortable as she's going to be once we land, which means she'll be even looser-lipped than usual with her criticisms.

It'll be a rehash of so many other family visits, like the week my cousins were visiting us from Taiwan. I was eight. She threw a plate of eggs at me and then told me to eat them off the floor, like the dog I was.

And you know, I did it, too, until my cousins, who'd been in what I think was a shocked silence, said, "Okay, okay. You've made your point. We think that's enough. She knows you think she's a dog."

I wish I could remember what I had done wrong. Maybe if I had righted the ship at age eight, life now wouldn't be so hard. (Maybe I'd be able to add scrambled eggs back into my culinary repertoire.)

I'm too tired to think about this. I still think I need a nap. We have something like eight hours until we land still, and I'm really hoping I don't have any more psycho bizarre dreams—or, worse, any more unattainable daydreams.

I wonder if they have any of that freeze-dried ramen anywhere? I feel in the need of comfort food. Or maybe that's just the last remnants of my hangover talking.

P.S. The airline attendants on this airline need someone to redesign their outfits. They look like little old ladies. If it were me, I'd do a darker green, to offset the livery, and get rid of the pinstriping. I might do a light-blue ascot tie, to play off what would be obviously British racing green, to evoke the sky, and then I'd do something sharp and modern, like waistcoats and trousers, not those terrible 1970s-looking skirt suits and pink Hello Kitty aprons. Whose idea was *that?*

TAIWAN, Part I

I feel like one of those cartoon characters with the really bulgy, bloodshot eyes. My head feels fuzzy, and all of my clothing feels too tight on me.

We're finally here in the southern part of Taiwan, where Mama grew up. The place smells familiar to me, all mothballs and moss and wet concrete. They build everything out of concrete here, since the humidity is so out of control. Like, it's so out of control that even the Eastern Seaboard can't compare.

The weird thing is, all Taiwanese seem to be in love with leather furniture. I finally asked a family member about this once, and they said it had to do with leather being a total winner in terms of status symbols. I buy that. I mean, heck, there's a reason people buy leather jackets—but honestly, how much of a status symbol can you be if you're on the floor because you're sweating so much that you've slid off your sofa?

Then again, I've also noticed that my relatives here never seem to be sweating. They walk around in long-sleeved shirts and pants all the time here, and they always look perfectly comfortable. Ridiculous.

Eldest Cousin picked us up from the airport today. He said he happened to be "in town," but Taipei is a four-hour drive from Rueitai, so I'm skeptical. Still, he looked happy to see Mama, and surprised—duh—to see me.

Mama answered the question fast: "Had to drag her home. She's running away from New York," she said, before he could even say hello to me.

Eldest Cousin lifted his eyebrows at me. He has perfectly shaped eyebrows, au naturel, and when he uses them to make remarks, his expressions are oddly deliberate, as if they were complete sentences.

I opened my mouth, but Mama cut me off.

"You don't need to hear it from her, she'll just lie to you like she does to everyone."

Eldest Cousin turned red. For me, presumably. "Now, Auntie, I don't think that's right."

"I'll tell you the truth. She got drunk, tried to sleep her way to the top, and screwed up so badly that they never want to see her face in New York again. I had to pay for her to come here with me. She doesn't have any money anyway."

Eldest Cousin said, "Ha?" and blinked, really fast. If we were in a sitcom, one of the other people waiting for their luggage would have leaned into frame and said, "*Awk*ward!"

You know, at some point during the flight I could have sworn that Mama came to see me after I had finally fallen asleep, despite my best intentions. I thought maybe she brushed my hair from my eyes, like she used to do when I was a little girl and I hadn't yet done too much wrong. But I must have dreamed it.

I try to hang on to these tender moments. Listening to her now, though, I wasn't even sure I could call it the same woman. How can she be so different from one hour to the next?

I was so tired anyway by the time we saw Eldest Cousin, everything sounded like it was coming from far away. It was like my reaction time was a few seconds slower than everyone else's. I'm sure I looked terrible. I felt like I reeked of airplane. Predictably, Mama looked as if she'd been in first class, where they apparently have showers and hairstylists. She looked perfect.

I could feel my shoulders drooping just a little bit more. Mama slapped me between the shoulder blades. "Stand up straight. Haven't you embarrassed me enough already?"

Eldest Cousin opened his mouth again, but Mama dumped her bag onto his shoulder and smacked it for good measure. "Let's go! I'm hungry!"

Where, where does she get all this confidence? I know for a fact that I didn't inherit it. It's like she's never second-guessed herself, ever. I read some book about birth order. Maybe it's because she's the youngest child? I don't know. Anyway, she never seems to care what anyone else thinks.

It's uncanny.

Ugh. Is only just past 1:00 a.m. where I'm from. Must stay awake. Ooh. They're calling for lunch. Thank goodness; was about to eat the blanket.

May 17, 3:36 p.m.
Guest bedroom

Have finally figured out what day it is.

Belly is stuffed full with things like sticky rice and fatty fatty sausages, with some of Second-Aunt-Married-to-Second-Uncle-on-My-Mama's-Side's amazing vegetables. (Taiwanese itself is more amazing than the vegetables, by the way: We have one word where I just had to write ten to describe someone's place in the family.) Had seven dishes on the table! Second Uncle is close to seventy but he eats like it's his business. Country life is good for longevity and hale health. Also apparently good for health: marrying a woman with fantastic cooking skills.

So anyway. When Mama went to the bathroom at the airport and while we were still waiting for the luggage, me trying to keep from falling asleep, Eldest Cousin cornered me.

"So what really happened?"

I tried to figure out what he wanted to hear. "She told you."

"Oh, come on, Mei Mei—no one believes what she says when she's angry." He pinched my elbow, and the memory of the staff member in Vegas doing the same thing, with the combination of his referring to me as "Little Sister" and probably me being pooped out of my wits, made my eyes well up immediately.

"Mei Mei?"

"Just forget it, Cousin," I said. I blinked fast, trying to control the tears, but that just made them fall. So embarrassing!

"No. No. What she said about you was terrible."

More tears. "Please, let's just forget it, okay? I can't talk about it anymore, and anyway, I'm tired, and it's not like I see you that often anyway, so why the hell should you care? I'm sure you probably don't even know where I've been working."

In my clunky Taiwanese, it probably came out a lot harsher than I meant it to be, because Eldest Cousin nodded once, let go of my elbow, and patted me awkwardly on the back. He didn't say anything else to me until Mama got back.

I felt like crap afterwards. I can't even do a homecoming right.

Mama looked all smug when she came back and saw us standing separate from each other, not talking. Or maybe I just imagined it. Either way, I'm going to have to do better. Eldest Cousin was just trying to be nice. Even if I know he's not as close to me as Mama is to him, that's no reason to treat him so badly.

And anyway, my cousins could very well be my allies here.

My brother, Ken, was here for lunch. First Aunt said he was only teaching morning classes, so it's not like he has such a terrible schedule that he can't come home for lunch. The university's only across the street from the main gate to The Compound, anyway.

He came in and saw Mama first, and he wasn't even really looking for me. I know, because it's not like he expected me to be home. So when he did finally see me—and, probably, finally, registered that it *was* me—he did a classic double-take and swooped me into a hug.

It's easy to hug me, after all. I'm his sister. I'm not the woman who gave him up at birth, just so her sister wouldn't be an old maid.

For years First-Aunt-Mama's-Older-Sister wanted a baby, but she could never find anyone in our village who wanted to marry her. The village lore is that she was just too damn smart—and prickly—for anyone to be brave enough to marry her, and that's probably right.

Either way, when my mother, youngest of a family of four, got pregnant with my older brother, well, she promised him to First Aunt, who then officially adopted him. So Ken grew up here, while I got to live in the States.

I shouldn't say "got to live." Ken is living out his life dream, with a parent who supports him and thinks he's the bee's knees (what the frick does this mean, anyway?), even if she's not his biological mother. I, obviously, am not the bee's knees to my mother. Or the cat's meow, even.

Mama always has a hard time seeing Ken. She can't look him straight in the eyes for a good long while—it might take two or three meals—and when she does, she does it from below her eyelashes, like she's ashamed of something, or trying to play the ingénue, I'm not sure. Maybe it's bad memories from the terrible fight she and Dad had over her giving up her first-born—a male, no less!—to her sister. Anyway, he just ignores it until she's ready to be normal again, but this time, all his attention was on me.

That might be why she flung herself at him. "Hello, son!"

I was still in the way, but she wedged herself in. I couldn't blame her. If I'd given up someone I loved, I'd want to hold them close every chance I got. Not that she would ever say that. (It is *so weird* that she still insists that he call her Mama. Or maybe it's a cultural thing. One more than the other, maybe. Hmmm.)

"Mama! You brought Mei Mei home!"

She ignored it. "You look so much older."

"Well, it's been two years."

She slapped at him. "You should call more often."

"Yes."

Ken is a genius at managing Mama. He just makes sure she's happy.

Would it be so hard for me to do the same?

Holy crap, how are they calling for dinner already? How? It's like we just ate.

But I should know better. The Taiwanese do everything over a good meal, and if there's a lot to be done, well, then everything is a good meal.

May 18, 7:00 p.m.
Guest bedroom

I am wide awake. I'd like to be winding down, since I know I'm exhausted on some level from that long-ass flight, but I'm all keyed up: it's the time I'd be getting up, where I live. Lived. Whatever. Getting up, and going to work, and oh, you know. Standard things that I can't do because I can't worry about standard things like an apartment or work anymore.

Everyone else has gone out, but I've begged off, claiming a headache. I do have a *little* headache. The quiet in this house is soothing, though. Outside I can hear the bats and the crickets, and if I turn on the lights in here I'll see the silhouettes of geckos as they rest up against the cooler glass of the windowpanes, every detail, right down to their little suction-cup toes. It's so peaceful here. It's nothing at all like New York, and—well, I'm not sure that's a good thing. People who write about creativity always say it's good to try something new every once in a while, but I'm not sure this is what they meant.

I was able to get up before Mama today. Second-Aunt-Who-Belongs-to-Second-Uncle was already sweeping the front courtyard, so I went around to our interior courtyard, where I played when I was a toddler.

When I was little, it had seemed huge. Now it seems quaint, two crosswalks intersecting, dividing the space into quarters of greenery that First Aunt keeps flush with random plants she decides to install on a whim, like her own private art project. Since I've been gone she's planted a pomegranate tree and a row of lettuce, which is weird, but then again, makes a peculiar sense: First Aunt is always trying something new.

The books say we should try something new after traumatic experiences, so I sat in the courtyard as the sun rose and allowed the mosquitoes to chew on me for a while as I visualized living the artist's life in Taiwan *and* keeping my mind off Chris and Stafford, both of whom I badly wanted to talk to. Okay, maybe one more than the other. One because I wanted to hear that everything would be okay; the other because I needed to hear from him that my career is over. Also, because I'm feeling a *little* bit guilty about dodging someone's calls.

I didn't feel any more grounded than I did before the sitting around and letting mosquitoes chew on me (actually, I think I was meant to be meditating), so I grabbed a spare key and went to the marketplace. It's not far, maybe a mile, but by the time I got there I was drenched. Humidity here is no joke.

I love the marketplace. The level of activity is outrageous. Everything is bright and cheery and there are lots of people around all looking happy, buying and selling and trading and shuffling along the narrow spaces between the stalls and the slow-moving traffic, bicycles and scooters and even the occasional cars. There are always little old farm ladies dragging carts full of fruit or vegetables, and lovely clothing of all different fabrics and types. In this part of Taiwan, merchants selling vegetables and fruit still wear the conical field workers' hats, and it's not unusual to see the older people in traditional dress, of gray or blue cotton, straight-legged pants that look like they might be pajamas but that are really just everyday wear.

I don't know what I was thinking when I went to the marketplace; I guess I was hoping to find some sign that this is a good place for me to be right now. I tried to talk myself into acting like I was on vacation, so I could assume a more relaxed mentality and try to figure out what the flip I was going to do with myself (*Vacation for Workaholics*, Strand, $19).

I stop at the very first stall I see that *looks* like it might be a step in that direction, one with clothing and fabric in it and a seamstress in the back, working away on a sewing machine. She's wearing headphones while she works and she's got them turned up and she's totally rocking out to them. I browse for a while until she finally sees me.

When she does, she whips off her headphones. "Ay!" she says, "why didn't you say something?"

I have to switch from thinking in English to speaking in Taiwanese. It always takes me two or three days to get used to people speaking my native tongue on the streets. "Oh, I'm just looking," I say, as casually as I can, hoping she'll ignore me. "Go back to what you were doing."

She shakes her head. "It's fine. I wanted to take a break anyway."

"Thanks."

I nod at her and smile, but she doesn't stop staring at me.

"Don't I know you?" she finally says, and now it's my turn to look closely. (This is terrible, but aside from my family, I have an awful time the first few days telling people from one another here when I've first met them.)

I shake my head. "I don't think so."

"I think I do."

"I really don't see how that's possible," I say, hoping I'm picking the right words, the ones that sound firm but polite.

"Your accent," she says.

"American," I say, disappointed in myself.

Her eyes widen. "I knew it," she says. "Your mother used to come by with you when you were young. You're Wu, right? From the old estate? You used to come all the time. It was my mother's shop then. And then your aunt came by with you, too. The one who's an artist. And after you and your mother left, your brother . . ." Her eyes widen even further. "Your brother still lives here," she says, sounding almost reverent.

Ah. Ken. The eternal bachelor, the scion of our family, the guy who's so cool that he goes by his American name almost all the time. Not because he prefers it, but because American names are very en vogue, and, I guess, because when your cool factor is sky-high, like Ken's always seems to be in town, well, you need a name to match. This is how nicknames are born, right?

Now I know why she thinks she's seen me before. She, like so many other single girls, has probably ogled my brother enough times in the marketplace that she gloms on to anyone who looks even remotely like him.

"Yeah," I say. "We look alike."

She studies my face some more, like she's comparing my every feature to Ken's. "What are you doing back here?"

"Just visiting," I say, and then I can't stop myself from trying something new. "Actually, I'm considering moving here. I thought I'd give it a try, anyway."

Her mouth drops open and she laughs so gaily that folks walking by her storefront look in. I smile.

"What's so funny?"

"Oh, Mei Mei—" I'd forgotten that everyone in this village calls me that, since I am, like my mother, the youngest of the extended family. "Mei Mei, you don't want to move back here."

"Why not?"

"It's too small for you! New York—aren't you in New York?" She uses its Taiwanese name, and I'm stunned by how foreign it sounds already. "New York must be so much more exciting. You'll die here. A big-city girl like you? You'll never make it."

"Well," I say, "I guess I'd like to try it."

"Well," she says back, "if you want. I wouldn't hold out too much hope, though."

I'm trying to keep the smile on my face, but it's not easy. I want to sit down on the concrete floor and cry.

She comes closer and pats my arm. "Oh—I mean, it's fine here to vacation. And you can always try, right?"

God. New York doesn't want me, and it seems that not even this tiny backwater on the island I thought I could sort of call home wants me.

What the hell is the matter with me?

So then I get this genius idea to visit Ken at his studio on the university campus. It's on my way home anyway. I remember it being wonderful in there, small but airy, since the windows were always wide open so that it didn't reek too badly of oil paint. The last time we were back, two years ago, Ken spent nearly all his free time hunched at his easel, muttering, looking exactly like a struggling artist should look, dabbing at something on the canvas, then taking a step back and looking at it before stepping forward and dabbing again. Deliberate. Earnest.

He was always working so hard.

Yeah. Visiting Ken *should've* been the right move, except it wasn't, because when I get to where his studio used to be, it isn't his studio anymore. Another struggling artist is in there, squinting at her canvas, and when I ask her where his studio is, she jerks her head in a vaguely down-the-hallway direction, so I go looking until I see his name on the plate beside the door.

I knock once and then I'm knocked way over, because the door opens under the pressure of my hand, and damned if Ken's new studio isn't huge.

Huge! And he isn't hunched over a canvas anymore, either, like some determined half-talent. He's working on a piece larger than anything I've ever seen from him. His style has changed—he's slap-dash going at the thing, something I can already see is going to be a gorgeous seascape with whitecaps and a rock at the south end of Taiwan that the locals call "Nixonhead," 'cause, well, it looks like Richard Nixon's head. The thing is massive in scope and sheer ambition.

Ken looks like a pro, a real pro. His work looks like a real professional's work.

Feh.

But oh! It gets worse. Because he turns around and sees me, and grins so big I think his cheeks are going to explode, and then he says, "What do you think of the new space?"

I snort. "You know what I think. It's gorgeous. How come you didn't say you had a new space yesterday?"

"I was hoping we could come over and see it together, but when I got up this morning Mama said you'd already left."

"I bet she didn't say it quite like that."

"No, you're right, she didn't." Long pause. "So."

"So," I say, at the same time.

"Um."

"Yeah."

"Where'd you go?"

"Just to the market."

"Any particular reason?"

"Yeah. I wanted to see if it'd be possible to make a go of life here. I wanted to see how the other people who work, um, in the arts do it, I guess." It sounds weird, to me. Can I even make a go of life "in the arts"? Is that a thing people do?

"And?"

I wave my hand. "Never mind. When'd you move into this space? And why?"

"Well, that's the other thing I was waiting to tell you. Mama, I mean. I was waiting to tell Mama when she got in, but we haven't had a chance to come over here together yet. And I guess I was going to call you and tell you after I'd told Mama, but you're here now, isn't that great? I can tell you my good news in person!"

I hate it when he goes all happy like this. He goes Pollyanna and you can never get any real information out of him. I flap my hand at him. *Go on.* Even siblings far apart can read basic signals.

"I have a solo show in Taipei!"

Oh, fuck.

"That's *great!*" I throw up my hands for good measure. "Fantastic!"

I can't even say now why I was so bent out of shape. I mean, what did I expect? Ken's been working at his craft for years. He's had the support and the backing and he's got raw talent. I couldn't possibly have expected that he'd be stuck in a beginner's rut all his life, or even a mediocre rut.

Damn, it hurt that he wasn't.

He looks closely at me.

"Seriously!" I yelp. "No more struggling artist!" My voice sounds strained. I grin so big my own cheeks feel stressed.

He's too happy to dwell on my weirdness. "Yeah! I mean, I always loved teaching, but not headlining a show wasn't helping me to get tenure or even get close to it. But someone finally took a chance, you know? I'm really excited." He pauses, looking earnest. I brace myself. "It's *better* than headlining, even," he says conspiratorially. Like that's a big secret or something.

"Wow," I say, and look around for a place to sit.

Ken clears off a bench for me.

"Oh," I say, trying to be witty, "don't bother moving your big important art for *me*."

It must come out funny, because he squints at me.

"Never mind," I say.

He pushes some more papers off and sits down next to me. "Mei Mei," he says, "what happened?"

I start yelling. "Would you please stop calling me that! I have a *name*. It's *Marty*, and I'm here because I really, really fucked up, okay, and I was kind of hoping that you'd at least understand what it was like to be struggling, just a little bit, but you're not struggling at all, are you? You're doing *awesome* things with your *awesome huge* canvases and your *huge-ass* studio that's bound to make Mama *so proud* of you. Really! There's no need for you to pretend like you're on anything but cloud fucking nine, okay?"

This last I say in English, good ol' swearing American, because there's nothing quite like dropping the eff-bomb in the middle of an idiom to prove your own point.

Which is that you are a jackass and that you are even incapable of being happy for your only brother, whom you haven't seen in two years because you are too wrapped up in your shit, which, by the way, you pooped for yourself.

On yourself. Barfed, even, on yourself. (Plus, I'm pissed off because First Aunt tried to get me to paint both last night and this morning, and I blew her off, and now I'm thinking deeply irrational thoughts about what would have happened if *I* had been the one who was left behind here, to paint and draw and be happy and make shit.)

Ken looks hurt. Fan-fucking-tastic.

He puts his arm around me. "Mei Mei," he says, "you're going to be okay. I'm sure it's not as bad as you think it is," and then I'm crying—again! God, when will I ever stop?—and I tell him everything, because even if he is going to be a rager success and that is going to make it even harder for anyone to even want me around, he is my only brother and probably the person who most understands what it's like to want to make our mother happy, even if he has another mother now.

I tell him about the firing and about the bad juju I left behind in New York, and I tell him about the girl at the fabric store—"Oh, yes," he says, "that's Shin Mei, and she's the town gossip, so I wouldn't worry about her"—and I tell him about how I'm pretty sure I'll never be able to feel like I fit in anywhere anymore, even if I am with my own family and in the place I was born.

Fuck.

So then after I've done crying all over him and me, he pulls a handkerchief from his shirt cuff—seriously?—and wipes my face and tells me I should take the day off and get over my jetlag and have as many naps as I want and spend some time wandering the grounds of the estate, which always made me happy when I was a kid, he says, and that if I want I don't have to come to the family dinner tonight, since that's where he'll tell our mother about the big show and he's pretty sure things won't go well for me if I'm around when she hears that.

I have a minor out-of-body thing where I pretend I'm Jody, or anyone else looking from the outside in, and I realize how fucking *crazy* it sounds that I shouldn't be around when my mother gets good news about someone who's not-me, and then I snap myself back to reality, telling myself it's not crazy; it's my life.

Perfect. Perfectly warped life, with a perfect older brother who has a perfect career too close to what I want, and his perfectly healthy attitude toward me, his fucked-up little sister.

Well. You can't get much worse than that, can you? So annoying.

But then the door to Ken's studio, which he'd closed after I started crying, flies wide open, and this guy, this guy who even through my tears I can see is drop-dead gorgeous in a Hong Kong movie star kind of way, all slopey exotic-or-whatever eyes and cheekbones so sharp you could fall off them, crashes in through the door, laughing at a remark made by someone just outside.

The whole thing is so Abercrombie and Fitch that I stop mid-nose-honk and check him out, noticing utterly despite myself the good jeans, the pinstriped dress shirt frayed at the collar and neck, the half-tucked shirttail, and the very good shoulders.

Yes, I am ogling.

I know, I am so smooth. I just keep on impressing myself.

The guy yells, "Ken!" and "Yo!" and I have to remind myself that I am not in New York or California, because he says these in perfect American English, and then he stops and looks at me, red-eyed and sniffling, and goes, "Oh."

"Oh" is the same in any language.

"Hi, Danny," says Ken, and tells me what Danny's Taiwanese name is, but I don't really care, because I am still staring at the guy and trying to be remotely cool about making sure I don't have any snot on my nose. "This is my sister, Marty."

"Hi there," says Danny.

"Hi," I say. "Sorry about this." I point to my face.

"Oh, you're gorgeous anyway," he says easily, eyes flicking over me. "Really." He grins.

"Uh. Thanks?"

Ken rolls his eyes and says, "Marty, Danny's one of my colleagues here. He teaches watercolor. Danny, Marty's just visiting for a few weeks."

"Yup." My conversational skills are failing. It's like once I got fired, I lost all salesperson capabilities.

Danny's looking at me thoughtfully. "What are you going to do while you're here?"

I have to blow my nose. I do so as quietly as I can and then I say, "A little bit of this? And that? You know."

Danny laughs. "No, I really don't. But if you want, I can show you around town and stuff. I mean, I know you've been here before, but Taiwan has lots of things to see and sample and taste."

This last he says with a tiny upward lift of the eyebrows, and I go irrationally mushy.

Ken says, "Dude, that's my sister," and Danny laughs, and it's such a good sound that I feel more lighthearted, and I think to myself, I should see more of this Danny.

And then Danny turns the grin on me, and I think, I must see more of this Danny.

Danny tells Ken he's just here to drop off the summer class schedule, and then he's out again, calling over his shoulder that Ken has his number, that it was nice to meet me, that I should call him.

Ken rolls his eyes, but I like Danny, and it could be fun to make a new friend here in Taiwan, especially one who looks like *that*.

After I was done snotting all over Ken's studio, I stopped by at the 85°C Café on the way home to check my email. Radio silence from Stafford. A sweet email from Chris asking where I'd gone to, and when I'd be back. I didn't answer that one, although it made me ache. An email from Jody with a funny GIF in it, some cartoon guy banging his head on his keyboard until his eyeballs flew out of his head and the head itself disintegrated into mush. I hiccupped a laugh and shut my laptop. Maybe I'd answer Chris later, when I could stand to think of the whole Vegas thing without wanting to dig a hole right where I stood to crawl into.

Later

Danny just texted. We're having coffee tomorrow.

May 19, late. Oh, god, so late

Urk. "Coffee" turned out to be Danny picking me up at ten on his motorcycle. Nice to see someone else besides my aunt and uncle and cousins, and also nice to see Danny on a motorcycle, dangling an extra helmet, idling in the forecourt of The Compound.

"Where are you going?" Mama called, and I told her I was headed out with a friend of Ken's, and that seemed to be good enough, because she didn't say anything else, but maybe also I was moving too fast to really care. I got the distinct impression I was fleeing again.

But then I was on Danny's bike, arms draped loosely over his hips, feeling cool for the first time in forever, and then sitting across from him at the local 7-Eleven ("Better coffee, I promise," said Danny, and he was right) while he settled in and asked me questions:

Did I like it here? Yes.

Did I miss New York? Yes? No? I don't know yet?

What did I think of Ken's awesome news? Oh, just dandy, isn't it? So proud, etc.

Danny peered carefully at me over the rim of his coffee cup and flipped open his notebook, started sketching.

"You're not drawing me, are you?"

"Yeah. Hold still."

"Why?"

"Why not?"

I shrugged.

"Hold still!"

"Sorry."

He glanced at me now and then, and I tried to be still, remembering what it was like to try and sketch someone who was constantly moving, and when he was done he flipped the book around toward me.

He'd drawn a funny little thing, a hybrid map and landscape, a beach. Nixonhead in the background.

"That's not a portrait!"

He smiled, pointed at the Nixonhead. "That. Is where we're going."

I looked more closely. "Now?"

"Yep. What else do you have to do?"

I thought about this. Avoiding Mama. Knocking around The Compound. "Nothing, I guess."

"Right."

"Hey."

"What?"

"Were you really drawing me, earlier?"

"Kind of. I just doodled where it looked like you'd want to go."

Oh.

It's two hours to Nixonhead from where we are, so I sent Ken a quick text telling him where I was going, and with whom, and then we left. No, I did not tell my mama.

South, south, due south, away from the village and the intervening cities and following the curve of the island until the water appeared on the right, me craning my neck to watch the waves as they broke on the shore.

Danny pulled over at a random stretch of road, white sand with black volcanic rocks here and there on the one side; Nixonhead off the beach in the near distance, and on our left side, a little row of food vendors. We bought lunch boxes and sat on some big rocks overlooking the beach. I thought of the canvas Ken was working on yesterday when I went to the studio, and marveled at the idea that people in Taipei would soon be seeing his perspective of Nixonhead. Yeah. I was proud of him.

Pork chops, pickled bamboo, rice, an egg, some bok choy. Taiwanese lunch boxes are not to be beat. And I was hungry. My phone pinged. Ken. I texted back I'd call him when I got home.

"My brother," I said, pushing my phone back into my pocket.

"Your brother's a good guy," Danny said.

"Yeah. How long have you known him?"

"Mmm. Lemme see. Maybe four years? I've been teaching at the university for ages, though."

"What's that mean, 'ages'?"

"Oh, practically since I graduated college."

I did the math. That was a long time, if he was Ken's age.

I bumped his (lovely, broad) shoulder. "That *is* forever. Are *you* headlining any shows?" And then I wanted to take it back, because why the frick would I say something like that?

But Danny laughed. "No, that's not my deal," he said, eating the last few bits of rice from his lunch box. "I just like to make watercolors. And teach other people how to do it."

"And then what?"

"Then they leave my class and they go on to more advanced techniques, with people like your brother."

"And then what?"

"What do you mean, and then what?"

"Well, what about you? Do you just do the same class over and over again?"

"Yep, pretty much."

"Aren't you bored?"

"Not one bit." He reached over and ate some bamboo out of my lunch box. "This life is too easy not to live it fully," he said, sounding sincere, and seeing him there, happily eating my lunch, utterly guileless, utterly guiltless, I thought, Yeah, he has it right.

"That definitely sounds like the right way to do it," I said.

Do one thing. Do it well. No need to struggle.

He stood up, brushing crumbs off his lap, and offered me his hand. "Come on, let's go."

"Where to?"

"Dunno," he said. "Look at Nixonhead? Sit on the beach? Who cares? We have the whole day."

Anyway. We just got back. I forgot to call Ken. I guess I'll try him tomorrow.

May 20, 5:15 p.m.
Guest bedroom

Have successfully avoided Mama another day. But had weird text exchange with Ken, like this:

KEN: Where were you all day?
ME: With Danny.
KEN: And yesterday?
ME: With Danny.
KEN: I meant to tell you about him.
ME: What about him?
KEN: He's not going anywhere.
ME: Isn't that a good thing?
KEN: That's not what I meant.
ME: Explain.

KEN: He's a professional loafer.

ME: Just what I need.

KEN: No. That is NOT what you need to spend your time doing. Plus, he's a womanizer.

ME: And hot.

KEN. LOAFER.

ME: Goodbye!

Enh.

May 21, 4:01 p.m.
Own room

There's a good reason I call this place "The Compound." It's like the Kennedys' joint, I'm sure, only in Asia. And in a smaller town than even Hyannis Port. It does double-duty in the coolness factor: it's foreign *and* it's home. It has big courtyards that all spill into one another by little contained alleyways, and Chin Dynasty–era rooftop designs, and hand-painted rafters and a great room where my ancestors hosted guests, and little anterooms where they hosted friendlier guests who didn't need to be given the whole formal-guest treatment. First Aunt has her own warren of rooms. So does Ken, and so do Second Uncle and Second-Aunt-Who-Belongs-to-Him. It's totally unlike anything you'd ever see in the U.S. But I think of it whenever someone asks me where I'm from.

I guess some things don't go away, even if *you've* gone far away.

I like this idea, of having one's own warren to putter in. As it is, I am in the guest quarters, across the courtyard from Mama, who's staying in a room on the upper level of Second Uncle's section. I haven't actually been with Mama alone at all, which is good, because I already feel like I have to prepare myself before I see her, even with other people around, and I do not have the energy.

Days go by so fast here. It's like the whole concept of time gets lost once you set foot on an island.

Really it probably has most to do with the constant stream of relatives who keep stopping by to say hello, or take us to meals. It's an awesome excuse to not have to think too much about no job, no best friend, angry embarrassed mother, and perfect, creative-genius brother.

92

Also probably has something to do with the fact that I have been out for the past few days with Danny. Danny! It's nice to have someone to hang out with, and I can't help but compare him to Chris, but he's nice to look at.

Really, really nice to look at.

Gotta go. Danny is coming to get me for dinner. And drinks. And karaoke.

Oh. Must mark down that angry embarrassed mother has been better than usual lately. Think this has to do with being center of attention. Everyone loves it when she comes home, and even she looks happy. What I guess I mean to say is that she is paying less attention than usual to me. Which is also good, because I'm trying not to be here for her to see.

Midnight
Own room

Most annoying conversation with Ken. Was waiting for me when I got home, can you believe that? Sitting in the chair that Grandpa used to sit in, hanging out in the Great Hall, looking like a photo of Grandpa, only he wasn't receiving any heads of state. He was receiving me, and I almost mock-kowtowed.

"Hey, brother."

"Marty."

"Um. Why are you still up?"

"Waiting for you. Didn't you get my texts?"

I pull my phone out of my pocket and look. Yep. Three texts from Ken, one per hour.

"What are you, my mother?" This is hilarious, but Ken doesn't laugh.

"We have to talk, Marty."

"Ohhhkay." I drag over a seat, making as much noise as possible, because Danny bought me two martinis over dinner and a beer or two over karaoke and I was a little loopy. Am still a little loopy. Still, Ken not bothered.

"Listen," he says, and I scoot my chair closer to him and cup my ear. Still hilarious! No reaction. Borrrrring.

"I'm serious, Marty."

Oh, frustration! "Ken! Let me have a little fun, will ya?"

"No, Marty. Danny is not a good guy. He'll never do anything in life and all he wants to do is mess around, okay? And I don't like the way he looks at you."

"Pffffft." I flap my hand at him. "*I* like the way he looks at me," I say. Not that it's embarrassing to admit this or anything. Anyway, the Danny-drinks have made me brave, and I feel like I've been resisting my impulses for far too long, right?

Ken finally figures out that I am in no mood to talk. He gets up to leave and shakes me a little bit.

"Go get some sleep. We'll talk some more later."

Why does everyone I trust have to be so party-poopy???

Sleep now. More later.

May 22, 3:05 p.m.
Courtyard, The Compound

The days are still ticking by, sure and steady. Ken and I sometimes have coffee together in the mornings at the little shop near the university. He sketches and I watch the street life. (He hasn't brought up Danny again, goody.) The scooters whiz by, many at a time, clustering at the stoplights like hornets, some of them with dogs in the footwells, and kids cross the street without hardly looking, just trusting the traffic to slow down.

That would so never happen in New York.

At lunchtime there's usually someone visiting, someone who's heard that Mama is home, and who wants to hear about America and what it's like. Or someone who wants to meet me and say something like "I knew you when you were *this* tall!" Like I said, it's a small village.

Obviously Mama doesn't tell them the same thing she said to Eldest Cousin. But I can tell she's frustrated. When people ask what I do—did!—in New York, she kind of rolls her eyes and says, "I don't think even she can tell you. Just some normal job, nothing special."

In rural Taiwan, we still defer to our parents. We don't argue in public, and we sure as hell don't correct them, even to defend ourselves.

As far as I can glean, the narrative is that I'm taking a break from the crazy world that is New York. But everyone in our family seems to know that we're not to talk about what happened to me.

In the late afternoons after his classes, Danny takes me out. We go to the coast and drive aimlessly, up and down. We drink. We laugh. Three days with him feels like forever, in the best way possible. Not oblivion, exactly, not forgetting. Just fun. Not dramatic, because not dateable. The guy sets off my Spidey senses. But so nice to look at. Heh.

Yesterday I went to see First Aunt. I hadn't seen her much in a few days, and I missed her, which is weird, because she's right around the corner and not halfway around the world, for now. I love her wit and her sense of moral justice. (These are some of the reasons Mama says she could never find a man. "Oh, your aunt," she likes to say. "Sharp tongue, sharp eyes, not a brain in her head for things like manners and being soft and sweet to men." Whenever she says that I want to laugh my ass off, because she's pretty much describing herself. But we do not laugh at Mama.)

First Aunt's studio is packed halfway up the walls, as usual, with her output. I've been over there a few times, since it's just a big room right next to her part of the house, but it's not like Ken's. First Aunt works in watercolors, and she sees things differently. Where Ken keeps everything flung wide open, she keeps most of her windows closed, because she likes to force herself to go outside, or at least go to work on the porch. She's had a few shows of her own, but she keeps on changing styles, and it's not like she has to work. Being the only unmarried girl in a family of four pretty much guarantees your father will make doubly sure you're provided for after he's gone.

But she loves to paint, so she goes on at it, selling a couple pieces here and there.

She's been trying to get me to paint, too. I keep on telling her that I'm no good at it, and I'm not that interested, but she won't stop asking. Each of the three times I've been over there she's met me with a brush in her hand and an extra smock. I pretend I don't see them. I fall into one of the chairs and tell her I want to watch her work.

Really what I do while she's painting is obsess over my bank account. I had an email from Stafford: No severance package. And I haven't found a subletter yet, and my credit card statement is due.

I gotta find some kind of work, fast. Rent's due soon, too. I guess I could ask for a loan.

No. No. Are you crazy? Remember what happened the last time you asked for money? It was, like, an hour of yelling about how worthless you were, and then another hour of screaming about the waste of a college education, and then a final half hour of keening about why bad daughters make decisions that hurt Mama.

Lesson learned: If you don't want to feel like you're getting your heart excavated with a butter knife, don't ask Mama for money. Ever. I'll just have to hope I find someone to lease my place. Airbnb? Ugh.

Anyway.

Today was an interesting experience. When I got to her studio, First Aunt was cleaning her paintbrushes. "Oh, good," she said, when she saw me. "Your mama was looking for you."

"What? Why?"

"Relax, Mei Mei. I told her to go look for you. I'm taking you two out for breakfast today."

I helped her to wash off her paintbrushes, and she and I and Mama walked down to the market, avoiding the fabric shop and seamstress. Ken must have told my aunt what happened.

It's like First Aunt knows everyone. All along the road to the market and especially once we got there, people called out greetings to her, or came to say hello. They all seemed happy to see her, and I remembered, with a pang, the way folks in my neighborhood do the same for me. The guy who sells me my newspaper and coffee asks after me, and my local bartender knows how I like my drinks, and the waitress at the diner where Jody and I have been a couple of times for hangover lunches on Sundays knows I like poached eggs on top of my corned-beef hash, not sunny-side-up.

And in the professional world I used (!!!) to move in, I could kind of say folks knew who I was. At least, they knew what the magazine was. And they knew how hard it is to sell the pages in it. But mostly, my peers were after the same dollars I was after, so it's not like I could say it was good to make friends with other salesfolk. And they don't know my name, really.

Here, everyone knows your name and where you come from and why, and a little something about your family. Everyone asked my aunt how her work was going. And they said things like, "Oh! You must be so proud of Ken!" And they made promises to take trips to Taipei to see his exhibition, promises I believe they will make good on.

It was almost life-changing to see. New York has its neighborhoods, sure, and its professional networking groups, but it's your friends who make up your community. Here, the community is all up in your stuff, and you might call a lot of the community your friends.

Everyone seemed to be watching me, like they wanted to ask some pointed questions, and they all said hello to my mother, and they all waited politely to be told how long we'd be staying for, and they almost all wanted to know what living in a big city was like.

Sometimes, Mama would let me say a few words. Other times, she said things like, "Oh, it's not like she hangs out with movie stars or anything, right, Marty?" Or, "It's not like you think. It's not like she's done anything you've ever heard of."

No one blinked. I guess I was right after all. Maybe all Asian mothers do treat their daughters this way. Hm.

I was just thinking that it'd be nice to find some work in a profession where folks not only knew your name, but where it was a group of, like, colleagues, you know? Where you could depend on each other and stuff. Surely there were groups like that somewhere, somehow.

We met so many people on the streets who asked after me, and time and again, as I wasn't allowed to answer for myself, I began to wonder how much she really understood about what I did for a living. What I used to do, I mean.

Maybe it would be easier if she just told people I was "between jobs." That would hurt less, anyway.

Breakfast was okay. I stayed quiet and ate as neatly as I could, feeling Mama's hawk eyes on me, and First Aunt did most of the talking. I could swear she was trying to keep Mama's attention off me.

Maybe I should try something in fundraising. Or public relations? Anything. Anything, just to feel useful. It doesn't have to be creative, even. It could very well be busywork, stuffing envelopes, or licking them, so long as I could find a job I can explain to her, one that she can describe easily to her friends.

Is being a consultant still a hot job these days? Maybe I can go do that. I could be a consultant to the perpetually plagued. It wouldn't even matter what kind of plague, or what size albatross you're lugging around, I probably know it and can consult with you on how to deal with it. Well, in a limited fashion, anyway. So far, my list of possible answers to any quandary looks like this:

1. Run to opposite side of globe.
2. Stay put; hide in apartment.
3. Pretend nothing happened.

Oh-kay!

Anyway. We'd just left the restaurant when I heard shrieking behind me. My mother looked over my shoulder, and her eyes got really big.

This tiny woman came right up to my mother, bypassing me like I wasn't even standing there. "I thought that was you, but I couldn't be sure!"

"Ai ya!" said my mother, and she looked genuinely pleased. "Zhang A Fun, is that you? It's been almost thirty years!"

It was indeed Zhang A Fun, and there was some small talk and the same requisite introductions and the whole back-from-New-York thing all over again, and then my aunt said to my mother, "Why don't we give you two some time to catch up?" and pointed them in the direction of a little restaurant where they could have tea and cakes, told my mother we'd be "around," and then dragged me away, quickly.

"I thought she'd never show up," First Aunt muttered. "She said she'd be there fifteen minutes ago. I want to show you something."

"Who *was* that?"

"Just an old friend of your mother's, and mine. We all went to school together, and she moved back from Japan last month. I told her where she could find us."

"Oh."

"I wanted to get you alone for an hour or so, is all."

"Wait." I shook off her hand. "Where are we going?"

She reached back and grabbed my hand again, without even breaking stride. "We're going where you need to go."

"No. I don't want—"

She let go and stood there in the street, feet shoulder-width apart, hands on her hips now, staring me down. "You don't want what?"

I almost laughed out loud. I could see how she must have been as a teenager, all legs and arms, with her hands on her hips just like that. She definitely would have scared off the boys of her time.

"I don't want to go to a museum or to that fabric store, okay? I don't want to see all of the great artistic things you're going to show me, to 'inspire' me, or whatever." I made the air quotes even though they don't translate in Taiwanese. My aunt blinked and waited. "I can't *do* anything or *be inspired* or anything like that because I don't have *money*. I need *money* first, right?"

My aunt has only good intentions. This is what almost everyone says about her. And yet, there's a side of her that can be so sneaky. She looks so sweet and so kind that no one expects it of her. And she often says artists are bad at lying. But that doesn't really mean anything. Lying's one of those things you might do for someone you love, according to my aunt.

It takes various forms. You know, like talking an old friend into meeting you in the market so you can walk away with a hostage of sorts.

She leveled her stare, calibrating, or something, and reached for my hand again. "For someone who's almost thirty, you are really, really young," she said. "Find what your heart wants first. I don't think you even know anymore. After that, the money is secondary."

She took my hand firmly in hers and dragged me through the marketplace before I could say something obnoxious about her having inherited enough to let her heart lead her life. We went past the covered meat market, deftly dodging puddles of bloody water and scraps of wilted vegetables. I let her take me. I couldn't argue anymore, and anyway, it wasn't like she'd have listened.

We wound around corners and into alleys and went past the fabric store, where Shin Mei looked up from her work just in time to wave, and then, oh, then, we ducked into another alley and out the other side and stopped finally in front of a storefront, and as my eyes adjusted, there they were, a set of traditional costumes, all on mannequins, and next to each one of them, lovely watercolor sketches—presumably, what the costumes themselves had started as.

Artists, my aunt says, always seem to know what they want, but sometimes they have to have it pointed out to them.

So I guess that's why I went hot, then light-headed. My skin started to tingle; the hairs on my arms went up, not entirely due to the blast of air-conditioning. I went and stood in front of each watercolor and compared it to its real-life manifestation, looking back and forth, back and forth between them. I touched them all—silk, and linen, and the designs appliquéd on in loops and swirls and squares, and the rich, deliberate embroidery. Some of it was plain cotton, overlaid with stripes and beads stitched onto or into the fabric. Some of it was more textured burlap or rough linen, speaking of hundreds of years of hard history.

I totally detached, except to look, and touch. I lost track of time.

I don't know what I was thinking, really, when I was doing it. I only knew that I wanted more.

It was so ridiculously, horribly out of reach. And I was undeserving, but I couldn't stop myself. My aunt was at the back of the store, greeting the proprietor, I suppose. I wasn't paying attention. I could hear them talking, much like you hear a conversation from the next carrel over in a library, or snippets of a conversation if you're on the subway, or maybe the rapidly dwindling murmuring of a theater audience right before the lights go all the way down—but it didn't matter. For the first time in a long, long while, I was riveted.

And not by weird pipe dreams either; not by thoughts of skinny little storefronts and twisted wishes for the one famous client who might make Mama happy and proud; not by ideas for marketing the place so that it might stand out among the hundreds of handiwork shops in New York City; not even by the thought of seeing one of my creations in the pages of *New York* magazine in a shoot about the latest gala event at the Costume Institute or in the fine print of the Playbill for a small but well-reviewed off-Broadway show.

No, for the first time in a long, long time I was paying attention to the beading, the cut, the fine chatter of the sewing machine in the back working its way through cloth. I paid close attention to the stitches, to the appliqués, if there were any, to the *intent* of each work, checking the watercolors and the mannequin and finally the swatches of fabric pinned next to each sketch, and the photographs that were pinned near the sketches, too, the ones that showed the costumer's primary inspirations, perhaps.

I looked at her notes, pinned, weirdly, next to the drawings, and skimmed them using my lousy Mandarin, and started all over again after I'd been past each of the eight mannequins that were out on display.

My aunt came to stand next to me, and the melancholy that rolled over me must have been tangible, because she reached down and took my hand and pressed each knuckle, something she used to do when I was a kid, and said, "It's almost time. We need to head back to meet your mother."

"Okay," I said, and then, because I couldn't stop myself, I turned on her. "Why did you bring me here?"

She shrugged, and we turned toward the front door, me dragging.

I'm not ready to admit that I love something so much, while it's still so far away. And yet at least I know where to go, now, so I can get a little of it, maybe.

Later
Own room

As long as I live, I'll never be able to comprehend the uncanny connection between a mother and a daughter. There are those who say it doesn't exist, that it's only imagined, or wished-for, even, and although I won't deny that both those possibilities have crossed my mind, with wistfulness being the primary culprit, I also am not able to close my eyes to the weirdness that is my mother always showing up at exactly the wrong moment.

"Ai ya!" and there she was, blocking out the sunlight (ugh—metaphor, much?), her hair looking frizzy in the sudden change from outside humidity to the relative cool and dryness of the store.

I snatched my hand back from the plastic holder by the door where the business cards to this lovely shop were. I hadn't even had time to thank the proprietor for letting me look, or even to know her name or greet her properly.

Uncanny.

My aunt immediately moved to stand in front of me— *cockblock*, I thought, and then started giggling—and my mother pretended that hadn't happened, pivoted, and greeted the proprietor instead.

"Don't I know you?"

"Yes, you do, I Sho," said the proprietress, and nodded. "We went to school together."

Mama nodded sharply and was immediately off on a brief recounting of her lunch with Zhang A Fun. They'd all been classmates.

"Your daughter has a good eye," said the proprietress, Ms. Liu, I was finally able to glean, and my mother snorted.

"Oh, she's just a dreamer." She laughed, for good measure. "Nothing ever comes of her dreams."

"Well, you'd be surprised. Sometimes dreams make the best futures."

"Not for her," said my mother, and something about her tone made everyone go quiet for a second.

I backed into a corner, near a mannequin. For what? Warmth? Jesus.

"Why not?" said my aunt, and my mother turned on her.

"You wouldn't know. You got the better of the two."

I bit my lip hard enough to distract myself.

The proprietress smiled weakly and meandered into the back room. I saw a brief glimpse of sequins, beads, satins, before she shut the separating door entirely. "Come back whenever you like," she called through it.

Everyone is afraid of my mother, I thought lamely.

My aunt shook her head. "You just love to do that, don't you?"

"She's only a kid," Mama said, and then she turned to me, still crammed into the corner. "You ready to go now? Back to the real world, where you can think about actually doing something respectable with your life?"

I guessed so.

What a day. It's only mid-afternoon and I'm exhausted already. You know that saying, about rolling stones gathering no moss? Well, I feel like I'm rolling around in a rut, expending all of my energy making a deeper rut that I'll never get out of. I don't have any of my books with me, and I'm tired of these lined notebooks. Maybe Ken has one I can have, one of those sketchbook things. Hopefully he's home, and not in the studio. I really don't feel like going anywhere very far right now.

Later

So it turns out Second Uncle had some blank books. Lookit! No lines! Wheee! *The Language of Paying Attention to YOU* says it's a bad idea to not complete things, but I say screw 'em. Anyway, a whole new country deserves a new book, don't you think?

Whatever.

Very interesting chat with Second-Aunt-Belonging-to-Second-Uncle, and Uncle himself, today. "Interesting" mostly because it was highly annoying. Also "interesting" because dear Mama crashed it again.

Un-freaking-believable. It's like the house is wired for video or something, except the place is over a hundred and fifty years old. They only just got modern bathtubs when I was in my preteens. How does she *know?*

I guess it's pointless to ask. The point is, she knows.

So. Ken. My happy-go-lucky brother, the better of the two, was sitting at his desk, shoulders hunched over, head crooked to one side, like he was studying the desk surface with one eye, when I went looking for notebooks. I'd have thought he was working on a complicated drawing, except for he was talking to himself, only he wasn't talking to himself, exactly, he was talking into his cell phone, which he had clutched between his ear and his shoulder.

"No, I can't, not now," he was saying, and some other variations on that; at least two before he looked up and saw me. He waved at me and tapped his watch, looking sheepish, with his eyebrows up.

I mouthed at him that I'd come back later and went in search of my uncle, a legendary pack rat.

I found him with his glasses sliding down his nose, reading the newspaper.

"Mei Mei!"

"Hi."

He folded shut the newspaper and waved me toward an easy chair. I sat, and a faint whiff of camphor floated up from the cushion. Mothballs. Love that smell.

"What do you need?" My mother's family is not known for beating around the bush.

"I need a blank notebook."

"I've got those."

He levered himself out of his chair and stepped to the bookcase at the far end of the room. He slid the door open and sighed: neat stacks of books, all lined up with the edge of the shelf. I wish my office looked like that, I thought, and then I went, *Oh, crap. I don't have an office anymore.*

"Weh! A Tsai!" my uncle bellowed in the direction of the kitchen. "What happened to all my blank books?"

Second Aunt stepped into the room. She has the most delicious cheeks—they're lovely and plump, always pink, and as she's gotten older her crow's feet have only added to her charm. "Oh, Mei Mei," she said, "are you hungry?"

I shook my head.

"Weh!" said my uncle again. "Books?"

My aunt bent to the lowest shelf and pulled out a stack of books. "Here," she said. "I put them on the bottom because you use these the least."

My uncle grunted and gestured to me. "Mei Mei wants them," he said.

My aunt held them out to me. "Take 'em all, or just pick one."

"How come you have so many?"

"People give them to your uncle as gifts. We can't use them all quickly enough, so they pile up. We've been saving them all, just in case. And now, look! You're here to use them!" She did what could only be described as beaming at me. The cheeks got pinker.

I chose one that didn't have vertical lines for writing in Mandarin in it—there were only three to choose from after I'd winnowed those out—and handed the stack back to him.

"Tea?" My aunt was already heating up the tea set. I nodded.

My uncle crammed all the books onto a random bookshelf and settled back into his chair. Behind him, my aunt set out the teacups and quietly rearranged the stacks of books. She sat, then, too, on the edge of a chair next to him, and gestured at me to take the armchair.

"So—" My uncle waved at my aunt to pour the tea. "What have you been doing with yourself?"

I turned myself sideways in the chair and hung my legs over the arm. "Enh. Not much."

"Really?"

"Well, we went to the shop where you can get a costume made, do you know it?"

"Oh, yes," said my aunt. "We are friends with the owner. She's a very smart woman, that one."

"I didn't get to talk to her much, but she was very nice."

"So. What were you doing there?" Uncle lit his pipe and looked at me over its bowl. Aunt poured herself, and me, some more tea. Taiwanese teacups are teeny tiny, an ounce or so. I've never been able to figure why. I think it's so people can keep their hands busy.

"Just looking," I said, trying not to take all my tea in one mouthful. *Girls should be dainty*, echoed my mother in my head, and I almost stuck out my pinky. *Always leave a little something in the cup*, said my mother, and I put my cup down. My aunt refilled.

"What did you think?"

"I liked it." I peered at my uncle. I wasn't sure what he wanted to hear from me. There's something very benign about a septuagenarian with glasses perched at the end of his nose, so I went on.

And on.

And on.

It was like I freaking couldn't stop myself. I don't even remember what I was babbling about. Something about the intersection of business, style, and art; something about woman-run businesses; something about color and texture and pretty pretty sequins—yes, really, OMG, to my aunt and uncle.

I finally stopped, and then my aunt said, "Well, you sound like you were really happy there."

"I guess so."

"So now what?"

And just like that, it was back to reality.

"Now I have to get a job. Back in New York, I guess."

She straightened, pressed her lips together. "It doesn't have to be that way."

"I like it there."

"But do you have the same kind of shops there?"

"Yeeeahhhh," I said, thinking about the crazypants rent and the outrageous competition.

"Not as good as the one here, it sounds like," said my uncle, and it struck me, sitting there across from them, that I might be getting tag-teamed.

"You don't have to make a decision now," he said. "Think about it. You have some time."

"Maybe," I said. "But I need to make money."

"You're with family. We can house and feed you."

My aunt nodded, her lips tucked in on one another. She looked determined.

Stupid me, I began thinking of the empty rooms in The Compound where the maids and servants used to live. Maybe there was room for me after all. I could picture the rooms, what a Manhattan real estate shark might call "cozy" and "intimate," but I wouldn't care.

There was a room off First Aunt's kitchen that led onto the forecourt. Maybe that could be my studio. And the windows are covered over with lovely bougainvillea vines that I can redirect around the panes, so I can get some light.

I could probably find some artist's materials for really cheap. I'd take Ken's castoffs, if he had any. I could maybe give art lessons to help pay the bills.

And then, my mother came crashing in. I don't mean she came crashing into my daydream, I mean that she literally came crashing into the room.

Yes, again. I swiveled, struggling to sit up straight before she could notice me lounging.

She leveled her finger at me. "Where. Were. You?"

Holy shit, what were we supposed to have been doing together?

"Uh. Right here. And then, in my room. And, now, back here . . . " I was babbling again.

"I flew you all the way here, and you don't even bother to spend any time with me? Don't you think you owe me that much? Brother, what has she been bothering you with?" She ignored my aunt.

"Nothing, I Sho. Just having a nice conversation."

She pointed at a chair in the corner, and I got up and brought it over to her, trying to not make too much noise. She glanced at the chair and sat in the armchair I'd been in, and I sat in the chair instead. "I seriously doubt that," she said, settling herself. "I bet she was telling you all sorts of horrible stories about how I treat her."

My uncle lit his pipe again.

"Wasn't she? Weren't you?"

I gave my uncle a meaningful look, but he hid behind a whole lot of pipe smoke. I sighed. "No, Mama. We weren't talking about you at all."

Quick as a snake, she whipped her hand out and backhanded me.

Shit. I grabbed my cheek and glanced at my aunt, who'd been busying herself with the teapot. She was holding her breath, I thought. Ridiculously, I had hoped no one had seen me get slapped.

I know. I'm an idiot.

My aunt narrowed her eyes and exited. *Great.*

"Don't talk to me in that tone. What's that supposed to mean, anyway? Like, you're too good to talk about me?"

I got up and stepped sideways, just to be out of reach. My damn cheek felt like it was swelling, and I tried to quell the ache in my throat that always preceded crying.

My uncle growled from his chair. "Stop. It."

I flinched, thinking he was talking to me, but he'd waved away the pipe smoke and was looking over his eyeglasses at Mama.

I stepped further sideways.

Mama settled back into the armchair. "Anyway. Whatever you were talking about, it can't have been of any use to anyone."

"Stop it," said my uncle again, and Mama turned on me.

"You see what you've done? Even here, halfway around the world, you bring your brand of discontent to my home. I wish you'd never come."

My uncle took his pipe from his mouth. "You're in my home now, and she can talk about whatever she wants to."

Mama ignored him. "She needs discipline. It's why she's a failure. I hope she wasn't telling you about her stupid plans to get everyone to play dress-up." She turned to me again. "Why can't you just do something *normal?* Look at your brother. He's doing something creative, right? But he's still respectable. Why can't you do something normal and *respectable?* Why is making me happy so hard for you?"

My cheek had started to sting. I was afraid to move.

"What we talked about is none of your business." Uncle crammed his pipe back into his mouth and jerked his head toward the courtyard. *Go.*

I went. My aunt met me as I crossed her kitchen. She handed me a bag of ice and guided me into the small room she and my uncle had meals in when it was just the two of them. "Put that on your cheek, Mei Mei."

She poured me a cup of warm soy milk and set it in front of me. The normality of it all—mother-like figure comforts distressed child with warm milk—made tears finally spring to my eyes. I sniffed, and she handed me a tissue.

My aunt busied herself scrubbing part of the wall.

"When I married your uncle, your mother was still in her late teens," she said. *Scrub scrub scrubbity.* "And I had to come here, and live with this whole new family, because— Americans don't do this, do they? They don't have their new wives come into their family homes, right?"

She glanced at me for confirmation and turned to a new spot on the wall.

"So I came into this family, yes? All alone, and having known only my own family. I, too, had a younger sibling, a brother, and he was many years younger than I was. He was truly just a baby, and he would always be just a baby. Coming here was, in many ways, just like staying with my own family." She glanced at me again, cocked her head. "Do you see what I'm saying?"

"Not really."

She sighed. "Mei Mei, your mama will always be the baby of the family. She has always gotten what she wants. But we don't always agree with her."

I sniffed again. The whole thing was hopeless.

"Oh, now, don't look so sad," said my aunt. She took the tissue out of my hand and leaned forward to check if Mama had left any marks. "You'll be okay. And you can stay as long as you like, no matter what your mother says, okay?" She winked. "She's your uncle's little sister, but he doesn't stand for too much ridiculousness, not even from her."

She sent me to my room.

The great thing about The Compound is that everything's walled in. So even if I had to go outside and across a courtyard to get to my room, I wouldn't have to explain to anyone I didn't know why I was walking around with puffy eyes, a snotty nose, and an ice bag pressed to my cheek.

My room, for now, is a safe place. But how much longer do I have before Mama claims all of The Compound for herself?

I have to find a way to get out of the house. I have to find some way to be useful.

I don't know what to do to make it better. How can I make it better? One thing's for sure. It's better I don't talk to anyone about anything that matters, for both their sake and mine.

And for Mama's sake.

May 23, 7:00 a.m.
Own room

Ugh. I might be out on a limb here, but I think staying up all night is *not* the best way to get over jetlag.

So last night Ken came into my room just before dinner. "What are you doing tonight?"

"Dunno. Going out with everyone else, I guess."

Ken raises his eyebrows. "No Danny?"

"Nope. New lesson plan. Working, whatever that means for him."

"Yeah," says Ken, and then he squints at me. "What the—"

I step back.

"Did she fucking *hit* you?" He reaches toward my cheek.

"Don't. It hurts," I say, and that shuts him up.

He shakes his head like he can't *possibly* understand how *that* happened, which is infuriating, because it looks like he thinks whatever it was is my fault.

"Okay," he says finally. "Well, given *that*"—he points at my cheek—"I'm betting it's probably a bad idea for you to go to dinner wherever she's going to dinner."

"Whatever," I say.

He puts his hands up. "No arguments. I came here to see if you wanted to go out, and anyway, I've already cleared it with Mama."

I snort. "She want me to punch out when I leave, too?" I ask, but Ken cocks his head at me, and I remember he's probably never had to deal with timecards. "Never mind."

"Do you want to go, or not?," Ken says. "Otherwise we'll pick something up and we'll eat here."

"Yeah, let's go. Wait. Who's 'we'?"

He grins. "My girlfriend! Time for you to meet her, don't you think?"

Boy, do I ever. For the first time since the whole Vegas thing, I feel like a normal person, getting excited about meeting her brother's girlfriend for the first time. Cool. Ken's already ordered a taxi, saying something about how we should celebrate (celebrate what? but there's no time to ask) and that after celebrating is not a good time to drive. His girlfriend is already waiting when we get there.

I like her, a lot. But that's not why I was up all night.

I was up all night because my brother's girlfriend is frickin pregnant. Holy crap! (Clearly this is the reason Ken thought there might be celebration.)

It's completely insane. We walk into the restaurant and there's this gorgeous girl sitting there, kind of like you expect Asian movie stars to look in real life, somehow professional and demure at the same time. She's reading the menu already and the light is hitting her cheek just right and she's wearing cashmere even though it's fucking eighty degrees outside. She's absolutely rocking the sweater, making it look like the most normal thing in the world, and then Ken calls her name and she looks up and smiles and you can tell it's like a movie romance from the 1940s, some Nick-and-Nora thing where you're pretty sure they spend half of their time bantering at each other, back and forth, batting around bon mots like nobody's business 'cause, hey, what else do you do on Sunday morning or a Tuesday night or whatever besides wear cashmere, sit in flattering light, and fling bon mots at each other?

And then she stands up and she's wearing a perfect dark gray knee-length skirt with hip kitten heels, because of course she's a working professional, and even if it's 7:00 on a Friday night, of course she's in her work outfit, because she's a real working professional, who's dedicated to her work and loves it and all of that stuff they say defines real leaders.

And then Miss Perfect, whose chosen American name, by the way, is Grace—*Grace!*—smiles at me from under her eyelashes—oh, yes, she has perfect eyelashes, not normal-Asian short stubby eyelashes—and puts out her hand and takes mine and pulls me into a perfect approximation of a New York City air-kiss and then says, into my ear and in perfectly non-accented English, "It is *so* nice to finally meet you. I think we're going to be *great* friends."

Oh, I hate her. She's too perfect.

Ken pulls out my chair for me and goes around the table, and pushes a little stray hair out of Grace's face and then taps her nose and smiles at her, and my heart, my heart fucking shatters, because I can remember when Stafford used to do something similar, even if we weren't ever really in love.

And I can too easily visualize Chris doing the same for me. He'd do the same if we were in a public space, with too many people around, like maybe at a work function. He'd have done the same if I had managed to keep my shit together in Las Vegas.

This I suddenly know.

Ken clears his throat, and I realize he's waiting for me to say something.

I say, "Hi, Grace. I don't know anything about you. I'm glad we're meeting."

Wow.

Ken laughs, a high-pitched hiccupping sort of thing, and part of me wants to snicker, but I say, "Sorry, it's just all so new, you know? I've never met one of Ken's girlfriends before," and Grace laughs, something generous and lovely.

"I know. It's a lot."

They exchange a look.

"Uh," I say, "what are we talking about here?"

If we were standing, I think Ken would have shuffled his feet like a kid. Instead, he picks at each of the appetizers laid out on the table—roasted peanuts, tiny dried anchovies, pickled carrots and radishes.

Grace and I watch him lay one of each on his plate and line them up, like mismatched toy soldiers.

"Uh," he says.

"You didn't *tell* her?" Grace's limpid eyes are narrowed, her eyelashes framing them. I make an unpleasant association with a Venus flytrap.

"Uh," Ken says again.

"Ai ya," says Grace. She shakes her head and scoots her chair closer to mine. "We're pregnant," she says, practically into my ear. She sits back and grins, bright and cheery, except that the two spots of pink on her cheek do not seem cheery. They seem panicked.

I do a take between Ken and Grace, and my uncharitable heart says, *Not so perfect, are we?* but I open my mouth and nothing comes out, which is probably a good thing. I kick myself for being such an asshole, and remind myself that Grace is the kind of daughter my mother would love, so maybe I should try and learn a few things from her.

Well, except for the whole pregnancy thing. You know.

"Wow!" I say.

Anyhow. Ken goes, "Yeah! We're pregnant!" and immediately flags down the waiter and orders bottles of Taiwan

Beer and some menus. I get that they're for toasting purposes, but I'm not sure we're really celebrating.

I am freaked out, actually, by how we're going to break the news to my mother, and then Grace says, "We have to keep it quiet for now."

"What, from my mother?"

She unwraps her chopsticks and separates them from each other with a neat crack before she answers me. "No, from everyone."

Ken giggles. This is not a pleasant sound, and I glare at him.

"What do you mean, from everyone? Don't your parents know?"

"No one knows except for you and your aunt. Ken's mother. I mean, not *your* mother, but his *mother*. You know."

"Yeeeahhh," I say. "I'm confused. Why can't we tell anyone?"

Ken laughs now, and it sounds a lot sharper than I've ever heard him. "Small town, Marty. Grace is the high school superintendent. And our families know each other. If people found out, Grace would have to leave the school. Her family would be devastated."

"Oh, come on," I bark. "I can't believe that."

Ken loses patience. "Where do you think we are, Marty? We're not in New York anymore, okay? This is Taiwan. In the country." He stabs at some more peanuts with his chopsticks, and they slip across the plate, miss the table, and land on the floor. I resist the urge to tell him that's not the way they work.

"Oh," I say.

Grace looks down at her plate. The beer arrives and Ken plays the jovial host for the sake of the waiter, just a guy having dinner with his girlfriend and his sister, a neat little made-for-TV family meal.

If Mama finds out, she'll go off the deep end.

This is awful. Why am I feeling smug? *Schadenfreude.* I looked it up recently. Still means exactly what I thought it did. I am a terrible person. But really, I couldn't help it.

Must brush teeth. Feel grimy.

Later
Own room, still

Everyone's gone to breakfast. They must have thought we

were out late drinking or something, because no one tried to wake me up. That's a good thing.

So anyway. It turns out Grace is a total pig. We ordered, like, seven dishes and she must have eaten most of each of them. I could hardly eat, myself. After the whole shock of new-family-member-times-two and, okay, let's face it, the temporary glee of the fact that the golden boy had finally, finally screwed something up, well, I was feeling a little sick to my stomach, frankly.

I mean, can you imagine it?

MAMA: Why can't you be more like your brother? He blah blah blah blah blah and is a bloop bloop blippity high-and-mighty et cetera and also has won every single award on the planet!

ME: He also got someone pregnant out of wedlock! And you haven't even met her yet! How's that for perfect son, hunh? Hunh? Hmmmm???

Oh, wheeee-ooo. That'd be a doozy, wouldn't it?

So anyway. After we'd ordered and the food had arrived (small talk was not easy, except that Grace is exceptionally good at it—of course she is!), I started asking questions. I'm sure it sounded like some kind of interrogation. I didn't care.

Q: How long have you been dating?
A: About a year.
Reaction: *Holy crap!*
Q: How come we haven't met you before?
A: Well, you haven't been back in two years. And we wanted to make sure it was something that would last. But all the other uncles and aunts have met her.
Reaction: *Oh.*
Q: When are you due?
A: In about seven months.
Reaction: *Oh.*
Q: How did you meet?
A: Some education thing.
Q: Why, again? Why won't you tell our mother?
A: Um, ahhh, errr ...

Yeah. So Ken couldn't tell me why he wouldn't tell Mama,

except I think I know why. I think it's because he's scared witless, and I told him so.

And then he was like, okay, fine, but I think we both know that it doesn't matter *why* he feels like he can't tell her yet; it only matters that he *won't*. And also that he isn't letting me tell her, either.

Great. So now we're both scared of our mother, and we have this huge secret. It's bad, isn't it?

So I'm like, Ken, we need to tell her you're going to get married. Because while we can totally predict what will happen when we tell her, we can't predict what's going to happen if she finds out some other way, or, worse, if you don't tell her until, okay, say, the baby is *here*, and then OMG what?

Ken ignores this entirely, and then he decides this whole pregnancy deal isn't complicated enough, because he says, "Guess what? Grace thinks she can help you."

And I'm like, "With what?"

And he goes, "She just *happens* to have an opening at the high school for a summer ESL teacher."

I glance at Grace, who shrugs and smiles at me. I lift my eyebrows, and she still doesn't give me the time of day except to flick her eyes at my brother, like he has all the answers. Ohhhkay.

So I squint at Ken. "What are you saying?" I ask. Like it's not totally obvious. But I want to hear him say it: I am reasonably sure that Ken is trying to sweeten the deal. As in, if I don't tell Mama Ken got a local girl pregnant, maybe Grace will find room for me at her school.

As far as I know, Ken's never had to bribe anyone to do anything before in his life. Maybe he's never wanted anything so bad. Either way, some petty part of me wants to see him squirm.

And he *does*. God, I thought that was something that only happened in movies. No, he actually squirms, and then he goes, "Like I said. She has an open position. And I think we can make it happen for you, since I know you feel like you're in need of some kind of income, or, at least, some excuse to stay away from Mama *and* something to do that you feel like she can be proud of"—*ouch!*—"So you know, why not just take it?"

I smirk. "In exchange for my keeping quiet, right?"

"Figure it out, Marty. You're smart." He stabs at the fish with his chopsticks. An errant eyeball sludges across the plate.

I look away.

Grace clears her throat. "You know, I'd give you the job anyway," she says. "We've had to hire people way less qualified than you before, and Ken speaks very highly of you. I just had to meet you, is all."

Ken looks at me and then back to Grace. Back to me again. "I'm not holding it over you, you know that, don't you?"

"Dude"—there is no Taiwanese word for "dude"—"I wasn't planning on staying here for longer than a couple weeks, you know. And Mama's supposed to go back about then, too."

"So? Time to stop letting her keep ahold of both your hands and feet, Marty."

I stare at him.

"You gonna keep on letting her hang the meat until the cat jumps so much it dies?"

I swear, Taiwanese idioms are *so weird* sometimes.

"Oh, Marty. What's the American expression—apron strings?" He lifts his eyebrows, checking with Grace, and she nods at him. "You have to cut the apron strings. You need to try and hunt down what will make you whole and complete. Mama isn't going to be able to do that for you. Why not just stay here for a while, even if it's without her, and find your own—you know, how do you Americans put it—space? Is that right? Space?"

The heat rises so fast to my face I feel queasy, and at the same time I'm wondering if *Ken's* been reading self-help books. "No, Ken, you're wrong. I'm not trying to make her happy, exactly, but she needs me—*us*—to keep on *looking* like we're at least trying to make her happy." Ken rolls his eyes at me, but I barrel on. "You're talking about her like she's a hopeless case, or something. She's not. And anyway"—I sit up straight—"anyway, if that were the case, you wouldn't be so damn scared to tell her about your new addition." I flick my chopsticks in Grace's direction. Rude, I know, but I'm pissed. "*And*"—I can't stop myself—"*and*, I'm not trying to fix her, or make her happy, or anything like that."

"Uh huh," says Ken.

I make a decision to not say anything. Grace quirks a very small smile at me. I ignore her.

Ken sighs, really loud and really annoyed. "You're missing the point, Marty. I think it's smart, is all. Look, put it this way: If you take this job, we'll get to spend more time together, maybe you can figure out what it's like to try and be creative here. Isn't that what you said you wanted before?"

I nod.

"Okay." Ken's on a roll now. "And, just to be clear, I don't know what it'll be like to tell her. You know her way better than I do. I'm just saying that maybe we can come up with a good way to tell her if we just give ourselves more time. Right? *And*, if we tell her later rather than sooner, maybe she'll just—I dunno—accept it. Especially if we tell her right before she leaves."

I narrow my eyes at him.

"Ha ha! Just kidding!" he says then, only it sounds weak. He covers it by reaching over me for the watercress, and then he says, "Plus, you'll have less time to spend loafing with the Loafer."

"Come on, Ken. Danny's not *that* bad." I don't say it's not fair, though, because Danny does loaf a lot.

"Oh, don't talk about your friend that way," says Grace, and winks at me. "He's awfully nice to look at, isn't he, Marty?"

Something about the way she talks makes me think she'd be great to work for. So I tell Grace I'll take the job, because now I want an excuse to stick around through the summer. To help with the pregnancy, you know. And I guess that means I've told Ken I'll keep his secret.

"You'll tell her before she leaves, though, right?"

He nods. I don't quite believe him, because it is really that hard to get Mama to come around to any idea she didn't have herself. And this is bigger than that.

So now I also need to be here to help Ken through the day when he finally, finally decides to tell our mother, and I need to be here for when she lets loose the hellhounds, 'cause we *all* know that's going to happen.

117

On the other hand, yay! New job! Money! Independence! And finally, at long last, a job I can explain to my mother! Also: new niece or nephew!

Win-win all around, right?

Right?

Later

Shite. No subletter yet, and I'm locked in here for three months. At least I'll be making some money.

May 24, 9:23 p.m.
Own room

My relatives are exhausting.

I fell asleep again after writing all that garbage down about Ken and Grace, and no wonder. I was pooped. (At least three of the self-help books I have say writing is supposed to relax you, but I'm not sure that's what they mean.)

Anyway. I woke up this morning to this frenetic, eager knocking on my door. I told whoever it was to come in. First Aunt flung open the door.

"Do you know what time it is?"

"Sleep," I said.

"Ridiculous. Get up. Time to paint."

"Mrrrrghhhpffft."

"Get *up*. Morning light is the best."

I sat up. "I can't paint," I said. "I have to get ready for my new job all today."

"Ken told me about that. It doesn't start until next week."

"Ugh," I said, and got up.

Okay, fine, so it was already ten. Okay, fine, so when I got to her porch the light really *was* gorgeous, and you could see how it probably was even better a few hours ago.

I stood there, hovering at the portico, enjoying the way the dust motes floated across the courtyard and landed here and there on the flowers, or were disturbed by the relatively few mosquitoes that were already out in the cool of the morning, and she started to get impatient.

"What are you waiting for? Light's being wasted."

"I can't do this," I told her, and really I couldn't. That same book that says that I have to write first thing in the morning also says the thing I love to do the most can also become a habit, something I can't let go of, almost like an addiction, and I don't have time for that now.

For now, at least, I didn't have time to not be able to stop.

"Don't be ridiculous. I've seen you draw. You're good, especially with figures." She's deliberately misunderstood me. "You haven't drawn a single thing since you've been here, have you?"

I wanted to tell her I had graduated to notebooks without lines, but that sounded stupid even to me.

"Look, you can't stop it, you know. Creating beautiful things is in your DNA."

I shook my head. "No."

"You're overthinking it." She waved a brush at me, flinging water droplets over the cement floor. They made irregular oblong ovals, almost serrated at one end from the force with which she'd gestured. "Come, now you're wasting my time."

I was, too; I could see it in the set of her free wrist, the way she was dying to get to her own palette and sheet of paper.

I reached out for the brush and sat on the porch, and I painted. I painted everything I could see: my aunt's one rooster, standing head and part of his wing above his harem of hens; my aunt's two lazy-ass dogs, one on its back, the other eating from its bowl while somehow still lying down; the guavas hanging sleepily from their leafy branches; the nascent pomegranates, still not heavy enough to add weight to the tree at all, looking jewel-like in places.

I moved to pencil work and drew my aunt, willowy and loose in her gestures, lips pressed into a thin line, working on her latest watercolor; a blurred set of motions in her wrist and arms to denote the speed of her work; sly eyes trained on the paper in front of her. Back to the dogs again, now scratching themselves, all motion and dusty bits flying, scraps of hair here and there.

Markers—oh how I love markers—markers are good for the stern lines of my uncle's part of The Compound, which you can see from my aunt's part of the house. Gray concrete offset with a brick portico and inset with mahogany doors and copper fixtures; plants, studiously watered and pruned by Second Aunt every morning, especially the bonsai in their pots, wired and strung to within their last needles. She saw me through the window and waved, looking happy and housewifely, even in her belted shirtwaist dress. (A woman should be fully dressed by the time her husband gets up, she once told me. I knew a bunch of feminists who might bristle, but my aunt ran everything around The Compound in her perfect outfits, and everyone knew it.)

We were at it until the sun was high in the sky. The light went flat in the studio and we moved outside into the set of rocking chairs First Aunt keeps out on the porch, ostensibly to rest, but I ought to have known that rest was never the sole point of a little time spent away from the work for my aunt.

"So. This job you're taking with Ken's girlfriend."

"You know, right?"

"I know."

"You know she's…?"

"Oh, yes, I know. We don't keep big secrets like that in our family. Well, it's harder to keep secrets when you live close to one another."

"Why don't you make him tell Mama?"

"I'm sure he'll tell your mother when he's good and ready. He doesn't quite, um, *trust* her, I don't think. He has to be ready to tell her."

"Why hasn't he told her about Grace at all?"

"Like I said, he doesn't quite trust your mother to react the right way. He doesn't want to hurt her. Anyway, there's time."

"Not much!" I say. Max, seven months, and then blorp! Baby.

"But that's Ken's problem." My aunt was on some kind of mission. "We're not talking about Ken right now. We're talking about you. Tell me about this job."

"Oh!" A change of subject. Perfect. "It's really fantastic! Grace says it's going to be students who are thinking about going over to the States to study, or maybe even teach English themselves here someday. The point is, they've never worked with a real American, so she says I'm the perfect choice. It's a perfect job for me."

"Is it?" Her rejoinder was so automatic that I was pretty sure she'd been waiting for me to take a breath so she could slip it in. I waited. Sure enough, she went on. "I mean, is it really? What are you *doing* here, Mei Mei? You're not here for vacation."

I told the whole ugly story a fourth time, surprised that Ken hadn't told her yet himself, and she nodded. "I thought so. You've been looking like you needed cheering up."

"Is that why you took me to that store?"

"No. Don't be ridiculous. I took you there because I knew you'd like it, that's all. Nothing about needing cheering up."

She rocked some more and I waited.

"Hm. So you got fired. And you're broke. Well, that's all too good to be true," she said, and I laughed.

"How is it at all good?"

She reached over and took my hand. "You're here, with family who can afford to support you for as long as you like. You should take some time, see what your options are, maybe see if you can get in good with the university's theater department. We have one, you know. And the shop rentals are a lot cheaper here than they are in New York, and the competition is so much less difficult to plow through—you could really stand out here, a lot faster than you would in America."

I pulled my hand away. "I'm going to go to work for Grace."

"Mei Mei."

"I *am*. I *need* to work."

"This would be work. But it would be *life* work, work you always wanted to do, not just some job you're taking because you're trying to impress your mama."

Well. There it was again. I stood up and faced her. "I think I could be really good at teaching," I said, trying to keep from getting too angry, and somehow, too sad, all at the same time.

She reached for my hand again and took it in both of hers. "I know you could. You could be really good at a lot of things. But you could be *great* at making costumes. Really, really great."

My vision blurred. I made some terrible excuse and left her. I avoided her the rest of the day.

I wonder what she did with my drawings. I think they were pretty good, actually.

I used to keep all these things. Whole notebooks of them. There's no reason I shouldn't doodle in these diaries, is there?

I went down to the university bookstore after lunch and bought some lesson-planning equipment and some pens and pencils. Those, at least, I could afford for myself.

I also got an email from Jody. She said Chris had emailed her from the contact form on her website, looking for me. "You should write to him," she wrote. "He sounds worried."

Maybe later I will. I asked Jody to please tell him I was fine and that I'd check in when I had better access to Internet.

Well, and what of it? He can't possibly really want to talk to me, anyway. Or maybe I just don't want to hear that I've probably ruined his professional career.

May 25, 10-somethingish p.m.
Own room

So much fun today! Spent day with Ken and Grace in the mountains. Had picnic! Played in creek. Took photos.

And then Grace dragged this enormous binder out of her bag and suggested I have a look through it. Thought it was papers to sign for school gig, but no. It was a *wedding* binder!

Geez, I didn't know anyone did those anymore. Grace wants to know if I can help her with her wedding dress, since Ken's said so much about my "skills."

After I'd done LOLing in my head, I said yes. Maybe will go back to visit Ms. Liu for tips.

Did not see Mama most of today. She was out to dinner with friends when we got back. This is nice, this not-seeing-her-so-much stuff.

May 26, 11:30 a.m.
85°C Café

Spent some time with Second Aunt and Uncle earlier today. Mama was out visiting yet another old classmate when I stopped in. Uncle was reading the newspaper. Second Aunt was starting the preparations for supper already, even though it was still morning.

She nodded at me and invited me to sit with her, gesturing, as the Taiwanese do, with an upturned open palm at the empty stool next to her. She was wrapping bamboo leaves into cones, filling them with parboiled rice, and stuffing that with egg and meat.

"Can I help?"

"I don't know—can you?" She smiled at me and held out two crossed leaves. "Wind them into a cone," she said, "fill them halfway with rice; add your fillings; top it off, and then wrap over the top to seal it off. Tie with twine."

"Uh."

She helped me through my first one, guiding my hands around the leaves and tying up my bundle for me, and then slapped another two leaves into my palms. "By yourself now."

She watched me while she resumed her own bundling.

"You know," she said after a little while, "your uncle and his brother used to take these to school every day for lunch." She tied off another one neatly and hung it from the bamboo pole propped across two chair backs.

"Oh?" I pictured it in my head: my uncle and his brother, his elder, now dead, walking the mile into school, when the streets still had mostly bicycles all over.

"Your mother always wanted so badly to go to school with them. More than once they spotted her, having run away from home, outside the school fences."

"Oh?" I said again.

"And when she was finally able to come to school, she was happy for a few days, and then she was miserable."

I kept my eyes on my rice-bundle, even though I know she was still watching me. "Do you know why?"

"No one knows why. Your mother is not the best communicator."

I snort.

"But from my point of view, I think it's remarkable that no one ever taught her to say what she wants without making her pout for it." She glanced at my mess of a bundle and took it from my hands. "You're terrible at that," she said, smiling. "I'm almost done anyway."

Funny, being told you're no good at something doesn't always hurt.

May 27, 11:24 p.m.
In Eldest Cousin's car

Busy sightseeing today. Ken came along. Really fun. Writing by flashlight. Things seen:

Black-faced spoonbill birds. Looked like awkward robbers, all legs and no talent for stealth. Endangered species or something; could only look at them through bird-binocular things. Very entertaining. Made up voices for birds. Hee! (For some reason they all spoke in British accents by way of Calcutta and talked mainly of bio-engineering the krill to reproduce faster.)

Very strange dinosaur topiary at rest stop on highway.

Lots of dogs on scooters.

T-shirts that mistake warning signs for in-vogue Americanisms. Nothing like TOXIC or BIOHAZARD, which might be kind of cool, but things like MY POULTRY AND LIVESTOCK ARE MARKED AND REGISTERED and IF YOU EXIT THE PARK GATES WITHOUT A HAND STAMP YOU WILL NOT BE GRANTED RE-ENTRY. No kidding. You can't make this stuff up. Shop girls were wearing them proudly until I told them what they actually said. Then I had to walk around translating T-shirts. They gave me a poultry/livestock T-shirt as a present.

Old Dutch settlement. Way cool. Clashing architecture with the rest of the island, mostly.

Lots of decrepit dioramas. I love dioramas, even the moth-eaten ones where the aboriginal Taiwanese are losing their skin tone and all the weapons have fallen out of their hands onto the "ground."

Things eaten:

Deep-fried dough sticks. For breakfast. Yum.

Eggy crepey pancakey things. Yum.

Pineapple shortbread. OMG yum.

Soupy dumplings. Yum.

Sautéed watercress. Yum.

Hot pork buns. Yum.

Dragon's beard candy, made right there on the street. *So yummy.*

Must stop. Am drooling.

Got picked up in morning. Just now returning home. Have successfully avoided Mama another day! Also avoided awkward weirdness with Eldest Cousin, as did not talk about airport argument.

Wish was one of those people who could just address something. Culture of quiet! And denial! So bad!! Did run news of job past Eldest Cousin. He said congratulations and that he was happy I was staying over the summer, and then he asked if Mama knew, and when I said no, he said, "Ah." And left it. Probably better.

So tired. Must nap now. Am going to have to put in extra laps around the track tomorrow to make up for piggy eating.

May 28, 10:21 a.m.
Bathroom, local school district offices

Oh, holy shit snacks.

Went to see Grace to hand in a missing piece of my formal application for work. Coulda turned it in after I started work, but I chose today. Today. Why???

When I got there she was up against the wall, and *Danny* was on her, and that same gray pencil skirt that I liked so much? His hand was up it, and she was moaning, and oh god.

Ohhh god.

Mama always did say I should learn to knock, but then *she* never did when she was coming into my room.

Am in bathroom because I don't know where to go right now. Had awful scene after discovering them and didn't seem to be able to stop face from flushing and also am pretty traumatized.

The Language of Paying Attention to YOU, again: Writing immediately after traumatic events can help take some of their power away.

Okay okay okay. Deeeeep breaths. Here's what happened.

Me, crashing open door. Grace, gasping from pleasure at Danny's hand up her skirt or whatever. Me, gasping, "Oh my *god* I'm so sorry," although why the fuck did I apologize?

Grace, pulling down her skirt.

Danny, grinning sheepishly, looking fucking annoyingly rakish and still hot, wiping Grace's lipstick off his teeth and then saying, "Oh, well. Guess that's the end of the road for *this* little affair."

And then walking confidently out the door, wafting along a combination of his usual cologne and Grace's perfume. I thought I was going to throw up.

Grace, looking as panicked as I felt just then: "Marty! Marty! Don't go!" because I guess I had turned toward the door and was trying to exit, and I'm reminded of Jody saying the same, and oh how I should have never come here.

"Marty!" says Grace.

"What!" I'm yelling, because the panic has given way to pure anger.

"What are you doing here?"

"*Paperwork, Grace!*" I yell, and then I'm panting and my knees are weak and I am seeing stars. That thing about counting to ten flashes briefly through my head and then I remember I'm supposed to count to a hundred when I'm angry, but I don't have time, because then Grace is telling me to calm down, please, and she's pushing a chair into the back of my knees while she's shutting her office door—so efficient!—and I'm sitting down, and Grace goes,

"You can't tell Ken."

"You're kidding, right? After what I saw?"

"You can't, please, you can't, it was just once."

I look at her askance, and even from that view, I don't see sorrow or regret on her face; I just see panic. "Oh, whatever!" I snort, and suddenly she's next to me in another chair, leaning in really close, and she says, and I swear I am not making this up—

"Tell him and you don't get to teach."

"What?"

"Tell him and I'm withdrawing my offer."

"No way, Grace. That is a load of total bull. You did *wrong* here." And then I say, "Wait a minute, the job starts *soon*. You can't withhold it from me."

"I can," she says. "I'll teach it myself."

And then, as I start seeing spots and racking up things to say to *that*, she finally starts to look a little bit contrite.

"I did. I did wrong, I know. I'll tell him, I promise. Just let me do it myself, okay? I won't get to see him until Monday, so just give me until then."

Holy shit! I mean, holy actual shit! Her eyes are bright; her cheeks are flushed; her lashes, those gorgeous lashes, are looking extra-dark and Hollywood starlet, and I can see how Ken fell in love, was beguiled, but all I can see right now is my heartbroken brother if he ever finds out.

I'm not sure I even have the cojones to tell him myself. I mean, can you picture it?

Setting: Int. KEN's Studio. Daylight.

KEN is busy painting, flinging globs of oil paint everywhere, including on himself. STUDIO AUDIENCE laughs at his antics.

MARTY walks into the studio, shuts the door, waves at KEN. SITCOM AUDIENCE claps, cheers.

MARTY: Hi, Ken.

KEN turns around in surprise and flings paint on MARTY. SITCOM AUDIENCE laughs.

KEN: Hey, little sis! What's up?

MARTY: The sky! What else?

Canned laughter.

KEN: But seriously, what's up? I don't have much time, you know. Gotta go meet Grace for our daily PDA!

MARTY: Yeah, so about that.

KEN: Isn't she amazing?

MARTY: Yeah. Anyway, I was going to say—

KEN: That she's beautiful?

MARTY: She is.

KEN: I'm glad you think so. She's the love of my life. Really. I'm going to paint a painting of her every day until I die.

STUDIO AUDIENCE: AwwwwwwWWWWWW!

MARTY: (*blurting*) I saw your adorable girlfriend putting her tongue down Danny's throat. You know, the Danny *you* were warning *me* about!

STUDIO AUDIENCE gasps.

Oh god, oh god, his face. It would collapse and his work would go to pieces and there would be mourning and then

Mama would find out eventually because Mama misses nothing, and then—

"Holy shit, Grace, is it even his baby?"

"Marty!"

"Just tell me."

Grace pauses, and in that moment I want to tell her to not say any more, but it's too late. "I don't know," she says.

"Fucking hell!"

"Just—I need some time." She looks sad for a moment, truly sad, and then she—I don't know, kind of *sharpens?*—and shakes herself a tiny bit, like a cat, and says, "We're agreed, though, right? You won't tell Ken, and we'll continue with your employment here as planned?"

"You *have* to tell him."

"I will." And then, "You know he's a grown-up, don't you?"

Ugh! So infuriating!

I can see my zero bank account and even more time spent away from home and away from my mother in favor of making that zero go away, and I still can't shake the image of Ken collapsing when I tell him about what I've seen, and so…

So I start Monday. Grace says she's going to tell Ken on Monday. Somehow I have to get through the whole weekend without saying a single thing to Ken about this…this…ugh. This *adultery*. Yuck.

Anyway, my application is complete. Now all I have to do is hang on until she does tell him.

May 29, 9:07 p.m.
Own bed. Cannot move.

Ohhhh. Am all bloated from massive dinner tonight. (Stuffing face so as to have excuse to not talk.) Wish could have ordered stiff drink just to calm nerves, but family mostly drinks weak and refreshing Taiwan Beer, and so would have been inappropriate, and obvious, *and* created Something to Say for Mama.

Told Mama about new job over dinner. Really can't say why I waited so long—is only two days until starting!—except I'm glad I did, because it gave me something else to focus on, other than trying not to think about Ken's love life.

Predictably, my gallant brother made me feel even *more* of an ingrate: He told Mama how lucky they were to have me, and how teaching at the high school would be a perfect extension of my personality blah blah blah and how now I could stay the whole summer in Taiwan and wouldn't that be great.

Everyone was very kind. First Aunt said she'd house me as long as I wanted, and Second Aunt said something about how lively it would be to have another young person to have meals with every night, if that's what I wanted.

The whole time, I watched and waited for Mama to start, and like clockwork, she did: Only people who couldn't make it anywhere else taught ESL in a foreign country. The pay must be for crap. They must have been really desperate to want me. She guessed, if I couldn't make it in New York, I might as well go crawling home to Taiwan, where I'd be hireable just because Mama had had the foresight to raise me in the U.S.

It was like she couldn't stop herself. She took an angry glance all the way around the table, sweeping everyone up in her glare, and steamrolled right into how the hell I was going to manage and how I should have asked her if I could stay and and and and.

God! I so wish Jody were there. Then she could see what a stupid, stupid idea it is for anyone to suggest that I should tell Mama anything. As it was, family all seemed kind of shocked for me. Was equally shocked that they seemed so shocked, until I realized it's not their fault they hadn't been there to witness the repeated Occasions of Mama that make up my life. It was Mama's decision to leave Ken with my aunt and take me to the States. Not their fault.

Anyway, tonight she was relatively tame. When Ken opened his mouth to protest what she was saying, I shook my head at him, and he took a big glug of tea instead. Eventually she wound herself down, ate some food, had a little sip of beer. In the intervening quiet space, someone said something about how Taiwan sure had changed since Mama'd lived there, and the conversation veered, thankfully, in that direction.

We were able to steer the topic away from my new gig for the rest of the dinner, except for a cousin who asked when the new job started. Couple of days, I said, and sat back, waiting for the blowup.

It never came. In the long silence that followed, I watched as Mama methodically lifted her chopsticks to her mouth until her cheeks pouched out with food. She wouldn't meet my eyes, and she didn't talk to me, but I knew what she was thinking:

You never tell me anything.

Her nose was red, and the rims of her eyes, but she didn't cry. She never does.

TAIWAN, Part II

Grace has still not told Ken.

I started work today.

These are the two things on my mind.

Am stealing a quiet moment to myself. I'd told Ken I'd meet him here, but he just called and said he wasn't going to make it, and you know what? I'm totally happy with that. I am really tired of keeping this secret from him. How much longer am I going to last?

I popped by Grace's office twice. No Grace. No Danny. Predictably, I haven't heard from Danny at all.

On the plus side: teaching high schoolers, even two hours a day, is exhausting in the best of ways. I mean, it's actually not so much an ESL class as it is an English conversation club, with guided conversation topics. And today the kids asked me if I would consider sponsoring an after-hours club, for the weekends or maybe after the regular school day, so they could talk about stuff that maybe wouldn't show up on the lesson plan.

(God, I hope no one wants to talk to me about sex in America or anything creepy like that. I think I'd totally freak out. And then, so would they, maybe. And then, quite possibly, end of teaching career.)

Teaching is a lot more creative than I thought it'd be, honestly. Every student is different, which means that I have to approach every student differently. (Wow, how's that for obvious statements? Teaching has made me stupid.)

But it's also funny to see how much they fall into stereotypes. Lee Bi-Kyum is the obvious ringleader. Everyone pays attention to him. He's got this Facebook page under what he wants his American name to be: Rip. His last name's Lee, of course. So when you read it out loud, it's Rip Lee. Get it??? Ripley? Argh!

(He says he's a huge fan of the Ridley Scott *Alien* movies. Gah, he was, like, twenty years away from being born when that movie was made. And Ripley was a girl. Oh, whatever.) Anyway, so he's big into movies. And he quotes lines, even if they're wacked-out translations. The other day he asked me if I'd ever seen *This Airplane Has Snakes on It*. I was all, like, what? And then—oh. *Snakes on a Plane*. So then Rip goes, "*Muthafuckaaaaa!*" at the top of his lungs, which makes the whole class bust out laughing, which is hilarious, because Rip's about as far from a big black Samuel L. Jackson as anyone. Rip is a lithe lean kid of sixteen. And he didn't know what *Muthafuckaaaaa* meant. He stopped saying it after I explained it.

Which was the thing that prompted the idea of an after-school club. And also why I think the kids might be interested in learning about more than just literature and movies and American history.

There are a few girls in class, and they're nice, but I'm having a hard time telling them apart for now. They all sit in a clump. They pay attention in class, and they're really sweet, but they all have the same long, straight black hair. And they all dress in the same skinny jeans and Jack Purcells the hipsters wear in New York, anyway. Hell, I could be in Flushing. So strange. They have a thing for Benedict Cumberbatch, when they don't have a thing for Rip. (Seems to be alternate days.) This tickles me pink. I want to giggle every time one of them pulls out a notebook and there's a big sticker of Cumberbatch's face on it. (Probably should not let on that female fans of Benedict are known as "Cumberbitches." Nope.)

Predictably, we talked a little about where English comes from. They all love English accents. I think they grew up with James Bond and Orlando Bloom and Keira Knightley and so are all very very excited to hear my crappy approximation of the English accent, and then I had to explain that British English isn't spoken in America, really, and they all became really disappointed because Rip had a friend who went to live in Hong Kong and all of his friends—and now, Rip's friend himself—speak gorgeously accented British English. Apparently they were all expecting me to have the same accent, since New York is the closest, geographically, to England.

Oh, also, Rip's great-grandma used to work at The Compound. Such a tiny, tiny town.

What the hell.

Anyway. That was the first day.

Oops. Coffee's here. More later.

So I walked in on Rip today, telling people about The Compound. I was about to ask him how he knew anything about The Compound, and then I remembered his great-grandma, and then I remembered about those pesky local history books that they must all have to read with our house and our family in it.

Was very weird, listening to someone else describe the place. I guess Rip's great-grandma used to actually work inside the house, while my mom was growing up, not just on the grounds. I think she was some kind of housemaid.

"Yeah, the house is huge, you know?" I heard Rip saying, and I ducked behind our classroom door just in time to hear him say some more. "It's kind of run-down, and it has lots of rooms and places to hang out and be alone and stuff." I could picture the girls in the room, eating up the emo.

"It's *old*," said Rip, and I couldn't fault him on that, and then he described the courtyard where I used to play, and the clutch of rooms in each of my uncles' quarters, and that's when I stepped in, because it was time for class to start, and also, it was just a skosh weird that someone else would know so much about my family's home.

Eventually we talked about New York and where I was from and all of that, and then later we talked about why I'd come back and where my family was from. They all already knew, of course. Apparently The Compound also has a small starring role in the "local historical homes" guidebook they sell at Rueitai's equivalent of a chamber of commerce. Aided by Rip's descriptions, nothing was a secret.

Small town. Almost way too small for anyone's good.

But I had a flashback to how awesome it was that First Aunt seemed to know everyone in the market, and then I had a silly pipe dream—yes! yes! right there in class!—that involved me doing my shopping on a Saturday morning and being greeted by all of my students, who would greet me with the Taiwanese honorific for "teacher"—"Good morning, Wu *lao shi!*" and then oh, if Mama and Ken were with me, and Ken and I would laugh about how funny and weird it was to run into your students in your off-hours, and maybe then I could tell Mama about my class and she wouldn't be mean, or embarrassed, anymore.

Blargh.

It's all been good. I've been so busy and so tired when I get home that I practically sleep my way through dinner.

Oh! Today someone asked me about Broadway. She wanted to know what it was like, mostly because the girl who asked had a relative who performed in one of the traditional Chinese operas, you know, with the puppet and the wailing string instrument and the little high-pitched drum? She—shit, what's her name? A Wang. A Chien. Wang A Chien, that's it—wanted to know if Broadway theater was at all like the theater her relative had performed in, and do you know what?

I got briefly homesick, but she didn't even ask about the costumes, which is what I'd been dreading. I'm not sure what I was scared of, now, but I know that I've been avoiding thinking about the store with the watercolors and the mannequins, and I've been so grateful for the busy-ness of this job, because I can hardly even find the energy to consider the life I thought I was so close to having.

All she wanted to know about was the way it worked—was it very hard for people to get a play on Broadway? I explained about off-Broadway, and off-off-Broadway, and all the tiny community playhouses that are everywhere, in every little community, probably much like the one at the university up the street. Practically everyone who makes it starts out in either a little acting class or a community theater, I said.

"Oh, I don't want to *act*," she said, "I want to write."

"Plays?"

"Yeah."

"Plays can be made into movies!" said Rip, but A Chien shot him a look and he shut up.

"Then you should write," I said.

She shook her head.

The room seemed to close in around us.

"She's really good," said one of the other kids, and A Chien threw an eraser at him, but she was smiling.

"Shut up."

"You are!"

I held up my hand. "Hang on. Why are you shaking your head?"

"My parents don't think I should write."

"Well, what do they want you to do instead?"

"Something useful."

"You can do something useful. But you should also always try and remember that you want to write."

"Writing takes a lot of energy."

"Yeah," I said, thinking of the night classes I took in figure drawing, and the weekends spent learning how to sew. "But you can still do it. I mean, look at me," I said, talking much faster than I usually do. "I teach here, but in my heart of hearts, I want to make costumes for people."

A Chien said, softly, "CoooOOOOoool." That word's the same in both Taiwanese and English. She made me smile.

And then Rip, bored out of his skull, perked up. "Like, *Alien* costumes? Can you make me into a big black man?"

The class cracked up. And time was up. And now I should go home. Must sleep.

Grace. Still dragging feet. Ken at conference in Taipei, though, so maybe that's why she hasn't told him. Ugh.

June 2, 6:33 a.m.
Own room

Mama just came in. Didn't knock, as per usual. Could barely get eyes open.

"Well, you might as well know that I'm going to have to stay here until you're done teaching, or whatever. Who knows what trouble you'll get into without your mama around?"

Slam went the door.

What just happened?

So sleepy. Can just catch a few more minutes before alarm goes off. Zzzzz.

Later
Classroom

I love it in here. School doesn't start for two hours. I'm making lesson plans, but really I just like to watch the light.

137

I'm imagining Ken, in Taipei, watching the same light before his conference starts. And Grace, still dragging her feet. I guess it wouldn't make sense for her to go up there to tell him, and over the phone would be horrible, so...

Oh, man.

Chris just called my mobile line. He had to work hard to get this number—I only told the HR people back at *Retirees' Review* so they could call me if anything came up that they needed me for. Like, say, if fairies came flying out of pigs' butts and Markham called saying he'd made a terrible mistake and wanted to place the deal after all.

Pigs did not poop fairies. But Markham does want the deal back.

I got all excited, but then I could almost *hear* Chris shaking his head over the phone. "Marty, I'm so sorry. He only wanted to work with *Retirees' Review* under the condition that you wouldn't have anything to do with the company. They kept me on the account, since they figured you were, um, baiting me. I mean, I don't feel like you were baiting me, but...you know."

Oh, hell. I could feel my stomach dropping, probably my heart, too, because I suddenly had to put my head on my desk—my desk! My teacher desk! From which I teach ESL, which is not what I ever thought I'd be doing, ever in my life.

"Chris, why the hell did you call me?" From my position flat on my desk, my voice sounds like it's echoing. It's so loud I can't stand it, and my nose is starting to drip. I pick my head back up again and prop it on my free hand.

"Aw, Marty, I wanted to hear how you are. You don't need that Irving deal anyway. We always knew you were going on to better things. Things you wanted to do."

I snorted.

"Sorry, what was that? It sounds like we have a crappy line."

"Nothing."

"Anyway, so you're in Taiwan! That's exciting! I know you have family there. What's going on? Are you in good with the local arts scene? I bet you are. I bet you're probably making a ton of friends and figuring out where all the best galleries are, right?"

I was quiet, and he went on.

"Maybe I can come visit. I'd love to see how you're doing, and we have an office in Taipei. How far is Taipei from you?"

I still didn't say anything, mostly because the last time I heard something this cheery, it was Chris, and we were on the way to Vegas, and everything seemed bright and happy and wonderful and I was on the verge of everything I wanted.

"Marty?"

"Taipei is about two hours on the high-speed rail, Chris. I'd be happy for you to come visit, but I'm not doing the things you think I'm doing."

"Oh! Well, tell me what you *are* doing!"

"Nothing exciting. Really. I'm working, teaching ESL. Living with my family. Just trying to get my feet back on the ground after what happened."

"Ohhh, pffft," said Chris. The long distance made it sound like a fizzling firework. "Marty, everyone in sales gets shit-faced and makes a stupid mistake. *Everyone.*"

I started laughing. "Chris, seriously? That's sweet, but I'm pretty sure you've never seen anyone crash and burn quite like I did."

"Well, I didn't see the actual *barfing*," he said, and then we both were laughing.

"Seriously," said Chris, after a while. "I think it's great that you're teaching. You could be passing on so much to these kids and not even know it. So you're going to stay on for a couple months?"

"Yeah—at least until the summer is done. Then I'll decide what else I should do. And anyway, I'm not doing at all what I wanted to do."

"That'll come. You just have to make sure not to lose it, you know?"

"I guess. I'm not sure I even know what 'it' is, anymore."

"Don't say that, Marty, okay? Remember? You told me?"

"You said I was loopy when I told you."

"Then I'll tell you again. You said that you wanted to open a little place that would let people step out of their skins for a while, even if it was just a night. You said you wanted people to feel like it was Halloween whenever they wanted, and that they could be someone else if they felt like it, just to be free. You said you wanted them to know what it felt like. What possibility felt like."

"That seems erudite for a loopy person."

"Oops. Hey, I have to take this other call, okay? I *would* like to chat some more, and I really *can* arrange it so we can visit, okay? Just let me know. Bye!"

He hung up before I could say anything else.

I could really, really love that man.

Day Is Not Ending o'Clock
Own room

The self-help books say you shouldn't ever let things fester. Something about disturbing your sleep. I called Stafford, although I wasn't sure why I wanted to. Maybe I really *was* homesick.

"Stafford Jones."

"Stafford, it's Marty."

"Marty! Hello there, love, how are you? Never mind; *where* are you?"

I couldn't really speak. In the split second between my hanging up with Chris and my dialing Stafford, I had somehow become indignant.

"Marty?"

"Stafford, why didn't you tell me Markham wanted the deal back?"

He didn't even pause. "You don't work for this company anymore, Marty. It's not your deal anymore."

"I know, but—"

"But what? Look, I like you, Marty. Everyone here likes you. But you terminated your goodwill with the company when you sabotaged the biggest deal we've seen for the alcohol and liquor category."

"But—"

"I really don't think you have much to say on that point, do you?"

"Stafford. I thought we were—"

"You thought we were what? You thought we were friends? Or you thought because we dated that you deserved some kind of special treatment?"

"Well, no, but—"

"It's just business, Marty. And as for our relationship, it's not like we ever thought we were going to get married or anything, you know? I never said I loved you."

All the blood drained from my head. I guess that's what it feels like to get told off. "That's not what I—"

"Was there anything else?"

"I guess not."

"Great. I have to go, Marty. Call me when you get back from wherever you are. We'll have lunch."

And then he hung up.

Wow.

June 3, 8:10 p.m.
Hiding in own room

Tried to talk to Mama about job. Went to her room and hung about in doorway until she noticed me. Or, uh, decided to notice me.

"What?"

"The great-grandma of one of my students used to work here. Isn't that interesting, Mama?"

She was sorting some laundry. "Yeah?"

Part of me always goes a little fizzy when Mama shows some interest. I think this is probably normal. Right? Who wouldn't be happy when their mother shows interest in them?

"Yeah!" I said. I stepped into the room and sat down in a rolling chair, scooted over to help her. "Do you know her?"

She smacked at my hands and I stood up again, not sure what to do with myself. I backed into the doorway again.

"Depends," she said.

"Well, *would* you know her?"

"We had several house servants back then, Mei Mei."

So far, so good. A conversation!

"Their family name is Lee. You know? I think she was probably a housemaid or something?"

"Oh, yes. She was a nanny here." Mama's eyes narrowed as she remembered. "They have several children in that family, two girls, a boy, several more offspring. How funny, you teaching the great-grandson of someone who used to *work for us.* What a reversal of fortune, *don't you think?*"

Maybe am imagining emphases. Made swift exit, citing digestive problems. God.

June 4, 5:07 p.m.
Own room

I haven't been able to stop thinking about what Chris said I told him about getting into costuming. (I know, it's sick that I can't even remember that conversation, really. I mean, I vaguely remember it, but it could just be one of those fabricated memories like kids make up when they really want something, or like suspects make up in those crime-procedural TV shows when they've been interrogated for too long?)

So today after class I went to visit Ms. Liu's shop again. I suppose it says something that I found my way there without too much trouble; *The Language of Paying Attention to YOU* says that our body sometimes knows better than our brains where our "north stars" are. Their wording, not mine.

Ms. Liu was sitting out in front of her shop, sketching something, when I got there.

"Hi, Mei Mei," she said, and hearing the diminutive from her didn't bother me. She pulled over another stool for me to sit on. "I heard you took a job at the local high school."

"Yep." I didn't say much else, and she went back to sketching.

"Do you want to come in? I have some new designs that I've been working on. Your aunt says you have an interest in costuming."

"Yep." Part of me couldn't speak. It was like being near the costumes made my head go spacey.

She closed the cover on her book and walked me into the shop. Same blast of air-conditioning, same adjusting to indoor lighting, as before.

She pointed out some books on her countertop. "So I'm working on this costume for a visiting storyteller," she said. "She wants it in red, and she brought in these books for me to look at, and these pictures. About the aboriginal people in the mountains." She smiled. "Turns out, they don't wear a whole lot of solid colors, but the storyteller is half aborigine, half from Taipei, and she wants to honor the lucky color red in our culture. So I will make aborigine designs on red cloth for her from beads, and I think she will be happy."

She showed me the different considerations she'd have to make—the aborigines were shorter and stockier than the storyteller, so their clothing was cut differently. And she had to be careful that the costume wouldn't look like a mockery of the aboriginal outfit, she said, because some aborigines felt looked down on by more recent inhabitants of Taiwan. Finally, she had to make sure she got the intricate beading just right on the costume—the aborigines place a great value on beads, so they had to be well chosen, precisely placed. Ms. Liu explained all of this to me in rapid-fire, excited patter. I wonder when I last sounded like that!

She left me with the books and pictures and disappeared into the back room. She came back wheeling a mannequin a few minutes later, guiding it around by the hips. On it was the muslin blocking of the costume the storyteller would eventually wear, the physical version of her sketches. Ms. Liu had pinned notes to it, for each color in its place. She'd sketched loose approximations of where the appliqués would go, and where the eventual beads would go.

The whole thing looked like a lot of work. But it was work that occupied real space, work that would eventually make someone really happy; work that would allow a storyteller to step into the skin of someone who might be miles away in space and time, adopt an identity, tell someone else's story without feeling too out of touch with reality.

She'd be able to tell better stories, I thought, because she was wearing a different skin.

Ms. Liu wrapped her hand over the shoulder of the mannequin, like it was an old friend, and smiled at me. "What do you think?"

"Yes," I said. "Yes to all of it."

Ms. Liu cocked her head at me and smiled, an inquisitive, friendly bird, and I thought to myself, *I would like to do this thing you are doing.*

I didn't expect to feel the pang that told me how badly I wanted to be back in New York again. I mean, not permanently, or *right now*, or anything like that. I just think I miss the place.

I mean, I know that Ms. Liu gets her inspiration from the things she sees around her—these are things that are familiar to her, after all, and they have a certain resonance. And besides, she has people who are coming to her with different requests every day, so everything stays fresh, and she must get all sorts of new ideas from the people who want to work with her.

My requests, from my students, are all about New York. Maybe all those philosophers were wrong. Maybe it's not so much about familiarity breeding contempt as it breeds creativity. Like, if you're comfortable in a place, aren't you meant to draw energy from it, or something?

I know! I can call Jody. Maybe that will make me feel better about missing home. I mean, I *do* have some news to tell her: I have a new job.

And I can tell her about the shop. She'll for sure want to hear about that. Maybe she'll even want to come and do a story on that storyteller?

How nice it will be to talk to her!

Ken gets back from his conference tonight, finally. I've been avoiding Grace, and I'm reasonably sure she's been avoiding me.

Later

Oooo. Phone conversation went like this:

ME: It's me.
JODY: Oh, hi there.
ME: Are you surprised to hear from me?
JODY: Not really. It's been awhile. We're due for a talk.
ME: Are you still mad at me?
JODY: I think I'm just hurt.
ME: Sorry.
JODY: Okay.
ME: Really?
JODY: Yeah. You were in a bad place.
ME: (*silence*)
JODY: So. What's happening?
ME: I have a new job!
JODY: Really? That's exciting!
ME: It is, kind of. I'm teaching ESL.

JODY: That sound good.

ME: It's fun.

JODY: High school?

ME: Yeah. They're a hoot.

JODY: How long will you be gone for, though?

ME: Couple of months.

JODY: Oh. I miss you.

ME: Uh. I miss you too. You should come visit.

JODY: Yeah, but...you should come back.

ME: I should, shouldn't I?

JODY: Just for the week. You miss it, I know you do. I bet we can get really cheap tickets if we look.

ME: I *do* miss it. The thing is, I feel short on inspiration here.

JODY: You're not short on inspiration. You're short on the thing all your crazy self-help books say you always need. You're short on closure.

ME: They're not crazy books.

JODY: Okay, fine. Anyway, that's what you need. You need to say goodbye to this place, say goodbye properly, even if you think you're coming back at the end of the summer. You know? Just do it right this time, instead of having the decision taken out of your hands.

ME: I *could*, I think. And maybe I should come home anyway to find a subletter for the two months I'll be gone.

JODY: Yeah. I'll look at some flights tonight and email you.

ME: Okay.

JODY: I need to go. I'm glad you're coming back. Can't wait to see you!

ME: Me too!

JODY: Bye!

ME: Yay!

Am utterly elated. Guess I *have* to go see Grace now, see if we can find some kind of substitute. Maybe she can take over, like she threatened to do. Ha! Ha! Ha!

Maybe will just email her. Don't think I can stand to see her, especially since she *still hasn't talked to Ken* OMG.

I mean, I guess there's still a couple of hours until he gets home, but…

I wish this were all over.

Later

Can't sleep! Very excited thinking about trip back home. Should I tell Chris I'm coming? Maybe should do that, just in case he gets a harebrained idea to hop on a plane and see me. Boy, wouldn't that be a doozy. I can just picture it: me, standing in front of the MediaStar office building, calling his line and getting this message: "You've reached the voicemail box of Chris Lincoln. I've relocated to Taiwan to pursue the love of my life."

And then, me: "Hi. It's the love of your life. I'm in *New York*."

Oh my.

And then, since I'm me and I have crap luck, it wouldn't be me who was the love of Chris's life after all.

Wow. What a downer.

Maybe will be able to sleep now.

Still later

Even given potential Chris-timing disaster, am happy at idea of visiting home for a while. Will make it a point to visit all appropriate galleries and shops, even that tacky Halloween joint on Broadway. Maybe will also pick up some nice coffee-table books at Strand, just to have them for inspiration for when I get back here. Also will get one for Ms. Liu. She's kindly.

I like idea of "stocking up" on New York. It's not like I won't be back there in a few months, but it would be nice to get closure, like Jody said. I mean, hell, I was me before I ever went to *Retirees' Review*, and I lived there way before I even knew Stafford. So there.

Will email Chris when get tickets. That should hopefully defer any major timing disasters.

Hm. Wonder if really could be love of Chris's life.

Silly!

June 5, 10:00 a.m.
Own room

Holy motherfucking son-of-a-bitch shit. I can't even wrap my brain around what just happened.

So Jody emailed me this morning, okay? She found some cheap tickets for next week that I can actually buy with my frequent flier miles, so I don't even need to pay for them. Awesome news, right? The day is going great.

So. I make myself some coffee; I'm sitting out in the courtyard; the hummingbirds are zipping around like they've had extra doses of fructose this morning. The lizards are looking extra-brave; two of them are staring at me with their beady little eyes and their weirdo plasticky tongues flicking in and out, like they want a taste of my coffee too, and the sun is out, but it's not too humid yet, okay?

And then, things go totally completely off the wall. What happens is this: I see my mother, my uncle, and my aunt moving around in the kitchen. I go in to tell them the exciting news, which I think is that I'm going back to New York for a week and then I'll be back, better than ever.

Instead, this is what happens:

My mother freaks the shit out. Like, seriously freaks out. Like I've never seen her this freaked out before.

Like, this is worse than the day she broke every dish in our cupboards because she couldn't understand why I was three "tardies" from not graduating—hello! senioritis!—or the night she called to disown me because I'd chosen a gig with an illustration firm as my first job out of college. That day, the screaming from down the phone line was almost palpable. I could swear it's responsible for my tinnitus.

This time, it was live and in person, and the very air seemed to shimmer with heat and a sense of violation.

Okay. So I go inside. She grunts at me. My aunt and uncle ask me if I'm hungry. My mother responds in normal fashion: "She's fat enough; she doesn't need to eat more; she's already spoiled enough here." Et cetera.

I clear my throat and my mother perks up. Probably my first sign that she was already spoiling for a fight. Ought to have saved it for another day.

Then I say the following fatal words: "Great news! I'm headed back to New York for a week, just to clear up some final details."

My aunt and uncle make appreciative noises: You must have missed it; when is your flight; when should we expect you home—home!—it will be nice to see your friends. And so on.

My mother doesn't make a sound. Predictably, ignoring the bad feeling looming in my chest, I open the gate further for her: "Mama?"

It's like she's been saving up. She lets loose. "You. Terrible. Terrible. Person. I flew you all the way back here, in the hopes that you would learn something from living in this amazing place, maybe learn how to respect yourself, get some self-esteem, respect your ancestors and where you came from, and you pull this garbage on me?"

"Mama?" Mewling, pathetic.

"Shut up! Don't you know by now that New York has nothing for you? You went to live in the big city and you were shamed from day one. No one wants you there, don't you know that? Can't you see no one is interested in what you do? Wasn't it enough that they fired you? Wasn't it enough for you to have been kicked out of the whole city in the most shameful way possible?"

She takes a breath. The room is a vacuum. My uncle and aunt can't find anything to say. But Mama only pauses for a very short time.

"You have lived in that pathetic apartment for over five years. And you can't even find someone to share your bed with. You give it away, like the whore you are, and you can't even make them stay by giving it away. Your friend—what's her name? Jody?—she only keeps you around so that she can remind herself of how much better than you she is. Can't you see anything? Why are you so blind? I only tell you these things because I love you. No one else would tell you these things."

Another short breath.

I can't think fast enough to think of anything to say.

"And now you tell me that you want to go back to that place! Why? Why? I've set things up so well for you here:

You have a home, a family here. You can do whatever you want. Lie around all day and eat chocolates! Spend all day hunting for a boyfriend, if you want! And finally, you got a job! A job that is well respected! People like you here, can't you see? You are back with your own people, people you can actually compete with. Why do you want to leave? Why are you doing this to me? For once I can be proud of you, and now you want to take that away from me. Why are you so selfish?"

(Holy fucking shit. No one but me will ever know how much that hurts to write down. When I have some time I am going to write to the authors of all those self-help books and tell them two things: 1. They were right, this is exhausting; 2. Practitioners of Write Shit Down should probably set aside a healthy nest egg for either vacation or therapy.)

Possibly here is where she pauses for a little longer, which is why I suddenly think of what I can and should say.

Possibly here is where I wish she'd paused for a split second longer than even that, so that I could think a little bit longer and realize that maybe only some of what I think to say should be said.

"What the hell!" This I say in English, because the only Taiwanese equivalent I can think of is really, really crass. "Mama, you are going to make me completely insane. You just told me when I started this job that it was for losers, that I'd never make any money. You just told me no one likes me and that not even my uncle wants to hear what I have to say. You tell me something like this every day of my life. So why would I want to stay here, anyway? Why wouldn't I want to go home, just for a little while? No. No. No," I say, because she has opened her mouth again.

I start to yell. "It doesn't matter what you say to me, because none of it is real. What world do you live in? What world is it that people are friends with each other just to make themselves look better? What world do you live in where it's *fucking okay to say things like this to 'people you love'?*" I lay on the sarcasm, and it feels good. The room goes quiet, except for Mama, who is actually trying to yell over me, but I don't hear her because I am yelling myself. Really, really yelling.

"This is all sick. Sick. You want to talk to me about self-esteem? Self-esteem? The only way I could possibly get any of that is to get away from *you!*"

"Then *go!*" Mama finally yells loudly enough to make us both go quiet. She roars it; her pupils have dilated, and I am scared stiff that she's going to have a heart attack or something crazy, but she stays upright, and then she starts in again, and I think that's what pushes me over the edge.

"*Shut up*, Mama. *Nothing* you say is any different than anything you've said before. You about to tell me you're going to disown me? Are you? Old news. You already tried that before. But I have something new for you. I do. You want to talk about how little respect people have for me? Well, how about this? Your son? The better of the two? The one you left behind? The one you wish you could take credit for, if only he were still yours? Guess what. He's having a kid. With someone you never met. He hasn't even married her yet. You proud now? *Are you? Who's the slut now?*" I take a huge, fire-stoking breath. "Know what else? He doesn't even want to tell you. You want to know why? Probably because you'll react *just like this.* Because you *never listen* and probably because you always sound *fucking insane.*"

"Fucking insane" actually has a Taiwanese equivalent.

It's about then that I realize what a huge, huge mistake I've made, because even Mama shuts up. She has nothing to say at all, which is what I thought I wanted.

Mama starts to cry, and my uncle looks at me and shakes his head. "Oh, Mei Mei. You shouldn't have told her this way."

Mama looks around. I know what her vision is like: blurred, annoyingly prickly. She's made me cry so many times that I know this feeling like the back of my hand, but I don't take much pleasure in seeing her cry now. "You *all* know about the girl?" she says, and my uncle says, "Not about the baby," but my mother has stopped hearing and doesn't care, and she finally, finally has a reason to feel wronged, and so she pushes past me, so hard that I fall, and we hear her pounding down the long hallway and up the stairs.

Taiwanese houses of that era are built with cement floors, but you can hear something like desperate footsteps no matter what.

The door slams. If it were just hysterical crying we might have all been able to stand it, but my mother starts wailing. I look to my uncle. He chews on the end of his pipe for a while, sighs. He presses himself to standing and shuffles toward her room. He glances back down at me, still sitting on the floor where Mama left me, and says, "Wait here."

We hear him shamble down the hall. Second Aunt pats my arm and pulls me up. She scoots a chair into the back of my legs and pours me some tea, pushes a bun toward me. "You need to eat."

I nibble, and it's right about then that the shouting starts. It sounds remarkably like what we've just heard from my mother, and I'm pretty clear it's all for my benefit, because then she shrieks that I should be kneeling at her feet in shame for what's just happened and that if I'd never come, this would have never happened. And who, who, Mama goes on to wail a third time, who had bought a ticket for such an ungrateful dog of a child in the first place?

"Maybe you want to go to your room for a bit?"

I think that's probably a good idea, since my room is so far away. I think suddenly of Rip: "In a Taiwanese house made in the early 1800s, no one can hear you scream, so long as you're across the courtyard."

My uncle shuffles back into the kitchen. He grunts, settling back into his chair, and re-lights his pipe. Something upstairs shatters. I stand up to go, and my uncle glances at me. "It'll pass," he says.

It always has before, but this seems so much worse.

"Go," says my aunt. "Things will be better later."

God. I can't even do a proper dramatic scene right. What I really should be doing, instead of reliving the god-awful memory of what's just happened, is hunting down Ken. He should probably know what I've done.

June 5, or Day That Will Not End, Redux, noontime
Own room

So it turns out my room really is the safest place to be, because when I went to Ken's studio, he was painting away, slashing at the canvas. I really did get paint all over me, just like in my little sitcom fantasy.

Ken was extra-energetic, happy to be back at his canvas after a long conference, and when I got there and saw that, I almost turned around and left. I mean, how could I tell the guy what had just happened? It's not like I haven't been interrupted enough times before (by Mama herself, of course) while I was in the middle of trying to make something, and those were just little annoyances. This? Kinda big. Okay: very, very big.

I am an idiot: I try to ease into the thing.

I do what I think is flouncing casually into the studio with a devil-may-care attitude and fling myself into the nearest chair, except the nearest chair is something ancient from my grandpa's time and made of wicker, and when I fling myself into it, the thing cracks underneath me with a horrible shrieking noise, just what you'd expect old wicker to sound like when it finally gives, and then suddenly I'm on the ground and my tailbone is killing me and tears are springing to my eyes. Part of my brain hears Ma yelling, "So fat! No one will want you!" and the other part of me just physically frickin hurts so much it can't be bothered to think.

Ken's at my side in a flash, trying to help me up by my elbow, except the way I'm feeling, it's better if I just stay there on the cold hard floor, but he's not having any of it, saying ridiculous storybook things like "There, there," and "It'll all be better in a minute when you get your breath back," and he pulls out that stupid gentlemanly handkerchief again and is trying to wipe my nose, but I swat his hand away.

This is like when you have the flu and all you want to do is lie on a cold hard surface. You want that because the flu puts you in a deep, dark, uncomfortable hole, and when you're in a hole like that, all you want is to know that there's someplace even worse you could be. Ergo: cold, unyielding, cruel floor, just where I am while Ken is trying to move me to someplace kinder.

I'm pretty clear that I don't deserve anyplace kinder, and I'm trying to tell him that, but he, my eternally, annoyingly, frustratingly cheery brother, isn't getting it.

So I let my temper get the best of me again, and I tell him, right there, though the snot and the whooping sobs (where did those come from?) make me barely intelligible.

"Ni tole Maba bebbeh Graaaaaaaace."

He draws his eyebrows up and starts laughing. "Oh, Marty. I can't understand you. Never mind, come on, let's get you off the floor."

I glare at him and swat his hand away again. Why? Why? Why did I not just shut my mouth? It's like a disease.

"I. Told. Mama."

I enunciate, for really really good measure.

Ken grunts. He's trying to lift me off the floor, and I am finally trying to let him. "That's nice, Marty. What'd you finally tell her?"

And then, "Oh, *motherfucker*, you didn't." Yes! There is such a word in Taiwanese. He almost drops me.

I wipe my face on my sleeve. "I'm sorry. I really really am." Ken prods me toward an armchair and I slump into it. "Ken. I'm so sorry."

"What exactly did you tell her?"

"You know. That you're having a baby with someone she's never met."

"*How* did you tell her?"

I squirm and try to stop hiccupping. "Well, we were having an argument at the time."

"Oh." His eyes widen. "*Oh.*"

"Yeah."

"So you pretty much said it just like that, didn't you?"

"I guess. I mean, with some other choice words thrown in."

"Oh, Mei Mei. How did this happen?"

Ken is sagging toward some kind of unreachable internal thinking process, and I'm desperate to get him out. Part of me is desperate to have him on my side again, and the other part of me is desperate to get him to tell me everything's going to be okay, that he had to tell her anyway, that, all things considered, this is the best way it could have been done.

Okay, maybe that last is stretching.

So I start talking, fast. "Well, she was hurting me." *Wow, that's lame.* "I mean, she said terrible things."

"She *always* says terrible things."

This comment stops the hiccups. "Oh yeah? How do you know? Like what?"

"Come on, Marty, does it really matter?" He starts pacing the floor. "It was a perfect plan, and now what? How are we supposed to mend this?" He stops pacing for a minute. "How are *you* going to mend this?"

I cannot believe what I'm hearing. "Are you really trying to dump this on me?"

"It *is* something *you* did, Mei Mei." He jerks his head, dismissing and totally confident. "Never mind, Mei Mei. Let's just start thinking about how we're going to fix it, okay?" He puts special emphasis on the "we," and I'm about lose it, because that's when it hit me.

Ken was *never* there. He couldn't really know what it was like. "So tell me, Ken. What do you think that means, 'She always says terrible things'?"

He flips his hand. "Do we really have to talk about it now? It's your status quo. Everyone talks about the horrible things she's done to you, and you always seem to be okay when we talk to you or when you come visit, right? You always come back smiling and happy, and you always come out on top. No problem!" He accentuates this last by brushing his hands together: Done and dusted. (Where did he pick that up from? So strange.)

Oh, man. I really could not communicate. Use whatever euphemism you want: wind knocked out of you; wind taken from your sails; knocked stone-cold sober. Whatever it was, it felt like it applied to me, right then and there.

"Wait. So you *all* know about what she's like?"

He cocks a sharp, short shrug and then seems to think better of the gesture. "I mean, we *hear*. But you're always okay. And you almost always seem to do something that sort of jives with what she wants, so maybe part of you wants to please her. Or knows she's only got your best interests at heart, or something."

"Dude. How?"

He's impatient. "How what?"

"How do you all know?"

He blinks. "She tells us, when she calls home," he says.

An unpleasantly familiar sensation is creeping up the

back of my neck and making the nerves there twitch and tingle, and then I realize what it is. I am mortified, just like I was as I was starting to piece together my behavior from the night I got so drunk at the sales event. I am just as mortified as I was in the seconds after I barfed on Captain Markham.

Everyone knows. Everyone knows the terrible things she thinks of me. Worse, everyone must know how I try to make myself as small as possible around her, and how badly I fail at it.

That's about all I have time to process, because Ken flaps the hand again. I want to cuff it to something. "Anyway, we need to talk about what we're going to do now."

"Stop saying 'we'!"

Ken huffs. "Well, you get to take some responsibility for this. You spilled the beans. Why was she yelling, anyway?"

I'm so annoyed I don't even want to tell him, but I do. "She was yelling because I'm supposed to go back to New York for a week, just to take the edge off the first time I left."

Ken shakes his head, slowly, like he's thinking something through.

"Wait, why are you shaking your head?"

"Marty, going back right now would be terrible for both of us, for both you and me."

"Whaaat?"

He pulls over a stool and sits on it, leans forward, talks at me. "Look. When I actually sit down to tell Mama myself, talk to her about this, she's going to really lose it."

"Man, you have no idea."

He ignores me, jumps up, starts to pace. I'm still slumped in the armchair. I can't and don't really want to move. Everything that's happened since I left New York just a couple of weeks ago is sitting on my chest. I am so very, very tired.

Ken is still talking. "How do I fix this? How am I going to tell her now? Do you think my telling her we're getting married will help?" He's talking faster by the second, pacing in tighter circles, and then his words sink in, and I realize it's obvious he hasn't talked to Grace yet. I stick out my foot and catch him in the thigh, trying to buy time so I can think up how to ask him without revealing anything.

"Ken. Stop. You're being ridiculous. You don't even know what you're dealing with. You've never lived with her or anything. Just stop for a second. Listen to yourself. You're just spinning random scenarios."

He turns and really looks at me. "You can't go. You *can't*. You need to see me through this."

Oh. Oh. I am so *sick* of being responsible for things. So tired.

I talk at him from my position in the chair, looking up at him. "This is not right," I say. "You all seem to think that I have some kind of hold on Mama." I think back to Second Aunt, spinning me long-ago stories about Mama, looking at me hopefully, as if I have some kind of key to the way Mama is. I think about First Aunt, willing me to seek out my own path, damn the consequences for my life with Mama if she were even to hear how close I am to finding something I like, god forbid. "Don't you people understand? It's *she* that has a grip on *me*, and *me* that is walking on eggshells all day, and *me* that needs to see *me* through this, okay? I don't have a clue how to do that, even, so for the moment I'm trapped, and all of you maybe should think about thinking about me and Mama as separate, and not stuck together, because you don't know *anything* about what my life is like. Not even a bit."

Ken shakes his head, refocuses. "What are we doing here? We have to go tell Grace."

I've run out of time. "No, no, no," I say. I push myself out of the chair and get in front of Ken. "You can't go tell Grace. I mean, you have to talk to her, but, I mean, well, *have* you talked to her?"

Ken shakes his head. "Why are you being so weird? Let me go. And no, I haven't talked to her. She called last night but I got home so late that I didn't call her back. She said she had something to talk to me about."

"Yeah."

"What?"

"Nothing."

"Marty. What? What did you do now?"

"Nothing. You need to go talk to her."

"Oh, Jesus, Marty, just out with it!"

Maybe I feel weak. Maybe I can't take any more. Maybe I am tired of lying, so I just tell him. "I saw Grace with Danny."

"Yeah, so what? They hang out."

"No, I saw her *with* him."

"What?"

"*With* him." I start doing something with my hands that might vaguely look like two people making out, but I can't make him understand. Finally I say, "You know. Kissing. Other stuff."

My nightmare becomes a reality. Ken's face goes utterly white and his lips part. His eyes goggle, and my handsome brother becomes a lost boy, right in front of me.

"Ken?"

"I *knew* it," he says, sounding flat. "I *knew* he was no good. Didn't I tell you?"

"You did," I say, and then I remember I have broken my promise to Grace, and now I have no job.

I feel a lot sad, but part of me also thinks I'm just too tired to do anything about it.

Ken tells me to go away, so I do.

First Aunt is the only person I think I can actually trust to not add any more to the insanity. Well, and Ms. Liu. But how pathetic is it to go leaning on someone you only just met? Someone whose full name you don't even know?

Ugh. How did I get here?

June 5, or Day That Will Not End STILL, 2:30 p.m.
Own room

This day is like one of those lousy days where you know you have so much to do that you should write down a to-do list (*Organizing Yourself to Be a Badass*, Amazon, $0.99), but you're still in that stage where you think you can keep it all in your brain? So then you just run around all day remembering random shit you have to do? Yeah, it's like that.

So I went to see First Aunt. She was in her studio, flicking color onto a sheet of paper.

"Hi," she said. "Heard you had it out with someone."

"Yep." I flopped into yet another wicker chair. This one didn't break under me, and I counted it as a point for me. "What'd you hear?"

"Just that you had a huge argument. That you tried to go home to New York and that she wouldn't let you go. That terrible things were said."

"Yep."

My aunt took a few more dabs at her work. She stepped back, dropped her brush into a cup, and dragged over another chair.

"So."

"Yep," I said again.

"What now?"

"She's *your* sister." Oh, I know. I sounded—and felt—like a real asshole. Could be good, to be one of those folks who's a perma-asshole. Whaddya call 'em? Misanthropes.

"Come on, Mei Mei. It doesn't work like that."

All right, so here's where the memory gets a little fuzzy. I mean, it's not like I haven't been traumatized too, during this whole thing. It's not like I don't get to claim a little bit of the victim here. I mean, hell, the yelling is just a tiny fraction of it, isn't it? It's what happens inside when the yelling gets to be commonplace. You start to believe the yelling, don't you? You start to sort of integrate it into your life, like it's something you either can't do without or you're not really sure how to disentangle yourself from.

Sooner or later you get to the point where you go to do something, say, like, okay, date. And you meet a guy and he's drop-dead gorgeous and there seems to be chemistry, I guess, and then you go on your first date, and part of you starts to whisper that it'll never last: he's just too pretty. So whaddya do? You start thinking that you might as well just have the one-night stand and see what happens the next day: if he really likes you he'll come back for more. He comes back for more. And then pretty soon you're stuck in a relationship that was never meant to be anyway, all because you gave up the cow with the milk, or whatever, and all because that sick little voice told you it would never last 'cause he was too pretty for you.

What the fuck.

Anyway. So I'm sitting there, trying to puzzle out what I'm supposed to do next. I mean, do I stay here? And what do I do with the whole Ken thing?

I get it. I get that it's my fault. But geez, Ken's just lucky he's a boy. If he weren't a boy, well, he'd be me, and I'll tell you what, if he were me and pregnant, it'd be pretty fucking obvious pretty fast.

Spoiled rotten, that's what he is. That's my story and I'm sticking to it.

I don't say any of this to First Aunt. I just sit there like a lump of poo (yes, that's a Taiwanese colloquialism), since I'm not sure where the heck I'm supposed to go next, or what I'm supposed to do. Do I go check on my mother? Do I go try to patch it up with Ken? I don't know anymore, and none of my decisions have turned out right.

So. Me: Lump of poo. Her: Staring at lump of poo. Then she says, "What do you want me to do?"

Which is unexpectedly hilarious, because that's what I was asking myself. I don't say anything, and then I come up with something intelligent. "I just need to hear from someone who actually understands what the hell is going on to tell me what to do. I'm completely lost. I want to go home."

"I don't think you can leave it like this," she says.

"Well, that's not good," I say. She cocks her head at me, which I ignore, because she's asking me what I mean, and I don't really know, can't even tell myself. I *know* I can't leave it, but I *want* to go home. And the worst bit of it is, I *also* want to help Mama.

After this useful exchange I think I must fall asleep, because the next thing I know, she's shaking me. "Hey. *Hey.* You need to figure it out."

"You need to help me."

"No. Just like you needed to figure out what you want from life, you also need to figure out what you are trying to get from your mother."

This is all too much. I think miserably to myself that this is the stupidest thing I have ever heard. Apparently the solution is to answer with something equally stupid.

I say, feeling whiny, "What I'm trying to get! I just want normalcy! I just want some time—an hour, even—when we can be near each other and I don't have to spend the whole time managing what I say. I don't want to have to lie anymore, and I don't want to have to listen to terrible things that aren't true. I don't want to have to hear them."

My aunt lifts her shoulders. "What's normalcy, anyway?"

I give her an "Are you for real?" expression and wave her off. "Oh, come *on*. Normalcy. You know. A little closeness between mother and daughter. A little baseline, so that we can be around people without her feeling like, every single day, she has to make me out to be the world's worst juvenile delinquent. What the hell is that about, anyway?"

My entire life has turned into a parody of a sitcom, something grotesque and vaudevillian. In fact, it wouldn't be at all bad if a big hook appeared and dragged me off stage.

My aunt pulls a lopsided smile. "Maybe that's her normal. Maybe that's just her way."

"That's the crappiest kind of normal I can possibly think of."

"You're right. It is a crappy normal. But it's what she has to live with." She puts her hand on my arm and waits until I turn to meet her eyes. "Do you hear what I'm saying?"

I *think* what she's telling me is that my mother's "normal" is way worse than anyone else's. I *think* what she's telling me is that Mama operates on a different plane from the rest of us.

What she's telling me is that Mama is completely off her rocker. Or, at least, she is according to my baseline measurement, and probably everyone else's too.

So I'm sitting there, processing this information slowly—dopily, almost. The only thing I really heard is that all these years, Mama has been dealing with some kind of bullshit voice in her head that tells her things are so much worse than they actually are.

And then, right on the heels of that comes terrifically sobering elation. Like, whoa, this might not be my fault. Like, maybe it's not me who's completely off-base all the time. Like, maybe I shouldn't have to try so hard. Like, maybe I should start paying attention to who I want to be, instead of who I think she wants me to be. Because maybe Mama is bat-shit broken. Maybe what she needs isn't for me to go around picking up the pieces, because I'll never find all the pieces anyway. Maybe that's what *you'll never be good enough* means. Maybe I never had the right stuff to begin with, because, hell, it was all in her head anyway for starters. It's never been me. She is sick, and I do mean that in the gentlest of ways.

And then, right on the heels of *that*, holy hell, why hasn't anyone been helping her? If they know this, then why on earth isn't anyone giving her any attention? That truth is too awful for me to imagine. I remember the way my uncle talked to Mama, the day that she said those horrible things to me, and now, instead of him looking like a savior to me, he looks like a ne'er-do-well where his baby sister was concerned.

And my aunt! What about my aunt! An artist's temperament; the woman who adopted Mama's son; the woman who even now is telling me things about my own mother that perhaps my mother should be telling me.

I consider the fabric store. Mama did not want me there. I didn't understand why. But could it have been as simple as wanting to have a little bit of her own with me? Could it have been simple jealousy that her older sister was seemingly taking yet another of her children, this time, her only daughter?

Could it be?

And then, in *her* normal—god. It must have felt terrible, watching her other child get sucked in by the same woman. She might have felt that her sister was being totally parasitic.

I sit there for the longest time, trying to put things in order. My aunt, who's feeling a little *predatory* to me now, pats my arm—I swear I flinch—and tells me that probably the best course of action is to sit a little on the situation and maybe have a bite to eat, and by that time maybe I'll have a better idea of what I want to do.

I *am* hungry. I shake her off, ignoring the surprise in her eyes, and I ask her, speaking slowly because I am still processing way too many things: "First Aunt, why? Why didn't anyone help her?" My aunt glances at me and slides her eyes away, quick, but not before I see something that reminds me of my father: Oh, horrible guilt.

"We—we Taiwanese—"

I wince. I am an outsider.

She goes on. "We Taiwanese don't see it that way. Help, I mean. We see it as interfering. Your mother married *out*, do you see? Women marry *out*. They become their husbands' problems."

Problems!

"I mean, I mean—" My aunt has seen my eyebrows go way up into my bangs. "What I mean is, we wouldn't talk about those things anyway. Your mother has a good life. It is a life of leisure. It is the life all women of her class get. It is as it should be."

Except she's *broken*.

Well, I think so, anyway.

Suddenly I am wiped out. I want to fall asleep again. (Is this what those fainting goats feel like all the time?) And First Aunt may be predatory, in my mother's version of normal, but her voice is soothing and I am hungry, so I do what she suggested in the first place, wishing I could unhear everything I've just heard. I have a little steamed scallion bun and warm soy milk, and then I go right to my room and I have a nap. I have another one of my predictably annoying dreams, where random people chase me around on weird mechanical implements (toy dinosaur, this time, with Ken on it) while pustules of guilt get pulled out of my skin in vines and on strings, yards and yards of them, all tattoo-stitched BAD DAUGHTER, and now I am finally awake and a little bit clearer and I know what I have to do now:

I have to talk to Mama. Really, really talk to her, even if I know I'll just find some way to make it worse. Hey, there's nothing like a track record for predictability.

I hear some noise coming from across the courtyard. For me to hear it all the way over here, it must be Mama yelling. Better go.

Still Day That Will Not—ohnevermind
Don't care what time—late, it's dark
Doesn't matter where

So. The yelling *was* my mother. Right before she flung herself down the fucking stairs.

Horrible. See? I knew something bad would happen if I tried to do anything. I *knew* it.

Okay. Okay. Must breathe. All the books say you should try and take a couple of deep breaths before you say or do

162

anything. Obviously this is something I am terrible at. But I am all alone now so there is no one left to upset. Might as well practice breathing breathing breathing.

Oh for fuck's sake. Never mind.

I mean, I know she didn't mean to hurt herself really. I think I know she was just being dramatic. But Christ, why did I think it was a good idea to tell her that?

Okay. Okay. So here's what happened.

I go over there, right? And when I get there everyone, including Ken—why is he not talking to Grace?—is clustered around something at the foot of the stairs. I can't figure out what they're looking at. A huge stain on the floor? Did one of the old tiles break? Did something crawl in here and die?

No—whatever it is, is yelling, and sometimes screaming. I get closer and squeeze in between Ken and my uncle. My mother is lying there, clutching herself, practically howling. I blink a couple of times and then do the only thing I can think of to do: I drop down beside her and try to hold her.

Why? Why do I not pay attention to the many self-help books that tell me to think before I do anything? When I get home I am burning them all. Except the ebooks. I don't know what I'll do with those—wave sage sticks at them in order to exorcise them from my system, maybe. Ugh.

Anyhow. Mama does exactly what I knew she'd do, which is swear at me and push me away and tell me I smell or something horrible like that.

Actually what she said was that I "reeked of desperation and insincere, obvious afterthought," and that I should "stay far, far away, maybe go back to the fetid pond you crawled out of."

Angry Taiwanese is incredibly dramatic. Or, Mama should've been a writer.

I try to hold her, but she comes close, I think, to hurting herself more as she's flailing, trying to get away from me. I'm still not sure what's happened to her, so I scoot back for a look.

Here's what I see: my mother, looking smaller than I've ever seen her. Her eyes are piggishly swollen from crying, and preternaturally bright due to the same tears. She's curled on the floor and I want to tell her that I know what it feels like, but that feels pretty much the same as trying to hold her, and since *that* didn't turn out so well, I just leave it alone.

I finally see that she's holding her leg. And that her foot seems bent at an angle that's just shy of—well, working. And it's already turning purple.

And that's when I finally find my mouth, and I say, "What the *hell* happened here?" Ken puts his hand on my shoulder, and I shake it off. "Gerroff me."

My mother gasps, "You. You happened here."

Something weird happens *to* me, right when she says this. I know for a fact that if we had been in New York, in a restaurant, in my office, at her house, I'd have clamped down and battened the hatches; just let her say whatever she wanted to say. I'd have listened to her tell me that there was no hope; that not seeing each other was the only way to go. I'd have known that, no more than an hour after saying those words, Mama would be on the phone again, asking if we could have lunch together the next day, or dinner that evening.

Mama never seems to mean what she says, but boy does she *say* it.

Part of me always knows that the only way to weather the storm is to let it run its course. Whether or not I get out unscathed is secondary.

But here's what I say now: I tell her to shut up, so I can hear what the hell actually happened. Hell, I've taken a first-aid class. Mama's not in shock, or anywhere near it. She's gasping and crying, but her color is good, and that flaming voice of hers is certainly strong enough.

So I tell her to shut up, just like that—"Shut up, Mama, with the stupid talk, so you can tell me what happened."

Ken does what I can only describe as fluttering. He bobs up and down and then he starts wringing his hands. The whole thing is ridiculous, and my world snaps into crystal-clear focus, so bright it almost hurts. I narrow my eyes to better see, and hear, and shut out everyone else, because they are just extra noise now, and I need to know what I'm dealing with.

I particularly do not need to see Ken acting like a twit. Ken seems to think this is new, or shocking, or something, and part of me wants to pull a Cher-in-*Moonstruck* and bark, "Snap out of it!" But I take a deep breath and hold my tongue, because it *is* all new to Ken, and he, sadly, is not as equipped as I am to Deal With Mama.

My mother glares at me, a wild animal in some kind of cage that is at least partially of her own making, I think, and then she says it again: "I told you—*you* happened."

Oh for Pete's sake.

When I was eight, I learned to roll my eyes from another kid at school. It seemed such a cool, *American* gesture that I immediately took it home, and the next time Mama said something outrageous I did it, and I got slapped so hard I saw stars. I haven't done it since then, because I got the message loud and clear: You'd better really want to piss someone off if you're gonna roll your eyes.

I have had enough. Mama is on the ground, still clutching herself. I still have no *fucking* idea what happened. I do the only thing I can think of to jar her into something even closely resembling reality: I roll my eyes, and she glares at me, and whips out her hand to smack me again, but I just rock back on my heels while she gasps in pain from the twinge she must have felt way down in her ankle from reaching for me.

I squint at her, just to make sure she hasn't done any more damage, but she recovers by going on, just like I knew she would. "*You* made me so angry I had to go upstairs, or do you not remember that part? You never remember anything that puts *you* in a bad light, do you? And then you didn't come to see me at all, even though you *knew* I was probably feeling bad, all because of *you*, again. You were gone for hours. You made me so angry I wanted to hurry and come find you. *You* are why I fell down the stairs."

I open my mouth to protest. I'd been gone *an hour*. And I'd been thinking of how to fix our problems.

But Mama rolls on. "You always are only thinking about yourself. You know that, don't you? It's why you'll never succeed. You *think* you know better than me, but I am your mother, and I get to say whatever I want to. You always want to play the wrong role. That's what's wrong with you. And all you want to do is hurt me. That's all you've ever wanted. Look at me now! At your feet, like a servant! Mothers are all servants to their children, but you're the worst of them all." She sniffs. "Even worse than Ken."

This is too much. "*Mama.*" It's sharp, louder than I intend it to be. Ken stops flitting. Second Aunt, who was on her way out the door, stops. Second Uncle takes a step closer to me. "Get a grip," I say. The Taiwanese equivalent of this is remarkably snappy, and is almost always conveyed with a narrowing of the eyes and a hitching equivalent to "why don'tcha?" I catch myself doing it just in time—that is, right after the words are out of my mouth.

I wait a beat. Mama doesn't say anything. *Good.* "You know, if you really wanted help, you could have asked. You could have asked Uncle to get me, or Aunt. Oh! You could have even called me. And we both know damn well that you could have yelled loud enough if you had really wanted to.

"Instead you chose to fling yourself down the stairs." *OMG,* I think to myself, *Mama is a drama queen.* I shake off the errant thought and go on. "So you chose to fling yourself down the stairs and *break* something, or whatever, and howl until we all came running, just like you've done all your life. That's not good, and that's not kind, and it's just not nice, or the way we do things, okay?" I look around. Ken's disappeared someplace, and my aunt and uncle are looking placid. Smug? It doesn't matter. My uncle shuffles to a side table and sticks his pipe in his mouth.

I point at Mama's ankle for good measure. "*That* isn't even broken, by the way. And yes, I would know," I go on, when Mama starts to protest, "because I've *seen* broken ankles. *That*'s just a sprain."

My uncle says, "Mei Mei," with a little warning in his voice, just as Mama bursts into tears. Really hurt tears now, and I feel immediately terrible. And *right.* And then she says, "My ankle hurts," and sniffles, and I feel totally annoyed, because I'm just dealing with a kid here. My aunts and uncle are dealing with their kid sister. And Ken is just—well, not dealing.

I bend down. I get behind her and lift her by the armpits into a position where she can hop to a chair by leaning on me. She can't push me away again without some massive force of strength or without falling, and although I wouldn't put either past her, she just flails and yells for a while, but we make it to the chair. I push over an ottoman and put her foot on it, trying really hard to be gentle.

I go to the freezer and get some ice. I ask Second Aunt for a towel to set the ice in, and put the whole package on my mother's ankle. I tell her not to move. I must sound firm, because she doesn't.

I look around for a pillow and lift my mother's knee, not asking her for permission. I ignore the whimpering and rearrange the ice pack. I don't ask her how she feels. If she wants to tell me, she can tell me.

"You're a doctor now, are you?" Mama sniffs. "Good thing I paid for your education."

I almost snap back that it was *Dad* who paid, but I bite my tongue. I know better now.

I'd have never guessed what would happen next. My uncle leaves the room. So does my aunt. And Mama and me, we fall frickin asleep, in side-by-side chairs.

But then, all naps must come to an end. And when I wake up, Mama is glaring at me. Like, really eyeballing me.

Here's how well I've been conditioned. I immediately sit up and fluff my hair, straighten out my shirt and run my tongue over my teeth to make sure nothing's stuck in them. (From what? The bun I ate hours ago?)

The sun is low in the sky and a set of clouds is pushing the daylight out of the room, but Mama's laser stare is enough to make me squint.

"Hi?"

"Well, don't you just know it all."

I sit up straighter, trying to gather my thoughts. My brain is still nap-fuzzy and everything feels like it's escaping me. I try and list the things we shouldn't talk about, the things we should talk about, and the things we have yet to talk about in my head, but it looks too much like a Venn diagram with virtually no overlap, and in the end I give up, because I remember that nothing I say will make a difference anyway. And, shockingly, this doesn't worry me. I sit back.

She sniffs. "You think you know the whole story, don't you?"

"I know you need help," I say, trying not to yawn.

"Is that what you think?"

Now we're getting somewhere.

"That's what your behavior is telling me."

"My behavior, hunh? When did you get a psychology degree? Finally figure out you weren't ever going anywhere without some proper schooling, right? I knew it. Oh. Oh. What's that? You don't have a psychology degree? Well then, I guess you'd better lay off the psychology talk, right? Uneducated cunt."

Every language has an approximation of this word. Why? Why?

I take a breath. Being fuzzy-headed is making the soaked-wick-plus-flame speed I've been reacting with these past few days impossible, and I'm realizing this is a good thing, and absolutely the way I should be treating all of Mama's statements from now on: slowly, impersonally, with great patience. "Mama, I'm just saying that maybe it's time we did something about this."

She leans back and shuts her eyes, looking exhausted. The sun is almost all the way down now. "I'm doing something about it," she says.

I lean forward. Maybe we *are* getting somewhere. "What, Mama?" I say, trying to sound nonthreatening.

Her eyes snap open. It's like something out of a horror movie, honestly, because then she says, "I'm going back to New York, too."

All the blood drains from my head. My ears start ringing, even over my tinnitus. I clutch at the arm of the chair I'm in and will myself to wait until she says something else, but she doesn't say anything. I force my heart rate back down and say, "Why?"

It's like she hasn't even heard me. "Yeah, that's right. I'm going to go back and start really looking after myself. I'm sick and tired of paying attention to you and your failures. *You* want to tell *me* what I'm doing wrong with my life? Ha! What a joke! I'm going to take care of myself."

I swallow. None of this makes any sense. "Well, Mama, that's great. When do you think you want to go back?"

She glares. "With you, of course. I can change my tickets to match yours. Since you created this problem, and you think you know so much how badly I need help, we'll just go together."

Well. This is an interesting twist. New York by myself I want badly. New York with Mama, all over again? Not so much. "But—"

"And don't think you're coming back here, either, Mei Mei. You're going to stay with me as long as I want."

Oh, deep breaths, deep breaths. "I'm pretty sure that's not what you want. I think you should just think—"

"Oh, you *think*, do you? I don't care. You think I need so much help? You get to help me. That's final. What's the point of a daughter, otherwise?"

My head is spinning. On the one hand, I get to go back to New York now. On the other hand, it sounds like I have to stay there. On the third hand (???), well, nothing's changed, has it? I stare at Mama for a long time, not taking my eyes off her, meeting her gaze, and I wonder when I've ever done that before. The answer is right there in front of my eyes, with Mama squirming a little under what I think is a pretty steady glare: I have never, ever looked her in the eyes for so long.

In my head I get a crazy vision of Jody with pom-poms: *You can do it!* I snarl at the vision, and Mama jumps a little bit. *Good*, I think.

I know I got myself here. And now it looks like I'm going back.

My mother leans forward again. She looks ready to push back, and she does. "I'm your mother. You think I can't make you do what I want?" She's wearing a linen shirt and linen trousers and I flash back to a photo I saw in an old *Life* magazine one time, of Katharine Hepburn sitting in a tree, wielding a chainsaw, looking just as determined as my mother does right now. I don't answer Mama, because there's no real answer to the question she's asked me. Instead I get up and I walk out of the room, as she asks a few more rhetorical questions. Turning my back on it feels good.

There's a week left until my flight to New York. I have that long to gird myself for what looks like a few months of practice with this new me facing the same old Mama, at least until I can screw up the courage—and the finances—to get back on track with figuring out what I want. I'm pretty sure it won't be in New York, with Mama.

June 6, 5:30 a.m.
Front courtyard

The air in the mornings here is so very, very still. It's too hot to be crisp, and humid enough to make the air over the rice paddies just in front of our house shimmer, all the way to the blue mountains in the distance. I wish I had my watercolor pencils with me.

I just saw Ken come back. Much the way I sometimes think I want my mother and me to have that mystical mother-daughter kinship that some of my friends have, I like to think that Ken and I have a sibling sixth sense, but today it just makes me sad that Ken was out all night, probably wrestling with this thing about Grace.

Sure enough, when he sees me sitting here, he comes over, shaking his head at me.

"Wow, you really know how to get into it, don't you?" he says, and I'm immediately reminded of my mother and her accusation that I bring my own cloud of discontent wherever I go.

I must flinch, because Ken pats my shoulder. "That's not what I mean. I just mean, you've only just arrived, really, and it feels like so much has happened."

"Yeah," I say, and then I ask him what I really want to know. "So, what did she say?"

"Oh, Grace?" Ken scratches his chin. "Oh. She said she's only been seeing Danny a little while. She said she's been meaning to tell me. She said—she said all sorts of things."

"Wait, a little while? Like...?"

"Yeah," he says. "The baby's not mine."

Oh. This is so indescribably sad. Ken looks utterly drained. "Ken, how can you know for sure?"

"We did the math. I was at an artist's retreat the month the doctor says she got pregnant."

"Oh."

"So is it Danny's?"

"I don't know. I guess so. Maybe?"

I'm outraged. "How could she do something like this?"

170

Ken sighs. "People change, I guess."

"So, are you still going to…"

"Marry her? Oh, hell no."

"But what's going to happen to her, then?"

"If she wants to keep the baby, she'll have to resign."

"No *way.*"

"Probably."

"Wow." I sneak another look at Ken. He's sitting up pretty straight, almost like if he let himself relax he'd just collapse into our driveway. "Are you okay?"

"Oh, I guess so. I mean, hey, it's not like there aren't other fish in the sea, right?" He smiles at me, but his eyebrows seem to be pulling his face down, and the whole effect is just pathetic.

"You know," I say, "you can be sad."

"Oh, I am. I just don't see any way to change it." He brightens. "Anyway, at least Mama can stop thinking that I'm a ne'er-do-well who runs around impregnating village girls. Ha!"

Ken barks this laugh, but we both realize how wrong it all is, and we sit there, watching the sun rise, and then he says, "Oh, Grace wanted me to tell you that she rethought and that you can still keep your job. What the hell did she mean by that?"

Ken's standing up now, trying to look like it doesn't hurt to recall every little thing Grace has said, but really, I know he just wants to lie down and have a nap, something dark and cozy with no dreams whatsoever. "Nothing," I say. "Don't worry about it. Probably something to do with my heading to New York. You don't care if I…?"

"No," says Ken. "Why should I? It's just a job, right?"

"Yeah. Hey, do you want to go get a coffee?"

Ken chews at his lower lip. "Actually, I think I really need to be alone right now," he says.

"But aren't you going in to see Mama?"

He smiles a little. "Yeah. I guess I mean, I don't really want to see *you* for a little bit, okay? I mean, I just need a little…"

All the blood leaves my head. I'm simultaneously embarrassed, angry, and regretful. "Oh, of course!" I say, brightly, agreeably, and then Ken nods and leaves.

He slopes back toward the house, barely picking up his feet. Right before he walks in through our front doors, he takes a breath and squares his shoulders, and I finally see the part of him that will always remember who and what our mother is. Even at this hour of the morning, he's putting on his best face, in case he bumps into her, just like I do, so she'll feel like everything's okay.

It's *not* okay, obviously. Somewhere on this trip I decided it was okay to throw my brother under the bus for the sake of getting my own back with my mother, and I'm not sure how to fix that, either.

I could still stay here and teach, and go back to New York when I'm ready. Not with Mama, I mean. Grace isn't going to fire me after all, but I'm not sure I can really work for her. And what do I do about Ken?

Later

Mama just hobbled out to inform me that she got tickets to match mine. Fantastic! Oh, I know, I know: sarcasm is the lowest form of humor. I don't care. I'm too tired to be ironic.

June 12, 2:28 p.m.
Classroom

I haven't written in forever. It's like I don't know what to say to myself. Like, I *know* now, I really really know it, that I could make a go of things here. I don't know how I know. It's just a feeling I have. But I also know that I'll never be able to forgive myself if I don't try and also make a go of things with my mother.

Except I'm still not sure if I can actually handle a New York that was foisted on me by Mama. I am going home, which is what I wanted. But I am not going home under the conditions I wanted to go.

I guess you can't have everything.

It's like I've crossed some kind of mental divide. Nothing I do will ever be the same again. What I was doing before couldn't ever possibly be good enough now.

Let's take a tally. My books say that lists are good.

1. No career.
2. No job, even.

3. No boyfriend, either. (Honestly, who am I kidding? I can't handle a boyfriend now, anyway.)

I've been thinking and thinking about how to make this go my way, but I can't. Not yet, anyway.

Okay. Let's review:

Top Six Things Marty Has Done Wrong in the Past Month:
- Barf on bigwig
- Lose gigantic deal
- Piss off best friend
- Ostracize self from entire freaking city
- Drive Mama halfway to total insanity
- Piss off brother

Yep. Ken's still not really talking to me. In fact, Ken is basically avoiding all of us as much as possible.

I guess he must have told Mama that I jumped the gun telling her about the baby, because she came into my room a little while ago and told me that she didn't know where I got my propensity to lying. And there was something else about being jealous of my own brother. Oh, well. I can't blame her.

For my part, I've been avoiding Mama, as much as I possibly can. I feel like what I need is time. I leave The Compound for long stretches. Second Uncle and Second Aunt don't say anything but the most normal of platitudes to me, and even First Aunt seems to have given up. It's like she knows I can't stand to think that I might have been happy here, just for a little while, even. We all take our meals together, except Ken, who's in his studio a lot, and Mama, who's insisted on having her meals brought up to her. We just eat. I don't say anything, really. The dining room feels like a mausoleum. Not that I've ever been in one.

I almost wish things were back the way they were before.

I wish I'd never seen Mama barely holding it together; I wish I'd never seen Ken fluttering like a lame bird; I wish I'd never—

Oh, hell. I wish I'd never come here.

I haven't even talked to Grace. I still don't know if I should work for her. Ken doesn't seem to care, but I think I do.

If I go back to New York, I can at least predict misery with Mama. And I can probably manage it.

Then again, I'm getting the idea that "I can probably manage it" is nowhere near ideal.

Didn't the Brontë sisters live with their dad, like, forever? Until they all died of consumption, or whatever it was Victorian heroines do?

I went to the costume store this morning. Ms. Liu let me wander as long as I wanted to, but I couldn't stay for very long, because I started to feel sad. It got worse when the storyteller came to pick up her aborigine costume. She saw it and lit up and couldn't say much more than "I love it" over and over again, and then she ran back into the dressing room with it and put it on and came out and thanked Ms. Liu profusely for it, using the traditional, formal version of the phrase, and turned slowly around in front of the mirror two, three, four five six times, looking at all the different beads and details.

She was enthralled, and enthralling, and that was even before she turned to us and asked if we wanted to hear a little of the act she was scheduled to put on. We did, and she smiled contentedly, almost to herself, and began telling us what she said was an old aboriginal tale about pit vipers. I nearly wept.

I left before she could finish, tapping my watch in a sorry attempt at an excuse. She nodded and went on telling the story, while Ms. Liu listened, looking happy.

I didn't tell Ms. Liu I thought I might not be back. She probably knows already. Gossip, small town, etc.

Only a little while now before the kids come back for their afternoon session. Better get ready.

June 13, 2:35 p.m.
Classroom again

Chris just called.

He sounds giddy and breathless. "Marty?"

"Hi, there." I know I sound flat, but I don't know how to fix it.

"Well, hello, cranky."

I sigh. "Sorry. Things are nuts here."

"Oh, are you busy? I can call you ba—"

"No, no. I really am happy to hear from you. What's up?"

"Listen! Listen!" It's like he can't contain himself. "I have great news, but you're going to have to make a big choice."

"What? Tell me."

"I have something really cool here for you. You have to come back to get it. Well, not all the way back. I mean, kind of. But kind of not."

"Chris. What is it?"

"Okay, okay. You're going to *love* this. My sister is doing some stage work for a community theater production of *Hamlet* in northern Westchester County. They need a costumer. Pro bono, practically—they barely have enough to rent the theater space, so it'd be a little stipend—but I thought I should tell you, just in case you want to—"

Something goes *pop* in my brainpan, almost like a revelation. This is nearly identical to the job Jody offered me to stay put. This is the job I probably should have always had; this is the job that is closer to my pipe dream than anything I've ever had before.

This is the job Mama will scoff at, but I find I really don't care anymore.

"Yes," I tell Chris. "I'll take it. When do I need to start?"

Chris is quiet for a bit. "Wow. I didn't expect *that*."

"I forgot to tell you I'm coming home anyway."

There's a longer pause now. "Whoa. Why?"

I shrug, forgetting that he can't see me. "It's complicated. When's the gig start?"

"Um. A week from now."

"So I'd have to get there ASAP anyway, right?"

"Well, there'd have been wiggle room. Like, you could have started procuring the costumes while you were there, you know, and then, when you were ready to come back—"

"I'm ready now."

"Marty, why are you coming home? Is everything okay?"

"It's as okay as it's going to be."

"And are you really good with this gig? It's not exactly what you wanted, I know. But it'll get you a step closer."

"I want it. Sign me up. Ink it. Do whatever it takes."

"All right, well, let me tell my sister, and she can tell the director, and he'll tell the—"

"Whatever, Chris."

"See you soon, right?"

"Yeah. Flight's in a couple of days, so I'll call when I get there. We'll have lunch."

"Or maybe—something like dinner? A movie? A date?"

Hunh.

"Yes," I say, and that feels good, so I say it again: "Yes. That sounds like a lot of fun."

He laughs, and that's all I need to know that this is a step in the right direction.

June 15, 5:00 p.m.
Classroom

Holy Christ on a bicycle. Like, on a big, huge, ridiculous penny-farthing-type number, because Christ on a penny-farthing couldn't possibly be more outrageous than what I've just heard.

I can't even—

Okay. So here's what happened.

When class starts, the kids are looking bright and peppy. Lately we've been talking about things they think are important, like movies and music and television shows. I let them bounce stuff off of me. We've been talking about Harry Potter, since most of them have read it in translation and seen the movies. I'm actually using it to talk about translation as a career, and they seem really interested.

I mean, hell, who am I kidding? These kids have been interested since day one. I am going to miss them like crazy. I guess they're going to miss me too, because when I tell them, at the very end of our club time, that they'll have a new teacher come Monday, they go really, really quiet. Even Rip doesn't have anything to say to that. He just sits there with his mouth hanging open, and then A Chien starts crying.

Great. Just great, because then I start to get that prickly feeling in your sinuses that means you're about to blow your cover as the cool, collected, foreign instructor.

A Chien's friends cluster around her, and Rip is still sitting there with his mouth open, and then he says, "Aw, come *on!*" in English, which is, okay, probably not something I should have taught them.

And then the class pops into noise. Like before they were in a bubble, maybe, and then the bubble blew and they were all a lot noisier than they'd been before. Ever.

They're all rattling off in Taiwanese. They sound bewildered and upset and I let them do that for a while until I hear someone say, very distinctly, "Lying is bad."

So that's when I physically step into what feels like a throng of students and hold up my hands like a cut-rate crossing guard and say, "Whoa, whoa, whoa," 'cause there's no real equivalent in Taiwanese, and they all screech to a halt.

"Who's lying to who?" I say.

Predictably, it's Rip who opens his mouth. "You are. You're lying."

I shake my head. "What are you talking about, Rip?"

"It's not just me! It's not just me. We all know!"

"Okay, *what* is going on here?"

A Chien looks like she's been holding her breath. "You're not leaving because you want to go back to New York," she finally says. "You're leaving because your mother is going back too."

Holy shit. I feel like someone's punched me in the chest. I'm scrambling, trying to figure out who told them. And then I immediately think that I can add "Letting Your Students Know Too Much about You" to the list of Shit Marty's Done Horribly Wrong in the Past Month. And then right after that, looking at the wide-eyed, anticipatory faces, I realize I've never once told them a single thing about my mother, because hell, this is still very much her place, her country, her village, and damned if I'm going to ruin it for her the way she's tried to ruin New York City for me.

I take a deep breath and go back to my desk. "Guys. *Guys.* Just sit down and tell me what you think is happening here, because I really don't have a clue."

"Rip's A-ma hears all the gossip," says A Chien. "Rip says his great-grandma heard it from someone that you're going home together."

I sigh and don't say anything. *Mama strikes again,* I think, and I can picture it in my head, Mama telling someone, anyone, that she tried to help her daughter to get a leg up in

Taiwan but that even that failed. I can *see* it, Mama balancing on one crutch, waving her free hand around in grand fashion: "Well, it's just as well she couldn't make it here. I need her to help me at home now that I'm hurt. It's just as it should be." I shake my head and get back to the students.

"Tell us why you're leaving." Rip is slouched in his chair, arms crossed.

I clear my throat. "Um. Not that I owe you anything, Rip, or any one of you, but I'm leaving exactly because of what I said: I miss New York and I want to go home." I don't say anything about having a job that I think is better for me there.

A Chien starts crying again. "*This* is your home too."

"Sure," I say slowly, drawing it out, trying to buy some time to figure out why the hell I'm even telling these kids anything, "but there are different levels of homesickness, you know." We covered homesickness last week.

Shu Ing, another student, throws out another gambit. "Your mother is going back, too."

Okay. Small village. Everyone really does know, and Taiwanese kids are notorious for wanting to know *everything*. "Again, not that it's any of your business, but yes, she's coming back with me." I take another deep breath. "Guys, we really shouldn't be talking about this. It's kind of inappropriate."

"Are you going back to be with your mother or not?" Rip is not the type to let up.

I sigh and give up. "Sure, that's part of it. She twisted her ankle recently and can't travel easily by herself."

A Chien speaks up. "It's true. All daughters should go with their mothers whenever they're needed and wherever they're needed."

Some murmurings from around the classroom. Rip steeples his fingers under his chin. He says he learned it from watching Robert Downey Jr. in *Sherlock Holmes*. "But shouldn't that only be true if your mother wants you to go with her?"

I go cold and then hot. "My mother needs me," I say, and that sounds pathetic, so then I say, "Everyone needs someone when they're hurt, and daughters are best equipped to know what mothers need!" I'm trying to be chipper and a little bit funny, but Rip isn't really listening.

He looks like he's pretty deep in thought. "My great-grandma says your mother doesn't even like kids," he says.

I totally freeze. "That's not true. I should probably talk to your great-grandma about this, Rip. Can you give me her phone number?" Somewhere in my memory bank, my mother screams, *I wish I'd never had you!* and I feel the sting of her slap again like it was yesterday. Except, oh, it sort of was yesterday. Last week, anyway.

"And"—it's like Rip hasn't even heard me—"she says it's amazing that you're such a good teacher and so good with teenagers, because she says your mother never even wanted kids."

I'm a little light-headed. "Rip!"

Rip goes on. "She didn't even want your brother, and who doesn't want a *son?*"

"That's enough!" I'm shouting, and Rip shuts the fuck up, finally, finally, finally. He looks a little bit smug, which suits the whole steepled-fingers-under-chin thing, except now he's stopped it and he just looks like a smug kid. I bare my teeth, just a little bit, and he sits back in his chair.

All I can think is *thank god thank god thank god* until I realize the kids are still staring at me, so I take four deep breaths (*Meditation for the Way-Too-Busy Woman*, bookseller by the N line at Ditmars, $1) and tell them there's no more discussing it.

The class is quiet, and I take advantage of the lack of noise. "Look. I'm sorry I'm leaving. I will miss you. But it's not up for discussion. Okay?"

I look at my watch. "You're all late to go home. Go. You can still send me email, okay? Even all the way in America." I write my email address on the whiteboard and draw a big star next to it on one side and a huge smiley face on the other, but when I smile at them my face feels like it's cracking.

A Chien is crying again, and she gives me a long hug. Rip is the last to leave. "I'm sorry I made you sad, Wu *lao shi*," he says, and I get a little pang, because I remember my daydream of bumping into my students on the street and having them address me just this way.

"It's okay, Rip," I say. "Good luck," and then, as an afterthought, "Rip, what did your great-grandma do at my house when she worked there?"

"Oh," says Rip, breezy as a spring New York day on the Hudson River, "she was a nurse, a—how do you say?— midwife."

Rip leaves, and now I know what the hell he was talking about.

Ramblings of a teenage mind aside, I'm pretty sure Rip was conveying the idea that my mother did not really mean to give up Ken to her unmarried sister.

I'm pretty sure the issue is exponentially bigger than even that, and I'm pretty sure it needs a lot more exploring. Actually, I think I just need to know a lot more than I've been told, especially now that I know more than I ever wanted to know.

I'm going to see First Aunt, because she knows more than she's telling, and also because suddenly, in my head, everything's gone pear-shaped, darling, as Stafford would put it.

June 16, midnight
Own room

Ohhhhhh I am soooo tired. I am so tired that it feels like I'm bubbly-drunk, like I'm talking and my brain is catching up a split second later. It's either dangerous to write this way or good. I can't decide which. It probably doesn't make too much of a difference. In six short hours we leave to get on the high-speed rail to Taipei, where we'll catch our flight home to New York. And only six hours ago I was trying to talk to First Aunt about all the shit that had gone down.

Turns out, "the shit was going down" in my own little pea brain. To everyone else, it was status quo. And I mean everyone else. *Everyone!* Except, of course, for me and Ken.

Oh, it was infuriating. You know, when you're angry at something, or generally frazzled by something, all you want is someone to at least be angry along with you, right? All you want is some damn empathy. But I didn't get that.

It's like, back in college, when I was doing cartoons for the school paper, right? I had this infuriating wreck of an editor who didn't understand the first thing about graphics. She'd say, "Words are my thing, girl, not pictures!" and I wanted to smack her, and so did the rest of the staff, but they were all so placid about it.

My best friend there, the managing editor, was this incredibly even-keeled guy. John always wore a preppy Lily-Pulitzer-type-color polo shirt, coral or pink, or blue or mint green, and his attitude was as casual as his clothing. "Heyyyy," he'd say, gripping me by the shoulders, "she doesn't mean anything by it. She just doesn't know any better." And then, when that didn't work, he'd get up on tiptoe so that all I could see was this broad expanse of whatever-the-hell-put-you-to-sleep-color he was wearing that day, and he'd say, "Callllmmmmm, Marty. Loooook into my shirrrrrt."

And we'd laugh and everything would be okay, but god, just for once—for once!—I wanted John to lose his marbles, too. "Yeah!" I wanted him to say. "Yeah! She's crazy! Worst editor on the planet! Let's mutiny! Make her so miserable she'll walk the plank! Argh! Avast!" Or something like that.

It's like that with First Aunt, too. She's eternally placid.

I ran all the way home from school and almost broke my key in the ancient lock trying to get it open fast enough, and then I bolted through the courtyard, almost killing myself on some loose stones, and I literally and very dramatically flung open the door to her studio and said, "Tell me about when Mama said you should take Ken."

Except she wasn't there. So now I'm doubly pissed. I'm firing shots across the bow of an abandoned ship, or whatever, and so I bolt into her bedroom, where she's lying propped up in bed, paging through some art books, just like the ones I was going to bring back for her from New York.

Just thinking that I was actually planning on coming back here stokes the fire even more, and so when I open my mouth, I'm practically yelping: "What *happened* to my mother? Why do you have Ken? Why?"

My aunt is apparently propped up in bed because she's feeling sick, a point she drives home by pulling a tissue from its box and honking loudly into it before she actually speaks to me.

"I told you," she says. "You really need to talk to your mother about this. You really need to sort it all the way out."

"This is ridiculous," I tell her. "No one is willing to tell me anything, and the one person who has all the keys to the questions seems to be incapable of seeing herself. What am I supposed to do with this?"

"Sometimes, we build our own prisons."

I just stare at her. She's sitting there, looking a little wizened, like some bed-ridden bodhisattva.

"Why can't you just tell me what I need to know?"

"Mei Mei, it's not my story to tell. And it's not our way to talk about these things."

OMG. I truly am about to lose it. "*What things?*" I yell.

My aunt doesn't really smile. I think she pulls off one of those "rueful quirks of the lips" or whatever. "These are your mother's issues, Mei Mei. If she chooses to share them with you, her daughter, then that is her choice, but it cannot be mine to make for her."

"Eurgh!" I throw up my hands and turn for the door.

"Mei Mei?"

"What?!" I snap my head back around to her. She's pointing at me.

"Mei Mei, you need to remember one thing." She holds up her finger for dramatic pause, or something, except I am way too impatient for dramatic pauses. I shuffle on my feet, and she glares at me. "Whatever you find out, remember it is not your story to tell."

Whaaat? Never mind. I can't *wait* to get back to New York, where it's normal to talk about mommy issues and therapy, and probably normal to talk about whatever the hell it is that Rip's great-grandma knows better than I do.

I do ask First Aunt about Rip's great-grandma. Here's what she said:

"Oh, that gossiping old toad. Always did love to tell folks she worked here." But there was a shifting look to her eyes. "Go. Go ask your mother. You need to know."

Right. Clearly I've reached need-to-know status.

So I go bolting off to Mama's room, where she is packing and repacking, forgetting if she's packed something, and doing it all over again. It's like she's addled by this incapacity to trust herself.

"Ma," I say. I'm too tired to add the second "ma."

"Oh, it's you."

"It's me. We have to talk."

(Part of me is thrilled, by the way. This is what happens in sitcoms! People get in a room together and have "family meetings"! They "hash stuff out"! They "come to terms" with things! Very, very exciting. Maybe I'll have something to tell Jody after all!)

She turns her back to me again and starts randomly stuffing things into her suitcase. Not a good sign. Mama usually rolls her stuff up very tightly before arranging it in her suitcase in neat rows. I press on, because now I really feel like I have to know.

"Mama. Mama. Look at me, please."

"What for? So you can tell me what else is wrong with me?"

"No, so *you* can tell me what is wrong."

This gets her attention. "I thought you were the expert."

"Just stop it, Mama, okay?" I'm tired of yelling. I clear a spot on the bed and sit down. "Why did you leave Ken with First Aunt, Ma? Really."

"I felt sorry for her. Her womb was like a rock. And she was incapable of ever finding a man on her own. Said it was something about the artist's temperament or whatever. She never could find a date." She says this without looking at me. "Whatever. Maybe she's gay."

I roll my eyes. "Oh, come on, Mama. You don't mean that. Why did you give up Ken?"

"Because I thought I would be able to have another child, someone who was just as good. I guess I was wrong."

"Mama."

"Because she needed me to."

"*Mama.*"

"*Because I wanted to, okay?*" The speed of her transition from trotting out routine lines to something sounding like the truth is stunning. She's stopped packing and is sitting on the floor, her bad ankle jutting out at an uncomfortable angle. She looks exhausted. Her lips are quivering. I feel terrible that I've caused this reaction. And I can't stand it, the idea that my mother is at my feet. I get down on the floor with her. She keeps on talking.

"The crying, the wailing, the constant pooping and peeing and coughing and fever and ugliness of a crying baby—I didn't want it. I wanted to give it back, but they wouldn't let me. I wanted to send it out for adoption, but they wouldn't let me. I wanted to give it to your father's sister, but they didn't want it. So I gave it away. I did. I didn't want it, so I gave it up."

Holy shit. I'm trying really really hard to think straight, but all I can think is that she can't even say his name, she can't even call the baby by his proper name.

"Mama," I say, as quietly as possible, "the baby's name is Ken. He's my brother and he's still your son, even if First Aunt has adopted him."

"No, no, it doesn't matter, don't you see? I gave it up, he's not mine anymore, I couldn't take care of it."

I swallow, trying to find a way to help her out of the hole she's in. "But you took care of *me*," I say. "I think I turned out okay."

She glances at me and keeps on talking. "It was so awful. It cried every single night. It would not stop. Your father was useless. He would always say he had to work late. I think he volunteered for the night shift at the hospital so he wouldn't have to hear it crying."

"Ken," I say again, a little louder.

"It was so hard all the time. I was all alone, in your father's mother's house, because that's what women who married out did back then, do you see? Your grandmother worked all the time. Your grandfather, too. Your father's sisters had married out. It was just me, all the time, with it. It and me, me and it. All. The. Time."

"Ken," I say, pretty loud now. "His name is Ken."

"It doesn't matter what we named him. I didn't want him." She sits back and wipes her eyes. "Ken. I didn't want Ken. There. I said it. Are you happy? Ken. Ken. Ken."

"What?"

We both turn around, and there he is. Ken.

Oh, fuck.

He swallows. "I heard you calling, Marty," he says. "And then—"

"How long have you been standing there?" My mother is panicked, predictably.

"A while."

My brain cannot believe it is hearing what it's hearing. The whole thing feels like a really bad after-school special on drug abuse: "How long you been standing there, Mom?" "Long enough to see you roll the joint, Billy." "I learned it from watching you, okay?" What a wreck. I guess I get my television show after all.

"Ken—" I go to stand by him, but he turns on me.

"Please stop saying my name, Marty, okay?"

I look at the two of them, checking first one and then the other. Back and forth, back and forth, like watching a tennis match. Man, this is some fucked-up shit. Ken was keeping what he thinks is a huge secret from Mama. The whole freakin' time, Mama's been keeping an even *bigger* secret from him for the entire thirty-two years he's been alive. The whole thing would be hilarious if it weren't so not-hilarious.

And it's not, because Ken looks totally shell-shocked. His face has gone completely white and his Adam's apple is bobbling like crazy, like he's about to start gasping for air. He says, "You didn't want me?" and those four words just about break my heart. My knees go weak.

Mama doesn't look so good herself: She can't meet his eyes, even though you can tell she really badly wants to look at him, and she's playing with the loose skin on her knuckles and running her fingers back and forth over them like they're some kind of human rosary bead set. The whole thing feels awful.

And then there's me. I'm standing off to the side, feeling like a tennis ref, only I don't know where the hell the court lines are.

I sigh. Ken turns to me. "I only came up here to see if you wanted to have dinner with me."

"Oh." Rotten timing.

Ken turns his back to Mama and corners me. "What did she tell you? What was that about?"

I make the call, just like a good ref would. "She's right there, Ken. You should ask her yourself."

I go to Mama and put my hand on her shoulder. "Mama. You need to tell him. It's not your fault. There's a name for it. It's called post-partum depression."

"You're an expert on everything, aren't you, Marty?" she says, but quietly, and the words have no bite.

"You guys have to talk."

"You can't leave, Marty." Ken looks like he's going to get in my way, but I sidestep him and am in the doorframe before he can block it.

"I can, and I need to. You guys won't be able to sort it out with me in the middle." I lean in to him. "It's not her fault," I say. I think of what First Aunt said. "Her normal isn't the same as ours."

He pulls back from me and narrows his eyes. "You're ridiculous," he says.

"Maybe," I say. "I need to go." I don't know where, but this isn't my quandary.

When I finally leave them, they're still standing, facing each other, not looking at each other.

Later

I've been downstairs for a while, helping Second Aunt to scrub the walls again and feeling marginally better, when I realize the lack of sound coming from upstairs. And then, when I get there and I find that Ken has slipped out somehow without saying goodbye and left my mother to fall asleep on a wet, tear-soaked pillow, I feel marginally *less* better. I pull the covers up over her and now I'm back in my own bed, where now we have less than a day before we fly off to New York again.

But I do feel better. A very very little bit better.

NEW YORK, Redux

June 20, 7:10 p.m.
Metropolitan Museum of Art, upper balcony

I have a glass of wine in my hand and the summertime tourists are out in full force. I haven't started that new gig at the theater yet, but everything is signed and sealed and I start next week, right on time.

I'm remembering the weekend in Las Vegas, which I think is the last time I was around this many tourists. Here, too, they are a day's worth of sketching—as they slouch on the benches, exhausted from art, or as they stand in front of the big paintings, some of them trying to look interested, some of them actually interested.

I can't believe it's been days since I've been back. I've hardly seen anyone, and today's the first day, even, that I've seen Jody, which is annoying, considering that I was supposed to be staying with her when I came back here.

Instead I'm stuffed into the spare bedroom at my mother's place, which really isn't a spare bedroom at all, just a little closet of a den type of thing. I'm in a twin bed, which is yuck.

It's not that I don't want to stay with Jody. It's that I don't feel like I can leave Mama. Navigating her narrow townhome staircase is hard on crutches. All day I'm upstairs, downstairs, up, down, up, down. Like a hamster. Oh well. At least I'm busy.

I haven't been back to even check out my place.

So lunch with Jody was okay, I guess. Predictably, we were thrilled to see each other. Not so predictably, she didn't have too much to say about my decision to come back here. So that part was really weird. Like, she kept on wanting to steer the conversation away from my coming back, aside from the fact that she was happy to see my face, be in my company, hear in real life what I was up to, instead of over email—whatever way she could say she was happy to be sitting across the table from me, she said it.

But she didn't say anything specific, like, oh, I dunno, "You crazy woman, what are you doing back here with your mother?" Or "Hooray! You've made such a smart decision!" Hm. I'm not sure which I'd rather hear from her.

Anyway, I couldn't stand it anymore, so I asked her why she wasn't asking.

And then she said, "Well, it's not like you've really wanted to hear my thoughts on that in the past."

"That's not true!"

"It is, Marty. You've listened very politely to me, but you've never really taken my advice or been happy with anything I've said, so I've decided to just keep my trap shut for now. It's your life, your relationship, so I'm going to leave it alone. Let's both leave it alone, okay?"

I thought about this for a while, as the waiter came with our lunches and refilled our water glasses. "Do you think I did the right thing?"

She sighed, giving in to me. "Dunno. Are you excited about the theater gig?"

"Yeah."

She peered at me. Seriously, just like Mr. Magoo, only she's not an old man. Also, not a cartoon character. Also, I'm pretty sure she sees more than he ever did in god-knows-how-many-episodes of cartoons. Okay, not just like Mr. Magoo.

Anyway, I said to her, "Oh, don't do that, Jody. I know what you're thinking. You're thinking, 'Hm, that doesn't *sound* like she's very excited.' And," I tacked on, belatedly, like the ungrateful wretch I can sometimes be, "I know it's just like the thing you set up for me earlier."

Jody shook her head. "It's not like that at all."

"But it is. Same small theater, same tiny stipend."

"Yeah. But you *chose* it this time, you see?"

"Not really."

She rolled her eyes. (Not like Mr. Magoo at all.) "Anyway. I was waiting for you to go on. Because 'yeah' sounds like you're going to say something else."

"Oh."

"So tell me more."

So I did. I told her about *Hamlet* and Chris and the tiny theater in Ossining (on, incidentally, the *right* train line, the one on the Hudson), and she listened and made appreciative noises and then she said, "It sounds nice. You'll need to let me know when the production happens so I can go see your handiwork."

"I will!" I said, mentally picturing the exclamation point so I could be sure I sounded like I was adding an exclamation point.

"So," she said then, running her finger around her glass, drawing patterns in the condensation, "you're living with your mother."

"Yeah, it just makes more sense."

"Do you have to go to the theater every day?"

"Nope."

"So some days you'll just be…with her?"

I nodded.

"How's that going?"

"She's been sleeping a lot. The jetlag knocked her out, I think."

"And the ankle?"

"Okay."

Jody was looking so eager, so earnest, trying to do something with her hands so she didn't pick at her nails, which she does when she's upset. There was an awkward pause between us that was new. It made me so sad I had to blink really fast and pinch the bridge of my nose to keep the prickly sinusy feeling from going too far.

I thought back to the last time we hung out together, when we got shit-faced and I had to tell her I lied to my mother about selling those ad pages, and how much fun we had even though we were mad at each other.

And then I decided that Jody deserved to know about everything that happened at The Compound, and what I found out about my mother and Ken. Heck, I deserve to tell Jody, and Jody deserves to know, so she can keep on being the friend I want her to be. *The Language of Paying Attention to YOU* says that you have to acknowledge and indulge your impulses every once in a while, so I did.

I told her all the stuff from soup to nuts, starting with Vegas and Chris, because I suddenly realized she doesn't know what actually happened, and this made me so sad that I wouldn't have actually been able to stop myself from telling her the story if I had wanted to. And somewhere along the line I found myself telling her about the garbage that went down when I was a kid, the confusion and the fear and the getting hit and the constant terror that something bad would happen, and then the bad stuff that still does happen every day. Jody's eyes got big and small, and I could see her pupils dilate and her nostrils flare and I knew I was giving her way too much information, but I also knew she could take it.

I told her about Mama and her normal, and Jody's breathing slowed and she looked like she wanted to say something, but she just tightened her lips and waved at me to keep going, even when I felt like I should stop.

Women Who Love Men Who Love Themselves does say people are a lot stronger than we usually give them credit for.

Hey, didn't I say I was going to burn all those books, anyway?

In the end, Jody did say something. She said, "I didn't know it was that bad."

Shit. Going to be late for train. Mama is going to freak out.

June 27, 9:20 a.m.
Guest bedroom, Mama's pad

God, I'm bored.

9:25 a.m.

Still bored. I know. I'm going to call Chris. One of those books I have floating around says I'm supposed to grab life by the horns and stare into its raging eyes, or something, so hell, why not?

9:35 a.m.

Why did I wait so long? He's free for dinner today, and he's coming up here to visit. Hooray!

Still have dress from Vegas, but he's seen that one. Plus, bad memories attached to that outfit. Maybe will just go to diner. No fancy dress needed.

Later

Chris lovely. Diner food yummy. Diner-wine, not so much. Oh well. Was all moony anyway so didn't need booze buzz.

I was so happy to see him. He brought me a nice bouquet of daisies. Even brought one for Mama. Did not let him stay near her long enough for her to say anything weird. Or embarrassing.

He wanted to hear all about Taiwan. He's been to Asia, but never to our tiny, yam-shaped island.

Was a little bit like a first date. Only wasn't, really, 'cause we've known each other for so long. But still, *was*, since I'm not working for *Retirees' Review* anymore, you see.

Hm. Anyway, definitely want to see more of him. Maybe will let Mama spend some time with him next time.

He seems capable. Of handling her, I mean.

Later

Ooh. Got good email. Someone wants to sublet my apartment for July, August, September. I need the money, so no-brainer, although had to think hard about whether letting a guy who owns two rabbits live in my space is a good thing.

Oh well. At least will feel less stressed about money. Plus, rabbits cute. He sent photos.

June 38, since month will not end. Don't care what time it is. Is dark.
Athenopolis Diner, Route 9, Ossining-used-to-be-Sing Sing or maybe am closer to Mahopac by now?

I am so pissed off that I have just consumed two massive bowls of matzo ball soup and two tuna salad sandwiches. (Somehow, I've gone from being a binge-drinker to being a binge-eater. My time in Taiwan must have rubbed off on me.)

Maybe I'm pissy from being around the pissy old crab who's our show's director. He bosses everyone around in the most condescending of manners, darling, and without being the slightest bit apologetic for it. ("It's a big, mean world, Marty, or have you not figured that out yet? It will not stop just because you cannot find les chaussettes pour Ophelia." Seriously, WTF.)

The other potential culprit is our prima donna lead lady, who is also a local dentist and has shockingly white teeth. Surely that is not normal, even for a dentist. Definitely is not normal for a twelfth-century Danish queen. We will have to do something about this for production.

About the only thing worthy about this production (today, anyway) is Chris's sister, who is nice and sweet and really kind to me.

No. No. I must be realistic. I'll tell you what the real problem is. (Matzo ball soup has made me honest.) The problem is the sad, ratty state of the few costumes we *do* have, and the very depressing standardization of costumes yet to be hunted down:

Hamlet—black tights, although start out in white at beginning of production so as to signify happier times [director's notes]. Dark green tunic with bell sleeves in horrible scratchy velvet. Poufy pirate shirt–type thing to go underneath tunic. Slippers. Gold or brass circlet around head [to signify royalty; director's notes].

Ophelia—floaty dresses, preferably in off-white. Especially good for simulating floaty death in floaty stream.

Polonius—see Hamlet, except for scratchy velvet cap of sorts with feather and no circlet. And beard. Must have beard. [Cast member is trying to grow self, but will not work.] Also probably good to have different color tunic.

Rosencrantz and Guildenstern—see Hamlet, except no circlets around heads.

Laertes—see Hamlet, Rosencrantz, and Guildenstern.

What a total lack of creativity. What a vacuum of joy. Of course, we don't have a budget, either. So all of this is triply, quadruply depressing, since I have to source icky old costumes from shut-down theater productions.

Worse, frustration with costuming is making me verbal. Told director was concerned lousy quality of clothes was going to show in bright stage lights, and that instead of sourcing old costumes, we should try and make ones from whole cloth. Wanna know what he said?

"Honey, unless you can sew and you have un petit massive trust fund, I'm not interested in hearing it. Did you get the slippers we needed? Try to get them as cheap as you can, okay?"

Ugh. So depressed. So frustrated. Maybe I should order a piece of pie before driving home. At least I will bring one home for Mama.

Had a big knock-down row with her today, by the way, although for once no one did any actual knocking down, or even lashing out. Was so tiring.

Am coming to grips with the idea that she might need professional help.

I am not a professional. Also, I am tired.

Maybe a piece of pie will make her feel better. Must remember not lemon chiffon; Mama hates lemons.

Going home now. Maybe Mama will be asleep.

Is actually July 1, but do not care. Soon will be Independence Day, but I am still dependent. On cranky director, on cranky Mama, on crusty costumes.

Later

Oh, wow. Wow oh wow. When got home Mama was on the phone. She paused long enough to tell me that it was Ken on the phone, and that I looked too skinny. Shrugged. Did not care about looking skinny. Cared a little more about Ken. Wondered how he was doing.

Started to go to room, went faster when heard beginnings of strained conversation. (I'm practicing denial, which all the self-help books say is useful sometimes.) I closed my door and checked voicemails. Chris! Squeee!

Talked to Chris, who made sympathetic noises and also plans for dinner next week. Joy oh joy!

Then I opened my email, because I had hatched an idea on the way home from the Athenopolis: I bet there are theater productions on Craigslist or something that are giving away their old costumes. I can sew, so why not try and patch these things up, embellish them a bit? I've heard even the Metropolitan Opera has costume sales sometimes. And up here, there may be smaller companies wanting to get rid of their costumes cheap.

Anyway, was immediately distracted by an email flyer from Ms. Liu's shop. It said something about that show that the aboriginal storyteller was involved in, and it had lovely pictures of Ms. Liu's design in full color, but I was more excited by an idea that seemed to come right as I opened her flyer. What if I could go work for Ms. Liu?

I wrote to her. And I'm not sorry I did. It feels like the best move I've made in a long time. Now, just to wait, and see what she thinks.

I want her to say yes, more badly than I've wanted anything in a while.

Oh, Mama is calling.

Still later

Mama wants to go back to Taiwan for Ken's opening show. She came in to tell me, casual as anything. Popped her head in. Did not bother with knocking. I am getting used to that and now wander around with a bra on at all times, even if am sleeping, so as to have the best chance of looking put-together at all hours.

"Your brother's big show is happening in six weeks. I am getting us both tickets," she said, and then closed the door again.

"Wait, what?" I opened the door and chased her down. She kept walking. "Ma! Come on!"

She turned halfway and said, "You know. Ken's big show. We should go and support him."

"Okay," I said. And then I added, "Do you want tickets to *Hamlet?*"

"That thing you're doing?" she said, and continued walking down the stairs. "In that run-down theater in Ossining, by the prison? Are the people in it criminals? Maybe."

Hmmm.

July 4, 8-ish or so p.m.
Closet-of-a-hovel-of-a-tiny-bedroom, Mama's pad

So tired today. Director was unbearable. Almost quit, but I thought of Chris and his sister and how they stood behind me so I could get this gig. Le Directeur made the entire company come in today for a reading, even though it's a holiday. He said *he* didn't observe it, so why should we? Hm.

Everything will be okay. Ms. Liu wrote back and asked me to be more, uh, specific about what I meant when I asked her for a job. What, like "Hi, Ms. Liu, It's Marty Wu. We met a few weeks ago. I am considering relocating to Taiwan and would love to come work for you," wasn't detailed enough, or something? Geez. Should have looked it over again before I sent.

Mama dropped the other shoe tonight, too, by the way.

She opened the door to my room just as I was typing a follow-up email to Ms. Liu about working for her, with, like, dates, and things I'd want to do with her and stuff.

"What are you doing?"

I couldn't think fast enough to lie.

"Uh. Um. Writing email to Ms. Liu."

"My friend?" This last, casually.

My nerves went all prickly, and I got defensive. "The woman you haven't talked to in thirty years? Yes. The woman who owns the costume store."

"What are you doing writing to her?"

"I'm *replying* to her." Defenses up in full force now. Panicky feeling in chest.

"What about?"

"A job." If I keep the answers short sometimes it helps. *Business and Bitch Both Start with B* says this is a good tactic.

"Here?" Mama must have read the same book.

"No."

"Marty." Oh, no. Here we go. "Please don't go there again."

"What?" I did not expect that.

"Don't go."

I've been practicing trying to keep from feeling too soft around her—you know, trying to remember that she's hurt my feelings many times, that maybe she needed a dose of some real talk. But she was looking down, picking at the edge of a pillow sham, and I couldn't help it. "Mama, what are you saying?"

"Just don't go. I'll support you. I'll give you all the money you want. You don't understand how much I can help you. Your father was very successful while he was here, and he's treated me very well, with alimony payments. And I have a sizeable inheritance. I can support you in your shop or whatever other idiotic thing you want. Just don't go chasing some insane idea again, okay?"

I opened my mouth. "It's not insane or stupid," I started to say, but then I looked more closely, past the anger and the frustration and all the hurt. She'd finally looked up, and away from the sham, meeting my gaze, like she really meant what she said. I ignored the part about the money. Somehow, it seemed secondary, even with my current tiny stipend and not knowing what Ms. Liu had to offer me, when I considered it next to spending a working life doing what I finally wanted to do.

Because what she was saying, around all the language and the totally unnecessary insults, I think, is that she didn't want me to go anywhere. Which was kind of a revelation. And also something I couldn't make fit into my life.

"I don't want your money, Mama."

"Too good for it?"

"No, Mama. It's just not what I want."

"What do you want?"

"Um. Your support?"

"Money is the ultimate support! I am supporting you!"

"Mama. I just want you to be happy."

"I can only be happy if you are a better person. When will you care about me?" She made an abrupt half-turn, all of her body language reading defeat and disappointment, and shut the door behind her.

????

Tired now. Long day today; longer day tomorrow.

July 5, 8:08 a.m.
Metro-North

Writing on trains: Rickety rackety bump blip. Good grief.

Headed downtown to talk to a tiny theater on the Lower East Side that posted on Freecycle. Something about "medieval costumes, FREE!" Maybe I can outfit our whole cast this way!

Very interesting morning.

Mama came into room again. At 6:00 a.m. Ugh. Was not even really awake.

She pulled all the covers off me and said, "*Get up.*" I thought I was having a horrible nightmare. I looked around for more weirdness: people riding dinosaurs or comets, maybe, or person-sized pencils and artistic implements with buck teeth leering at me. No such luck. Weak morning light came in through the windows and my stupid underwire pinched a nerve in my boob or something when I sat up. It hurt, so I knew I wasn't dreaming or asleep even.

"Wake *up*," she said, sharply. "Listen, Mei Mei. You have a responsibility to *me*. You need to stay *here*, with *me*. I deserve at least that. I gave you life and I get to tell you what to do with yours."

My bra was really bothering me, so I unhooked it under my shirt, pulled it out from one of the sleeves of my T-shirt, and flung it across the room, where it landed on my suitcase.

"Sloppy wench," she said, but I had stopped caring.

I squinted at her and snapped on the light. I yawned, not covering my mouth, and stretched for a good long while before I answered her.

Yes! Yes! Seriously. Like there was a switch and the pinched nerve in my boob had flipped it. "Mama," I said, "you're being ridiculous. When we can both be happy for each other, then we can call each other responsible."

Yeah. I'm not even sure where that came from.

She glared at me and then she left. She didn't even slam the door, just left it wide open.

When I had brushed my teeth and went downstairs finally, she was not home.

Am meeting Jody for lunch.

2:12 p.m.

Lunch with Jody blazing success. Went like so:

ME: So, I've been thinking I shouldn't live with my mother anymore.

JODY: Duh. You can stay on my couch, since Rabbit-Boy is living in your place.

ME: Really? For the entire month?

JODY: Yeah. As long as you like, or until you find another place, which will never happen, between the play and managing your mama.

ME: Aw, thanks.

JODY: No sweat.

Jody's so cool. But she's smiling pretty big as she says it. Excellent.

Later
Mama's pad

Mama was on the phone with Ken when I got in again tonight. Looked happy.

I just told her I was moving out. But I also told her I thought we should go to Ken's show together. And also I told her I was going to take a job in Taiwan. I didn't mention Ms. Liu, since I haven't heard back from her yet. Mama said, "I guess I should think about going back there too, then."

I waited for her to say something mean, but she didn't. And then I opened my mouth to protest, but instead I heard myself saying, "Whatever you think is best for you, Mama. I'm going to stay in town, but I'm sure you can stay at The Compound."

She looked past me and sniffed. "Don't you think I know my own hometown?" she said.

Words are just words, after all, aren't they? Sometimes we say things just to have stuff to say, and sometimes we can really mean them, but it's probably better to not put too much stock in talk.

Who knows what she means? Who cares?

Rob, the guy with the rabbits (RobwiththeRabbits), wants to sublet my apartment for a while longer. I can't blame him; it's a nice space. But he's asking if he can move some more books in from storage, which means I'd have to clear mine out.

It's nice that he's a reader. I wonder what he reads? Rodent maintenance manuals? Ha!

EPILOGUE

August 30, 6:08 p.m.
Ms. Liu's shop

Start new job tomorrow and so am settling into apartment above shop.

Mama went home today.

Get this: She found a support group for ex-pats back in Bronxville. She was on the computer at the 85°C a lot of the time, IMing with her friends, while we were here. I met some of them while we were still in New York. Coffee every day if she wants to with these ladies, and always someone to talk to.

It's all kinds of women of all ages, some who work still, some who are retired, some who never worked.

Hm. I keep telling her it's not enough to just keep busy, but we never talk about the whole post-partum depression thing. I guess when she's good and ready she'll say something. If she doesn't, I guess that's okay too. For now.

RobwiththeRabbits wrote to me to thank me for "letting" him sublet the apartment for a while longer. Chris and I went out to meet him and we both liked him. We had to pick up a bunch of my books, to make room for his. It turns out he doesn't read rodent maintenance manuals, he reads Tolstoy.

I donated most of my books to the library. Well, the ones in my closet anyway. I chucked *Business and Bitch Both Start with B*, *Women Who Love Men Who Love Themselves*, *The Language of Paying Attention to YOU*, and some others too. I mean, I'm glad *TLPAY* made me start these diaries, but on the whole, I think I missed my sketchbooks more than anything. Good thing Ms. Liu laid in a whole pile of them for me. They do say art fills a void, after all.

Hamlet ended up being one of those rewarding experiences that was also a massive headache. I lugged my sewing machine out from the attic storage space in my apartment and took it to Jody's, where I spent most of my evenings sewing on ruffles and beading and piping, trying to give the tired old costumes I eventually found some kind of life.

So many feathers in all the caps; so many yards of piping on the dresses; so many faux-fur bits and plastic medallions. In the end, I think it turned out okay. The director, though, just looked at them and said, "Nice additions," and you know, he was right. They were just additions, and even though I think they made things look better, I kept on comparing them in my head to the stuff Ms. Liu was inevitably turning out, making up out of whole cloth, while I was sewing and gluing and pinning.

I think that's what convinced Ms. Liu to take me on. The portfolio I eventually sent her showed "before" and "after" of the *Hamlet* costumes, and she wrote back that she was impressed and that she'd take me on as an apprentice until December, see how it went.

Tomorrow we start on my first-ever client. It's a young lady in Taipei who wants something to wear to a masquerade ball. Coooool.

The opening night of Ken's show was awesome. What a party! We didn't get to see him for very long, and he's still in Taipei now, but he'll be home tomorrow and then we can talk. He did look really happy to see us both, and, well, recovered from the Grace-mess. Although he looked thrilled in general. There was a big turnout. The entire faculty was there, and some journalists, and some photographers. Danny was there, too, looking louche and very cool, as if he couldn't give a damn, and I truly believe he didn't.

Ken nodded at him from far away, which I think was about all he could manage.

Grace was nowhere to be seen. I haven't asked what happened to her after all. I guess there's time to find out later on.

I think I wasn't prepared for how incredible Ken's work looked there on the huge white gallery walls, with concise curatorial notes in English and Mandarin pasted next to each one. They'd even written up a biographical note about Ken and his work and screened it onto the wall at the beginning of the exhibition. My brother is making some kind of splash.

Ooo. Text message. It's Jody, planning her visit to Taiwan. Jody is up way too early, planning this visit. Clearly is excited.

Ooo. Another message. Is Chris. Says he'll visit over Thanksgiving. Not so far away, if you think about it.

For now, must continue moving in.

Acknowledgments

My friend Roz once said to me, "Writing is a solitary sport, but publishing is a team effort." Many, many thanks to the members of my team:

Kate Schafer Testerman.

The Chicago Five, my first-ever real critique group: Roger, Allison, Nancy, Sue, Tabitha.

The Home Team: Peter Bilton, the real Jody (who is nothing like the Jody here), Larry Curran, Lara Taylor, my brother Bor, my parents. My parents-in-law, Marilyn and Jim Sr. John and Ann Brantingham. Jen Helé. Jim Jr., my husband and steadying influence. Marjie, Subbie, and Suzanne, bolstering neighbors.

The Away Team: Roz Ray, Alex Clark-McGlenn, Chels Knorr, Andy Seiple, Bruce Holland Rogers, Ana Maria Spagna, Iris Graville.

The Home-Away-from-Home Team: Camille Griep, Kelly Davio, Joe Ponepinto, Rachael Warecki, Kelly Grogan, Stefon Mears, Doyce Testerman, Tom Greenman, Stephanie Hammer.

Additional thanks to Stafford Sumner, who let me use his name and is also nothing like the Stafford in this book. My ShelterBox teammates, for listening to me bang on about this book and writing in general whilst we were on deployment.

And Rosalie, for obvious reasons.

Beyond these, there are still dozens of people who helped on this road to publication. I am grateful for the grace and generosity I've encountered since I began writing.

The interview with the professional costumer Marty references is part of a real episode of RadioLab. Marty quotes June Ambrose, costume designer to everyone from Jay-Z to the Backstreet Boys. You can listen to the whole thing here: http://www.radiolab.org/story/dust-planet/.

EGG HEAVEN: STORIES

Robin Parks

Short Stories

Lyrical tales of diner waitresses and their customers, living the unglamorous life in Southern California.

"Illuminates a world entirely its own"—*Kenyon Review*

"A skilled and elegiac storyteller" —René Steinke

Paperback, 150 pages, $16.95, October 2014

HER OWN VIETNAM

Lynn Kanter

Novel

Decades after serving as a U.S. Army nurse in Vietnam, a woman confronts buried wartime memories and unresolved family issues.

"Compassionate and perceptively told"—*Foreword Reviews*

Silver Award, Indiefab Book of the Year, War & Military Fiction

Paperback, 211 pages, $18.95, November 2014

WHITE LIGHT

Vanessa Garcia

Novel

A young Cuban-American artist distills her grief, rage, and love onto the canvas.

"A lush, vibrant portrayal"—*Kirkus* (starred)

Listed in NPR's Best Books of 2015

Paperback, 284 pages, $28.00, September 2015

THE FEMALE COMPLAINT: TALES OF UNRULY WOMEN

Edited by Rosalie Morales Kearns

Short story anthology featuring nonconformists, troublemakers, and other indomitable women.

"Spellbinding... A vital addition to contemporary literature"—*Kirkus*

"The stories sing off the page" —Rene Denfeld

Paperback, 327 pp., $24.95, November 2015

Shade Mountain Press
www.ShadeMountainPress.com